SOUL'S BLADE

LEGENDS REBORN SERIES #2

EVA CHASE

ISBN-13: 978-0995986510

To the wizards at heart

I

After killing my first dark fae, there hadn't been much to do other than head home. The five of us were piled into a van tricked out for fae-hunting, which I'd borrowed from a man who was probably dead. It didn't make for the most peaceful atmosphere.

And yet, for a couple hours squeezed in the backseat beside the young man I'd risked everything to keep alive, that space somehow felt cozy. Priya, my roommate and tentative friend, was humming cheerfully at the wheel. Darton's friends—Izzy at his other side and Keevan in the front—looked relaxed for pretty much the first time since we'd taken off on this chaotic road trip nearly three days ago.

Darton himself had his arm around my shoulders. I'd let myself lean against his well-muscled chest, where the rise and fall of his breath could remind me at regular intervals that for all the mistakes I might have made in the recent weeks, I'd done one thing right. I'd saved this incarnation of my king from a fate that might have destroyed his soul completely. And I'd wiped myself out rather thoroughly in the process, so this position was totally acceptable.

Even great wizards needed a break from time to time.

By all appearances, the guy who was also my liege liked taking my weight for a change.

Possibly I liked it too. The heat of his body seeped through his cotton shirt to the side of my face. He smelled like warm musk and the earth of the forest where we'd confronted our greatest enemy—of this life, at least. I closed my eyes, soaking it in.

"You should spend the night at my apartment again," I said. "Even with the mercenary gone, the glooms will be on the prowl for you. Tomorrow we can figure out the best long-term plan."

"That works for me." His thumb stroked over my hair where it lay against the nape of my neck, just barely skirting skin-to-skin contact. Just barely avoiding jostling loose from his mind another memory of his original life. I swallowed hard, resisting the urge to nestle even more closely against him.

The more memories he awakened, the easier the glooms could find him. I'd risked a lot when I'd thought we were pretty much goners anyway, but I was going to have to go back to my usual, more cautious ways now.

Priya pulled up by the campus gates for Keevan and Izzy, who lived in the residences—and didn't have to worry about the dark rabble cutting *their* lives short. Keevan gave us his usual rakish smile. "It's been real... and also completely bizarre. Thanks for a wild ride, Emma. And I'd better see you soon, Art." He saluted to Darton and me with one dark hand and hopped out.

Izzy squeezed Darton's arm. "If you need anything..." She glanced past him to where I'd straightened up. "Either of you. Just let me know, all right?"

There wasn't a whole lot an ordinary mortal could do

against a fae enemy, even a mindless scrap of darkness like a gloom, but then again, she and Keevan had proven themselves awfully useful in the past day. I wasn't going to forget that. I nodded.

"All right."

She swept her pale auburn waves back from her face and slipped out. The breeze made her loose trousers ripple around her legs like one of her usual flowing dresses as she walked into the lengthening shadows of the evening. She looked like a wavery, flighty girl, but that shell hid a will strong as steel.

"And onward," Priya said, spinning the wheel. Technically she was an ordinary mortal too, but raised by the light fae like a changeling, which one had to guess was why she'd taken our recent adventure so much more easily in stride.

As she turned onto our street, a sense of relief settled over me. Home. We were almost home. And in that home was my bed, where I could properly rest my weary body for the first time in far too many days. I started to sag into Darton's embrace again—and my gaze caught on a movement in the shadows.

I jerked upright. "Stop!"

Priya didn't ask questions. She hit the brake hard. I pressed my hand to the window, staring at the buildings beyond. "What—" Darton started, and I motioned him quiet.

We'd stopped just a couple doors down from our apartment building. In the shadows along the edges of its neighbors and between them, thicker patches of darkness were creeping. Glooms. Some of them drifted aimlessly, but others slunk through the shadows toward the same place we'd been headed. And the shade in front of our building was rippling with them. My heart sank.

"The apartment building is full of glooms."

"What?" Darton said. "Why would they go there?"

I bit my lip, my mind whirling. "The mercenary summoned them all back to him, but most of them hadn't made it close to the forest when we destroyed him. All that extra energy and sensitivity he was lending them died with him. So they must have gravitated toward the closest place where they sensed your essence, if they could sense it at all. And for a bunch of them, that was here. This is the last place you spent an extended amount of time before we took off."

He'd been in there several hours, sleeping on the couch and then having breakfast, just before the first wave of them outright attacked.

Darton stiffened. "Will some of them have gathered on campus then? Keevan—"

I shook my head. "Keevan will be fine." Even though he shared the dorm room where Darton had slept most other nights in the couple months before now. "They're not going to hurt anyone if they don't see any point in it."

"They tore up the campus plenty on Friday."

"Because the mercenary had them all stirred up, and because those people were between them and you." Because it was him they wanted—just him. Or rather, my king's soul lodged inside him.

"Speaking of which," Priya piped up, "it looks like we're not keeping quite a low enough profile."

She was right. A few of the glooms had changed direction. They wriggled along the edges of the shadows on the road just a few feet from the van. My body tensed.

The daylight was already fading. In a handful of minutes, it might be dark enough for them to make that final leap to us.

"Are we just going to run again?" Darton said. The frustration in his voice reverberated through me. I frowned at the creatures lurking beyond the window, and a sense of resolve rose up in my chest.

"No," I said. "The mercenary did us a favor. Now we've got a whole bunch of the local glooms collected together in one spot. I'm better off taking care of them all now rather than giving them time to scatter."

The fewer I left in our vicinity, the longer we could go before enough amassed to truly threaten Darton again.

I pushed open the door and stepped onto the pavement. Before I had a chance to tell him to stay in the van, Darton had shoved himself out the opposite door. "Darton," I said, but he didn't so much as hesitate as he strode around the van to join me.

I felt absolute loyalty to my king, but I could still note that at times he displayed an idiotic lack of self-preservation.

He halted in the thin sunlight beside me. The dagger one of the light fae had given me—the dagger I'd forgotten he'd been holding onto—glittered in his hand. He squinted at the shadows.

"I can see them, just a little," he said. A reminder that the glooms *were* still slightly super-powered, thanks not to the mercenary but to other dark stirrings I didn't like to think about. Otherwise only my fae-touched sight would have been able to make them out.

"And they can see *you*." I motioned at him to get back. The glooms were churning in the shadows now.

More were starting to seep from the edges of the windows and doors on our apartment building.

Swine crud. I darted to the young maple growing in a plot of soil set in the sidewalk, part of the town's initiative to "keep the streets green." Right now it could keep me supplied with fresh twigs so I could work my magic.

"So what are we going to do?" Darton said as I snapped off finger-lengths of wood from the lowest branch. "Are you sure you're up for another—"

The sun dipped just a sliver lower, and the nearest glooms sprang.

A cry broke from my mouth, but Darton's reflexes kicked in. His hand whipped through the air, slicing the fae dagger across the patches of darkness leaping at him. At the touch of its blade, they shattered into the air like burst balloons.

Darton stumbled backward with a rough inhale. "Okay," he said. "I guess I should be glad for all that fencing practice after all."

I wasn't sure if it was his time in fencing club or a deeper instinct that had guided his hand, but it didn't much matter now. More glooms were pouring out of the apartment building and rippling across the road. I waved Darton out of the way and smacked my palm against the trunk of the young maple.

"Sorry," I murmured to it. And then, to Darton, "Be ready to catch me." The last thing I needed was to split my head open on the sidewalk when I fainted. And I could already tell a faint lay in my future.

I closed my eyes, reaching my awareness into the tree, into all the living energy thrumming beneath its bark. The bright green pulse of it shimmered against my eyelids. I sucked in a breath, and yanked, hard, thrusting my other hand forward at the same moment.

"*Darkness begone,*" I called in the ancient tongue that was my first language.

The tree's life ripped through my body and shot out from my hand. It blazed across the street, searing through every gloom in its path. Searing through the walls of the buildings and on into the rooms and hallways, eating up the glooms there too.

Lights blinked out in apartment windows with the tinkling of popped bulbs. A startled yelp carried from the main doorway. A woman walking her dog stopped in her tracks, gaping at me, as the tree trunk turned cold and dead against my hand.

A chill rushed through me too. My head spun. My legs crumpled, and the world around me fell away into blackness. Yeah, I might have pushed myself a *tad* too far.

My eyes blinked open what felt like ages later, although judging from the faces leaning over mine— Darton's and Priya's—I hadn't been out for more than a couple minutes. They looked concerned but not panicked. Darton was gripping my shoulders. I staggered as I tried to push myself to my feet, and his hold tightened.

"Em," he said. "Take it easy."

"Are you okay, Emmaline?" Priya asked.

I swiped at the sweat that had beaded on my forehead and gathered myself. Not a single gloom remained around us that I could see. But we had a different sort of company now. Several of our neighbors had emerged from the apartment building. The woman with the dog was talking to one of the men and pointing at me.

I didn't normally blow my cover quite this blatantly.

In the last few days, stealth had mattered a lot less than survival. Concealment was another habit I was going to have to get back into.

"We'd better go," I said.

"Inside?" Priya said. "Where do you want to stash the van?"

I shook my head. "Not here. I mean, you should go home. You'll be fine. But even if I exterminated all the glooms that were in the apartment, they'll have left their mark all over the building. It's not safe for Darton anymore." I gave another heave and managed to balance on my legs this time. Which was a good thing, because apparently I was going to have to wait a while longer before I got that sleep I'd been looking forward to.

"Come on," I said to Darton, suppressing a yawn. "Back in the van. We'll grab a hotel room for the night and figure the rest out in the morning."

Because if I'd learned anything about the dark fae over the years, it was that there were always more.

2

I'd swear the beds in the hotel room we stepped into half an hour later were just begging to be collapsed into. Unfortunately, my work wasn't quite done.

I dragged in a lungful of air that smelled like ambiguous floral freshener. "Sit down," I said to Darton. "We've got to make you harder to find."

He sank onto the second bed. It was a good bed, no squeak or creak, just the faint rustle of the duvet. I'd chosen the hotel well, at least.

"I thought that the... glooms, and the other dark things, were only following us because of the mercenary," Darton said. "Now that he's gone—"

"No such luck. They're always drawn to you once you start waking up. They've gotten us plenty of other times before"—*every* other time before, to be exact—"without any of the higher fae involved. It just usually takes them longer to gather enough numbers to do real damage. I'd rather avoid them even knowing where to gather for as long as possible."

"How can you do that?"

I dropped the duffel I'd carried up from the van onto my bed and unzipped it. The twigs I'd gathered earlier today would still hold enough life to be useful. By tomorrow, I'd need a fresh stash.

I snapped several of them, letting loose the sharp green smell from within, and lay them around me on the floor.

"I can cast a spell that'll dampen the impressions your soul gives off. It should keep them from noticing you unless one brushes right past you. And there are ways we can make it less likely they'll do that too. Give me the dagger."

He handed it over. I ran my fingers over the polished wooden handle. The living energy sealed inside it wouldn't last forever, but at least it wouldn't drain simply with the passage of time, only through usage. It was the one helpful thing my light fae sort-of brethren had given me in this life.

I stepped closer to Darton and raised the blade to carefully slice off a small lock of his gold-blond hair. He looked up at me, but I didn't let myself meet his eyes. My skin was already tingling with the awareness of his presence, of the privacy this room afforded us. I couldn't afford those kinds of distractions.

My fingers closed over the golden strands I'd cut off. I brought the dagger to my palm and dug it into the flesh. Darton winced as the blood welled up.

"I hate seeing you do that, Emma."

"Says the guy who had me slice open his entire forearm a few hours ago." Remembering that moment, the rush of blood after, made my stomach go wobbly.

"Hey," he said. "I'm pretty sure that move saved the day."

It had. But I'd hated doing it all the same. I'd hated

knowing that if the gambit didn't work, if it didn't draw the dark fae mercenary into our trap, I'd just killed my king.

I sucked in my lower lip. "Well, this move might save us a whole bunch of days if I do it right. And doing it right needs some wizardly blood. Now stay still."

He sat stiffly upright as I squeezed the locks of his hair against the cut on my palm. Words in the old tongue rolled from my mouth in a steady whisper. I grabbed one of my few remaining wands—cedar, that was a good fit for my purpose—and dragged the tip across my bloody hand.

"I managed to get rid of some of the glooms with the dagger," Darton said. "Even though I don't have 'wizardly' anything. Maybe I should keep it on me from now on, in case you're not around to save my skin. Unless there's a better weapon I could use?"

"One brief battle and you're already wanting to upgrade your weaponry?" I teased. "If we have the time, I can try to make you something better. Just keep in mind we're talking a *lot* of time. It took me a couple years to get Excalibur ready."

He perked up at that. "Excalibur was real?"

I ignored his question as I drew a circle around him with the wand. "*Like mist conceal, and never reveal.*" I repeated the chant again and again, and finally pressed my palm, blood-smeared and hair-flecked, to Darton's forehead. He twitched, but managed to restrain a full flinch.

The threads of my magic wove around him. Around the soul I could feel like a pulse of energy beneath his skin. Another magic lingered there, tangled so deeply in his essence that I couldn't pick apart where one began and the other ended. But it was that spell that had kept returning him to life, in new bodies and new times, after each time the creatures of darkness had overcome us.

A shiver of some other sensation—thicker, almost stuttering—ran through the pulse. I'd felt it before, casting magic this closely on his past incarnations. My brow knit. That part, it didn't feel like my king. Was it some sort of damage that had come with the wound he'd been dealt, that would have caused his first and only death if I hadn't intervened?

If it was, it didn't really matter. It hadn't changed over the centuries, and as far as I could tell it hadn't harmed either of us in any way.

I let the chant fall from my lips again, and then I pulled back my hand. "You can wash off your forehead now. Sorry. I know it's kind of gross. And yes, there was a real Excalibur. I haven't paid enough attention to the more modern tales to know whether the reality would meet your expectations, though."

Darton got up and ambled over to the bathroom. He left the door open so we could keep talking.

"Did I really pull it from a stone?"

My lips twitched upward. "No. That's just fanciful thinking. I commissioned it from the best craftsman in the kingdom, and I worked magic over it for those two years until it was so attuned to your soul it was almost magic itself. When you held it, it was as if it was part of your living body, your life energy glowing right through it."

"Sounds pretty intense." Darton splashed water on his face. "I don't suppose we could pick *that* up for the next time the glooms come calling?"

My smile turned into a grimace. "No. It was lost. In all our early lives, I never got old enough to go looking for it properly, and by the time I did, I had no idea where it'd ended up. I've asked around among the light fae over the years, but no one's had a clue. At least not one they could be bothered to tell me."

"This isn't what you expected, is it?" he said, coming to the doorway. Damp strands of hair framed his handsome face. "From the spell you cast, when I was— when that really powerful dark fae tried to kill me. You wouldn't have wanted us to be stuck in some weird cycle of getting attacked by the glooms and the rest, dying and being reborn, over and over."

"No, I didn't." Suddenly I felt twice as exhausted as before. "I told you before, I only had a split second to act, before the Darkest One would have done even worse to you. All I know is I threw out all the magic I could summon with the intention of keeping you alive, keeping me with you so I could help you stay that way, and keeping the Darkest One as far off as I could manage. And I guess it did all those things. But... this isn't how I'd have wanted it to go."

It had been a very long fifteen hundred years, let's just say.

Darton rubbed his mouth. I was getting to know this version of my king, his quirks and habits, well enough to see whatever he was about to say mattered to him a lot.

"So is this what our lives will be from now on?" he said. "Running and hiding and fighting when we have to?" His voice came out strained.

Oh, my king. Oh, the young man carrying him. My stomach twisted.

If I'd been more careful last week, he might not have even started to awaken yet. He might have lived on in full, blissful ignorance for another year or more. I couldn't give that back to him, but I'd do whatever else I could.

"No," I said firmly. "You'll go back to classes tomorrow. I told you we'd figure out a more permanent solution, and I meant that. You should have a normal life... for as long as you can manage it. And I think we can manage it at least a little longer."

And maybe between guarding him and dealing with whatever glooms wandered our way, I'd finally find a way to untangle that hasty spell of centuries ago. To release us from the cycle of lives and deaths the Darkest One was bound up in too—without letting her go free.

Okay, so I'd been trying to do as much for most of those centuries and hadn't gotten close before, but it was at least *slightly* possible. A wizard was allowed a little hope.

The pressure of all my responsibilities settled over me. I couldn't restrain a yawn this time. My eyelids had started to droop. I might have swayed on my feet. Slightly.

Darton's expression softened. Gods, he could melt me from across the room with just one look like that.

"Get some sleep, Em," he said gently. "You've saved my hide at least three times in the last twenty-four hours. I think you've earned it."

"Well, if you're going to make it a direct order, my liege," I mumbled, and climbed onto the bed. I didn't bother with sheets or duvet. The second my head hit the pillow, I was out.

* * *

My king followed me into sleep. Somewhere in the depths of my slumber, a memory from our first life together swam up, vividly sharp.

The fire crackled in the hearth, the pungent scent of pine smoke drifting through the air of Arthur's bedchamber. The light flickered over the smooth-shaven face of the newly crowned king. He leaned forward in his brocaded chair and lifted the crown from his head. Holding it in his hands, he studied it as if he'd never looked at it before.

"Is everything all right, sire?" I ventured from where I sat on the other side of the hearth. Normally I wouldn't have been hesitant to speak. But up until five hours ago, I'd served a prince, not a king. And I'd never seen his expression quite like this. Set and yet somehow uncertain.

"What if I can't do it, Merlin?" he said, quiet but steady.

"Do what?" I said. "Order people around? Make sure those people have food and work and relatively few other people trying to kill them? Debate with the lords about how exactly they should do those things on their lands until your head aches? I'm pretty sure you've been doing all of that for a rather long time already."

A hint of a smile darted across his lips and was gone. "It's different. Before I was one of many voices. Now I'm the last one. The final decision-maker."

"Right. Because you had so little authority when you were just the crown heir. I wish you'd told me that earlier, so I could have ignored you when you dragged me on all those sodding horse rides."

He rolled his eyes at me, the least king-like gesture I could imagine. Yet somehow Arthur managed to make even that look regal. My pulse stuttered. Damn him.

No, damn my foolish heart.

He lowered his head to consider the crown again. "I just want to do right by them. I want to do right by all the people in this realm. What will happen to them if I fail as a king?"

I kicked out my legs and crossed my ankles as if this conversation was nothing more than shooting the breeze. "I suppose some other fellow will come along who wants to take on the job.

Hopefully one who's generous with his food and his wine."

Arthur shot me a look. "Are you implying I haven't been generous enough?"

"Of course not. You are exactly the king I came here to serve." I dug a twig from my pocket and cast its energy toward the dancing shadows along the wall. They shifted into human-like figures, bobbing their heads down in a bow. "And look, I've brought a whole bunch of minions who think you're the best thing since spoked wheels too."

This time, the smile that crossed his face stayed. "Merlin," he started.

"Sire," I said. "You were a great prince, and you'll be a greater king. Do you really think I would waste my talents around here if I didn't believe that?"

He chuckled, and the last of his tension left his shoulders. "No, I suppose not."

When he hefted himself to his feet, I stood as well, ready to take my leave. But instead of dismissing me immediately, Arthur moved toward me. He clasped my shoulder. The warmth of his hand bled through my tunic, and my breath caught.

"I'm still not sure how I was lucky enough to end up with you at my side," he said. "If I've been great, it's in large part thanks to you."

"I'll be sure to remind you of that the next time you propose we go riding somewhere," I tossed out, but the heady sensation in my chest had tightened into a knot.

I'd never told him the full story of why I'd sought him out. I didn't even know the full reason. But I knew my father had raised me for this purpose, to watch over Arthur, not just for the king's protection but for my people's as well.

He'd never said it outright, but I knew it all the same: Something about the man before me had made my father afraid.

3

Someone was shaking my shoulder. My eyes popped open, my fingers grasping instinctively for a twig, a wand—anything with power that might be in reach. All they caught on were the folds of the sheet now draped across my shoulders.

Darton was leaning over me. I pushed upright, shaking off the last shreds of sleep. "What's going on? Is there a gloom? Did something happen?"

"Hey," Darton said, raising his hands. "Everything's okay. My first class today starts at eleven. I thought it'd be nice to grab breakfast with you before I left. I wanted you to at least know I was heading out, anyway. We haven't had a chance to talk about what precautions you think I should be taking now and all that."

"Right." I blinked at the clock, which insisted it was quarter to ten—in the morning, obviously, given the bright autumn daylight streaming through the hotel room window. My head felt muggy, as if it'd filled with rain clouds while I slept. I rubbed my eyes. My mouth tasted like ash and sour wine, even though as far as I could recall I hadn't consumed either in a rather long time. "When did

I go to bed?"

"Like, seven last night." Darton frowned. "Should I have woken you up earlier? I didn't mean to throw you off somehow. It just seemed like you really needed the rest."

"No, no, it's okay. I'll be all right." My body was catching up after those three days of barely snatching more than a few hours rest here and there, not to mention the multiple intensive castings on top of that. I probably could have happily slept until *tomorrow* morning. But I wouldn't be much use to Darton unconscious.

"So you haven't seen anything at all that was unusual or made you concerned?" I checked.

Darton shook his head. Then he paused. "I did have a dream—one I think was actually a memory. I'm not sure if it meant anything significant."

"Well, now that you've mentioned it, you might as well tell me the whole thing."

He sat back on his own bed, his gaze going distant. "I was lying on... I guess a mat, in a big tent. And I had the most awful pain in my side. Not where the Darkest One—" He cut himself off with a gesture to indicate the spot below his rib cage where the greatest of the dark fae had dealt her would-be fatal wound. "Higher, just below my shoulder. Anyway, it burned like hell."

"If you were in a tent, it was probably a battle wound," I said. "In the last few years, one of our neighbors decided they liked what you'd done for your kingdom so much they wanted to take it for themselves. You were not on board with that idea. And you were right there with the army driving them back. You were never one to stand aside while others were fighting on your behalf."

Darton nodded. "You neither. You were there. I mean, as the Merlin before. You were chanting something that made the burning ease off. And you had some paste you mashed onto the spot—something to help it heal, I think. I'm not sure. I was kind of hazy by that point."

"Hmmm," I said. "That doesn't really narrow it down. You did have a habit of getting yourself injured alarmingly often during those battles. Probably because you were always running to the front of the fray with that sword I enchanted for you."

Darton's brow furrowed. "I think it must have been a really serious wound this time. You were... very upset. I swear you sounded like you were holding yourself back from crying at one point. Or maybe that was just in my head."

A lump rose in my throat. I could think of two or three times I'd felt that panicked over one of my king's injuries. I hadn't realized he'd ever noticed how frantic I got when I wasn't completely sure I had the skill to save him. He'd never mentioned it afterward. Never pointed out that my reaction was more intense than one would generally expect from an attending wizard patching up his liege. But then, we'd also been friends.

He'd been my only real friend. And more than that too. Had some of that other emotion shown through without me realizing?

I swallowed the lump and made myself shrug as if it wasn't of any significance. "Well," I said in my best flippant tone, "if you'd kicked the bucket on me, I'd have been out of a job. Finding another would have been incredibly inconvenient." My stomach gurgled. "And I think we'd better get that breakfast before *I* kick the bucket out of hunger. Just let me take a quick shower first. I'm wearing more of the road than I'd really prefer to."

It was more than breakfast I needed. I had to come up with some sort of plan. I stepped into the hotel bathroom's glass-walled shower stall and turned the water control to close to the hottest setting. The near-scalding water battered my skin. I scrubbed soap over it, my mind spinning off in other directions.

I had my standard techniques. The spells like the one I'd cast on Darton last night, or the salt boundaries I'd laid down before to alert me when a gloom came near. Simply staying near him, ready, as much as I could worked to a certain extent.

But those strategies had never been enough in the long run any life before. And I wasn't likely to make any progress on untangling the spell that both bound us in these repeating existences and drew the darkness back to Arthur's soul if I was standing guard over him every minute of the day.

My thoughts slipped to Jagger—the man who we'd ended up connecting with while fleeing from the dark fae mercenary. A man who'd hunted fae himself, at least the lesser sort. It was his van parked in the hotel's underground lot.

He'd blown up his entire home to kill off an onslaught of glooms and buy us the time to get out of there. We hadn't seen him since. I didn't see how he could have survived the explosion. It was hard for me to imagine the gruff, no-nonsense man with his silvery hair and face etched with scars giving up just like that, but maybe he hadn't seen it as giving up but giving over. His life for ours.

The thought made me uncomfortable. I turned off the water and grabbed one of the towels, directing my mind to more practical matters.

Jagger had given me some new ideas. Ones I hadn't considered, thanks to technology that grew by leaps and bounds while I was busy getting through yet another childhood. Solar panels could capture sunlight and contain it for at least a little while, to use as a weapon or as a shield. In a dire situation, we could make use of the flame throwers the van had come equipped with. I wasn't sure how I could adapt the fae hunters' science to Darton's everyday life, though.

The old ways might be old, but I knew them through and through. The mercenary had been a fluke. And now that our battle with *him* had destroyed a sizeable population of glooms and other shadow creatures, it might be months, even years, before enough amassed again to cause any real damage. We could start with the basics, and I'd build a consolidated strategy from there.

I was still mulling it over when I stepped back into the main room. I gave my hair one last swipe with the towel, tossed that onto the bed, and combed my fingers through the damp strands. Then I noticed the way Darton was looking at me.

He was sitting on the end of his bed, shoe in hand as if he'd been about to pull it on, but he'd frozen. His gaze was fixed on my face with an expression like he was surprised to see me. Like I hadn't been right here talking to him all of ten minutes ago.

"What?" I said, lowering my hands.

A hint of a flush crept into his cheeks. He lowered his eyes, but they leapt back up to me the second he spoke.

"You just—something about your hair, and maybe the light— You almost look like you. Like Merlin."

His voice came out low. Was I imagining it, or was there an almost *husky* note in it? As if he were pleased by what he saw?

The sound sent a tingle over my skin. It seeped right into my chest with a flutter of hope I should have suppressed. But I could also be idiotic at times, especially when it came to my king and my heart.

I took a step closer, tilting my head in whatever approximation of *coy* I was capable of, and let my own voice drop. "Do you like that?"

Darton blinked. For a split-second, I really thought he was going to reach for me, grasp my hand and tug me to him the way he had more than once in the last few days, with desire hazing his eyes. Then he rubbed his mouth and really looked away, with a muffled laugh.

"It wouldn't make much sense if I did. You were a *guy* back then."

The words raked through me, scraping open a scabbed over pain I really should have left alone. I sucked in a tight breath and formed some manner of smile.

It wasn't only the rejection, although that was the sharpest part of the hurt. Hearing him say those words rubbed me as wrong as if he'd said I'd been a genius horseman or a force of darkness. I hadn't felt particularly like a "guy" back then, any more than I felt particularly like a woman now. I was Merlin. This body's parts or that one's, it wasn't of much consequence to me.

But this wasn't the time of a debate on that matter. I wasn't sure my king would ever understand. *He* was too solidly a man.

A man who had clear tastes and preferences.

"I was *me*," I said simply, and moved to my duffel bag. The sting of humiliation kept prickling through my chest. I dug out my last wands and transferred them into the backpack where I could keep them more easily at hand once we left the room. I'd look for a tree or a shrub to claim some fresh twigs from on our way out. And sometime very soon I'd need to make a visit to my storage locker, although that too was becoming depleted of supplies much more quickly than I'd prefer.

Thank the light, Darton didn't push the subject. He watched me in contemplative silence. His phone pinged with an alert, and he picked it up.

I hefted the backpack over my shoulders. I'd have to keep a proper distance from him from here on. In the last couple days, with our next death nipping at our heels, I'd let my sense of caution slip. What did it matter if he woke up a little, if my heart broke a little, if we were going to die an hour later anyway?

I'd given in to the want in his eyes and his voice. We'd kissed, we'd touched—we might have done more if those early memories hadn't thrown him off course every time the skin-to-skin contact had continued more than a few minutes.

Thank the light for *that*. Because we weren't dying, not yet. I could control myself. I'd done it before, if not always *well*.

"Who is it?" I asked. A report from Izzy or Keevan, maybe? Darton had already typed out a response to the texts.

"My little sister," he said, with surprise and clear affection. "Asking for tips for her college applications.

And she wants to come down here to visit and check out the campus."

4

"So this barrage of glooms just never stops?" Izzy said. "They keep coming after Darton—Arthur—you know, over and over, until..."

She trailed off uncertainly beside me as I twitched my wand toward another meandering gloom. "*Darkness begone*," I murmured.

A magical spark ate away the scrap of darkness, leaving nothing.

Keevan stood a little ahead of me, and Priya had paused at my other side. I'd found a chunk of time in the middle of the day when they were all free, and now they were rearranging themselves around me as we patrolled the campus, blocking my wizardly activities from view so I didn't cause another public stir.

The breeze whipped around us as I scanned the grounds. The chill in it stung my cheeks. By all appearances, we'd cleared out the central square of any remnants of the mercenary's dark forces.

"Yeah," I said. "But reducing the gloom population buys us more time. We just want to make sure none of that population runs into Darton first."

I directed us toward the athletic fields. Technically *I* was supposed to be in class, but my Organic Chemistry lab didn't feel particularly pressing when various glooms were still drifting around campus. The fresh alert boundaries I'd laid down this morning weren't going to give me any warning of dark creatures already within them.

"That's where the cleanup crew comes in." Keevan rubbed his hands together. "Is it just glooms, or are there more of those weird shadow animal things around too?"

I couldn't tell whether the thought made him eager or nervous. Maybe a little of both. "There aren't so many of those in the world in the first place. And they're more averse to hanging out around people when they aren't... motivated to do so. They probably wandered back to their original haunts as soon as the mercenary stopped pressing them."

A shadowy form wriggled through the corner of my vision. I corrected myself. "Most of them, anyway. Over here."

My grip on my wand tightened. I strode toward the snake-like creature of darkness, gathering the life energy inside me too. Exterminating the bigger beasties took more magic than the glooms. I *really* needed to get back to my storage locker and retrieve more of my stashed wands.

How many did I even have left there? I'd burned through more in the last week than in at least five past lives before now. But it had been worth it. My king and I were still here.

And being mildly tired and stressed about supplies beat fleeing for our lives any day.

"*Darkness begone,*" I muttered at the shadowy snake, pushing an extra umph of energy through my wand. The beastie disintegrated before it could slither around the corner of the building it'd been hugging—and so did the wand. Hog's balls. I wiped the grit from my hand onto my jeans and reached for another.

My last one. After this, until I made it to my storage locker, I'd be relying on scavenging living wood from the local trees.

Izzy's head twitched. "There's something," she said, pointing with her chin.

There was. Another gloom was skirting the stands by the football field. She'd noticed it from twenty feet away. My gut clenched as we headed over.

Priya was tracking it with her gaze. "You can still see them too?" I said to her.

She shrugged. "I could always see them a bit. Just, like, a sense of them—you couldn't really call it *seeing*. I must have picked up a sensitivity growing up in the enclave."

With all those light fae around her. That did make sense.

"The feeling's definitely gotten more muted since we got rid of the mercenary," she added. I guessed it wasn't too hard for her to figure out what I was worrying about. "And it doesn't look as if anyone else is noticing them."

A couple of freshmen strolled right past the gloom without a flinch, even when it darted into the girl's shadow to trail along behind them. I flicked my wand toward it before they carried it any farther away. A couple of whispered words, and it was gone.

The tension in my gut remained. "Can *you* see them at all now?" I asked Keevan.

We started to circle the stands so I could check the

shade beneath them for hints of movement. Keevan cocked his head. "Only a bit. Like, if you point one out, and I focus really hard, I can get a sense of the shape of it. So maybe I always could have and I just never knew to try before." He nudged Izzy with his elbow. "Izzy's always been the sharpest one in our bunch."

Izzy rolled her eyes. "I don't remember noticing them before you showed up, Emma. But I guess maybe I wouldn't have made the connection. The first few times I got a sense of one, it was just a shadow that seemed *off* somehow, but I couldn't explain why."

I didn't know whether that should reassure me or not. She didn't seem to have any trouble identifying the things now. She *had* been burned by one in our earlier travels. I'd healed the wound, but maybe the close contact had increased her sensitivity. Or was it simply what I least wanted to believe—that a different dark force was now lending them power?

"Don't sell yourself short," Keevan said lightly, grinning at Izzy. "I was going around without *any* clue there were little bits of darkness coming after Darton."

"I don't think a talent for noticing dark faerie things is going to do me a whole lot of good anywhere else," Izzy replied.

"Oh, you never know. You could carve out a new little niche for yourself."

Izzy shook her head with a laugh. Keevan's grin widened, his eyes so bright you'd have thought it made his whole day to have amused her. He kept watching her, his normally jaunty expression turning almost tender, when she turned to make some comment to Priya. I glanced from him to Izzy as the realization settled over me.

Oh. How had I managed not to see *that* all this time?

To be fair, I'd been rather preoccupied with the whole not-getting-killed thing for most of the time I'd been around the two of them. And it didn't look as if Izzy had noticed the shade of longing in Keevan's expression either. I guessed her excuse was still being hung up on Darton. Not that I could blame her there.

"What's the sack for?" she said to me then, startling me out of my speculations. My fingers had twisted into the fabric of the empty, herb-rubbed bag I'd been carrying under my arm. I forced them to relax.

"If my plan works out, it'll be for containing one of the glooms. When we've pretty much cleared the campus, I'm going to bag one of the last ones. They're useful for testing spells on."

Keevan perked up. "Spells for destroying dark fae?"

"Spells for binding them," I said. "If I break the spell I cast way back when that's kept the whole dying and being reborn cycle going, Darton—and I—could live a normal life with what we've got now. But that magic has also been keeping the very powerful dark fae who tried to kill him imprisoned where she can't hurt us or anyone else."

"So if you free the two of you, you free her too," Priya filled in.

"Right. And then even if removing the spell meant the glooms weren't drawn to him anymore, which I'm not sure of, she'd probably pick up right where she left off." I grimace. "I need to come up with a spell that'll keep her bound without our souls being tied up in it. But we're talking about a fae tens of times more powerful than that mercenary we only barely managed to stop. It's not easy."

"And you can't just adapt the original spell?" Izzy said. "I guess you'd have done that already if you could."

"Yeah." It seemed easier not to mention that I wasn't entirely sure how I'd cast that spell in the first place. It certainly hadn't turned out the way I'd been imagining in my surge of panic as I'd raced to my king's side all those years ago. "I'll just need a place to keep my test subject. I don't really want to be keeping a gloom anywhere near Darton."

If one of my experiments failed and the vermin got a taste of him during its escape, we'd have a new onslaught on our doorstep in days.

Keevan rubbed his angular jaw. "Can't you stash it in that dorm room you're going to be squatting in?"

Before everything had gone to hell last week, I'd found a room in Darton and Keevan's residence building that had been left vacant while waiting on repairs and magically taken it off campus records so I could use it for myself. It meant I'd be closer on hand if something went wrong in the night, but—

"That's still closer than I feel comfortable with. I don't want to take any chances."

"Hmm. What you need is a place like Jagger's."

He waggled his eyebrows as he said it, but it wasn't actually a bad idea. Jagger's home had been a fortress against the dark fae: set apart from anything that cast a shadow, drawing all its power from solar panels, bordered by gas jets that could burn off any of the dark rabble that approached it. Forget experimental glooms—if I could stash *Darton* away someplace like that...

No. For one thing, even Jagger's setup hadn't stopped the dark rabble when they'd been stirred up enough. And more importantly, there was no way Darton was agreeing to that big a disruption of his life. I was supposed to be helping him get back to normal, at least for a little while.

"You could keep it in your old room in our apartment," Priya said. "I don't mind taking on a new roommate."

My lips quirked up, but I shot her a questioning look. "Are you sure?"

She waved off my concern. "You said you'll still pay your half of the rent, after all. I can keep an eye on it. I'll be happy to help."

Some of the tension inside me loosened. One of the biggest ways this life differed from most of the ones before: I had actual friends this time around. Friends who really did want to help. And maybe the circumstances Darton and I were facing now weren't all that different from what they'd been before the mercenary. I'd brought us back to baseline, hadn't I? Which might be as close to normal as we could ever get.

No more glooms lurked under the bleachers. I zapped away a couple we came across lingering near the campus theater building where Darton and I had taken a stand at the start of this whole mess, but it was looking as if the pickings were getting thin. Good. I was more than ready to be done with them.

"Loner at ten o'clock," Priya said, motioning to a patch of darkness wriggling along the hedge by the horticulture department's garden.

The last time I'd been out this way, a bunch of hacky sack players had been using the garden as a playing field. Now that stretch of autumn-shriveled greenery was empty except for the gloom and a guy with hunched shoulders cutting through—late for class, based on his hurry. I veered a little to the right so he could pass before I got down to business.

He ducked through a gap in the hedge, swung left— and hesitated.

His whole body stiffened for a second, his gaze fixed on the spot where the gloom was lurking. My skin went cold. His brow knit. He blinked, and then shook his head and hustled on. I watched him go, my spirits sinking.

It wasn't just Priya and Izzy. It wasn't just sensitivity brought on by experience. That guy had no connection to the fae at all, no reason to be "sensitive" to their kind. The gloom should have been completely imperceptible to him. And yet it had clearly drawn his attention.

"He didn't really see it," Priya said. "He got an impression, but not enough to be sure of himself."

"Small comfort," I muttered. It didn't matter what about the gloom had caught his eye, only that it had. And I couldn't blame that fact on the mercenary's powers now.

I tugged the sack out from under my arm. I might need that new binding spell for more than just creating a more stable life for me and my king. The mercenary had sensed the Darkest One's intentions. With each new piece of evidence, I couldn't ignore what my instincts were telling me. Even with our souls still bound, she was stirring. Which meant she might break free on her timetable, not mine.

"Okay," I said, shaking the bag open. "This one I'm taking with me."

5

Just to be clear, I loved my parents, even if they were only the most recent set in a long line spanning centuries. They'd given me my space when I'd needed it. They hadn't freaked out too much over all the quirks you'd expect to see from a child growing up with a knowledgeable wizardly soul merged with her body. They'd always shown they had my back when I needed them there. That being said, they sometimes had the worst timing ever.

My phone's ringtone jangled, and I scooped it up from the cafe table with a jerk. I didn't want to distract Darton from his little sister—or draw her attention to my presence watching over them. They were sitting on the other side of the campus cafe, but it wasn't as if I were invisible. Or inaudible.

"Hi, Mom," I said quietly.

"Hello, dear," Mom's warm voice carried through the line. "Is this a good time to talk? You sound a little strange."

"No, no, I'm fine." I cleared my throat. Darton hadn't even glanced over. That was good. He knew I was here, of course, but I'd rather he forgot I was as well as he could. He hadn't seen his sister since the summer, and a normal visit wouldn't include a wizard bodyguard hanging around. "I'm just doing some reading on campus. I don't want to disturb anyone talking too loud. What's up?"

"Oh, I texted you a question over the weekend and didn't hear back, so I wanted to make sure everything was okay over there."

She'd texted me? I must have missed it amid all the chaos. "I don't think I even got that message," I said. "What was the question?"

"I found a box of your old high school notebooks. I wanted to make sure you didn't have any use for them now before I put them in the recycling."

Darton's sister—Audrey, he'd said her name was—ducked her head as she giggled at something he'd said. She had her back mostly to me, but I'd seen enough to know they looked a lot the same. Her hair was a matching wavy golden blond, her figure tall and athletic. The jacket she was wearing proclaimed that she was a member of her high school track team.

Darton smiled back at her over his cappuccino. Then a woman brushed past the back of his chair, and he tensed as if restraining a flinch.

He'd been jumpy all day. Considering recent goings-on, I couldn't blame him for being a tad nervous about his sister's visit, but I'd hoped it might give him a welcome change of pace. A sense that things *could* go back to normal. I was here to make sure nothing got out of hand, after all. And I'd only seen a couple of lingering glooms since clearing the campus earlier that week.

"Don't worry about it," I told Mom. "I don't need that old school stuff anymore. Go ahead and get rid of them." Any notes I'd made that were of real importance, I had stashed either back at the apartment I'd shared with Priya or in my storage locker.

"All right," Mom said. "Sorry if I'm hovering a bit. I'm still getting used to you being so far away."

I smiled with a pang of bemused affection. "It's not like I visited more often when I was at Yale."

"No, but I could drive to see you in a few hours if I wanted to."

Thank the light she hadn't been able to just drop in to check up on me over the last week. Trying to explain even half of the stuff I'd been up to would have taken some major mental gymnastics.

"So are you going to tell me more about this boy?" she added.

My shoulders stiffened. My gaze leapt to Darton automatically. "Boy?"

"Don't pretend you don't know what I mean," she said in a teasing tone. "The last time we talked, you had to get off the phone because a boy was calling. You think I can't tell from your voice when it's someone important?"

Oh. I'd almost forgotten I'd used that excuse. I'd actually needed to get off the phone so I could run off to protect Darton from a rambling gloom. I rubbed my mouth, my chest constricting. My relationship with my fellow college student and long ago king was one more in the long list of things I couldn't talk to her about. That list was only going to keep getting longer now that my liege was waking.

"He's just a friend," I said. The standard stall.

"Hmm. Is that all you want him to be?"

"*Mom.*"

"It's just a question."

I rolled my eyes, but I couldn't help smiling again. It was such a regular, Mom-like thing to say. As if I *were* a regular college student making eyes at a cute classmate. "We'll see," I said. "I promise I'll tell you if anything major happens."

That doesn't involve magic, reincarnated souls, or faerie beings, I added as a silent addendum.

The waitress brought Darton and his sister the sandwiches and fries they'd ordered. When Mom said her good-bye, I settled in at my table for a long haul. My stomach gurgled. I should probably get myself something to eat too.

As I signaled a waiter, a familiar face appeared by the cafe window. Keevan raised his eyebrows at me, changed course, and strolled inside.

I suppressed a sigh as the lanky guy ambled over to my table. Keevan hadn't always been my biggest fan—he'd kind of outright blamed all the trouble we were in last week on me. But then I had been lying about quite a few things to him, so I guessed we were even there. And he'd helped plenty since then.

Keevan glanced over and noted Darton's presence before dropping into the chair across from me. "You look like you could use some company. Is this some super spy wizard stake-out?" He grinned.

"I'm just making sure Darton has nothing to worry about other than showing his sister around campus," I said. "He didn't exactly like the idea of her running into a bunch of glooms or worse."

"I thought we took care of all the glooms and other beasties on our patrol."

I shrugged. "We got most of them, at least. But, you know, he's pretty protective of Audrey."

Not that long ago, when we'd been getting to know each other—before he'd known who either of us really were—he'd told me the story of how he'd saved her from drowning in the family pool when he was nine. Dragged her out and performed CPR on her until she started breathing again. He'd thanked Boy Scout training for his quick thinking and the ability to pull it off, but I figured some credit should be given to Arthur's ingrained determination too.

I don't know how I'm ever going to do anything better than that, he'd said, talking about how aimless he'd been feeling in his life recently. My fingers curled around my coffee mug. We hadn't talked about those feelings since. Since he'd found out he probably had less than a couple years left of this life, because of the soul he was carrying and the dark forces intent on claiming it.

"So he asked you to put him on surveillance for the day?" Keevan said.

"Yeah. Did you figure I was just stalking him for fun?"

He spread his hands. "I don't know. *You're* pretty protective of *him*, in case you haven't noticed."

"For good reason," I muttered, and took a sip of my tea.

A bluster of autumn leaves gusted past the window near Darton. His arm jerked, knocking into his cup. Audrey's hand shot out. She managed to catch the glass just before it tipped over the edge of the table.

Darton laughed, making an awkward gesture as if joking about his clumsiness, but his sister's brow knit. If I could see the strain drawing lines at the corners of his mouth, she had to too.

Keevan's smile had turned crooked. "Aw, come on, you love it. Saving him, getting to be his defender. Don't tell me you don't."

"I don't love the fact that I need to." I sure as hell wished Darton could have relaxed right now. But then, we'd only been back for a few days. The truth was still sinking in.

"Fair." Keevan shook his head. "I really don't get the relationship you two have. It's like you're soul mates or something, but then at the same time you're... whoever you already were, right now. At least he is. Because he only just got onto the whole Arthur thing, right? You've known who you are all along."

I tensed again, despite my best efforts. "I have," I said. "But the kind of body, the kind of brain I'm in has some influence. I still had kid-like impulses when I was a kid and all that."

"Really? I would have liked to be around to see that."

Maybe you will, I stopped myself from saying. *If I don't come up with a brilliant solution to all our problems in the next year or two, we'll be dying and starting all over again. Although maybe the second part only if we're lucky, given how things have gone in this life so far.*

Keevan leaned his elbows onto the tabletop, looking over at Darton again. "It must be hard for you, huh? Even now. You know all this stuff that he's hardly even remembered yet."

"I'm kind of used to that part of the cycle."

"Yeah, but..." He turned his gleaming eyes on me. "It's not just about doing your job or whatever. You've got a personal stake. You haven't followed him around all this time, going through all those deaths, just 'cause you worked for him once upon a time."

Maybe he didn't know what a sore spot he was poking, but my hackles rose all the same. A retort fell out of my mouth before I'd had a chance to think it through. "And why do you follow Izzy around, Keevan?"

His mouth snapped shut. Oh, so there were ways of shutting him up. But I didn't feel particularly vindicated, watching the slump of his shoulders. Keevan and I had our differences, but he wasn't a bad guy. *He'd* only been looking out for Darton, in his own way.

"It's not that pathetic, is it?" he said hoarsely. "I don't—I mean, I try not to—"

"It's not," I broke in. "I didn't even notice until a couple days ago. I'm sorry. I shouldn't have brought it up."

He rubbed the back of his neck. "I guess I shouldn't have been hassling you about Art either."

"I get it," I said. "I know it's a weird situation. I'm not used to having to help people outside of it understand how it all works."

"Yeah." He looked at his hands and then back at me, his expression suddenly serious. "I've been glad when it's felt like there was something I could do that might make a difference. But I don't really know how I fit into his life anymore. How do you keep a friendship with someone who's... becoming someone else? Can you?"

I turned that question over in my head. "Who Darton is—his personality—he's always *been* Arthur. He's not becoming someone different, only realizing why he is who he is. Before, he just didn't know the history, why he felt certain ways. So he's not going to change that much."

But my throat had gone tight. *Who* Darton was might not change a whole lot, but his priorities had already taken a major shift. I didn't know how much longer there'd be room for friendship, honestly. I'd never been able to find much space for it in my own lives. And I had no idea how to tell Keevan that, or if I even should.

"I can't help thinking—" Keevan started, and a dark twitching caught my eye. My back went rigid. Keevan fell silent, following my gaze.

In the shadow under the order counter, a dark fae creature was creeping in Darton's direction. Its long, sinewy body and pointy head brought to mind a weasel—a big one. My hand dropped to my shoulder bag, to the wand I'd been carrying in there.

I hadn't gotten any warning. It must have already been within my protective salt lines. We'd missed this one in the other day's trawling of campus.

It was just the one, though, and it didn't look as if it had much sense of purpose. It was moving vaguely toward Darton, but it hadn't turned its head in his direction once. Maybe it simply sensed something potentially intriguing awaited in the room, with no real idea what.

I had time. I could do this slow and careful, with a minimum of disturbance.

"Keevan," I said, readying myself to stand, "could you—"

I meant to ask him to go over and say hi to Darton and his sister, so they'd be otherwise occupied while I dealt with the shadow vermin. But apparently Darton had been watching *me* more closely than I'd realized. Before I could even finish my sentence, his head jerked toward me and from there to the dark creature. Then he was pushing upright with a rasp of chair legs against linoleum.

"Art!" His name burst from my lips as I scrambled to my feet. He was already moving, heedless of my protest. The fae dagger I hadn't known he was keeping in such easy reach glinted in his grasp. He dodged the other diners and lunged down to slash the blade through the shadow creature's head.

I'd only managed to take a couple steps toward him when his blow hit. The creature shuddered and disintegrated around his strike. Darton straightened up, a breath stuttering out of his mouth.

His sister had gotten up too. Audrey stared at Darton, her face paling beneath her tan. Her gaze dropped to the knife.

"What are you doing, Darton?" she said. "What *is* that?"

Darton took in his sister's expression, and the determination etched on his face faltered. He jabbed the dagger into its sheath and shoved it in his pocket. I took another step toward them, my pulse thudding. Was there anything I could say that might reassure him or her or both of them?

Darton's gaze shot to me. His jaw tensed, and he gave me a brief shake of his head. One swift movement, and a sensation like clenching fingers squeezed around my heart.

He didn't want me getting involved. Did he think I'd make the situation even worse?

He hadn't even trusted me to take care of the creature for him.

Keevan came up beside me. Darton turned to his sister, touching her arm, saying something in a low voice.

She was frowning. Her chin trembled when she answered.

I could have calmed her, at very least. Suggested an alternate explanation for her brother's bizarre behavior. But even though Darton's mouth had twisted with guilt, he didn't look at me again. It was like he wanted to pretend I wasn't even there.

I'd wanted that, before. But I'd also wanted him to believe he could count on me.

"What's going on with Art?" Keevan said in a hushed voice.

"I don't know," I said.

Audrey strode off to the restrooms. As soon as the door closed behind her, I couldn't hang back anymore. I hurried to Darton's table. He'd sat back down, his shoulders slightly slumped.

I leaned over beside him. "What are you doing?" I demanded under my breath. "I was going to take care of the creature. That's what I'm here for."

Darton blinked up at me. Another flash of guilt passed through his eyes. But his mouth set.

"Then why hadn't you? You'd seen it, and you were still sitting there."

"It wasn't an urgent threat. I was getting ready to handle it in a way that wouldn't freak your sister out. Isn't that what you wanted?"

A choked laugh slipped out of his mouth. "I want to know she isn't going to get hurt a lot more than I'm worried about freaking her out."

"I wouldn't have let her—*or* you—get hurt."

He looked back at me steadily. His voice wasn't angry or accusing, just softly matter-of-fact. "How do you know that for sure? They got past you in the end all those lives before, didn't they?"

A chill settled over me. I'd *seen* in his jumpiness that he hadn't felt safe even with me here, even if I hadn't wanted to admit it.

Why should he trust me? Hanging around near him, laying down warning lines—those were all the same strategies I'd used in the past. In the past, when a fae mercenary had nonetheless managed to target him and nearly kill the both of us. And, as he'd rightly pointed out, in all the lives with all the deaths before that.

I'd been trying not to interfere too much, but *he* was going to screw up the normal life he wanted if I couldn't give him the confidence that I'd be ready when he needed me.

"I know," I said around the tightness in my throat. "I can do better this time. I'll show you."

6

I started to tense as I turned Jagger's van off the two-lane highway onto the local road that led to the construction site. I hadn't told Darton much about what to expect. Hadn't wanted to give him the wrong impression in either direction if I chose the wrong words.

He looked a little tense himself, but he straightened in anticipation when I turned again, onto the driveway. The fur ruff along the hood of his bomber jacket rustled against the seat. I studied his expression as he took in the view through the windshield.

The place wasn't much to look at yet—not that it was ever going to be a beauty of a house. I was going for function over style all the way down here. Construction tarp drifted across the unfinished walls of the single-story structure. They hissed in the breeze as we stepped out.

Darton tapped his foot against the sprawl of hard concrete. "This is an interesting take on lawns."

I glowered at him. "Grass makes shadows—shadows the dark rabble can hide in. We can't count on the desert heat baking the plant life away like Jagger could, so a concrete yard seemed like the safest bet."

I wasn't taking any chances there. The ground thirty

feet from the house on every side was solid, flat cement. A chalky smell hung in the cool air. The construction team had only just finished pouring it yesterday. Beyond the edge of the concrete stretched yellowed fields, nothing thick enough to provide a lot of shelter until they reached the farmhouses or the patch of forestland some half a mile away.

Darton turned, surveying the grounds. "How much of this land is yours?"

"Ours," I said automatically, even though technically I'd paid for it. But I'd kept my accounts, the ones my careful records and magical beacons led me back to life after life, mainly to fund whatever my king might need, so really the money was his as much as mine. I hadn't done much to earn it in over a century, other than let it sit and snowball with interest. "The full lot is about a couple square miles."

Darton gave me a startled look.

"It wasn't *that* expensive," I said. "Just some old fields no one had found much to do with in a while. I guess the soil isn't great for farming."

He shook his head and ambled over to the house. "I can't believe you pulled this all together so quickly."

I couldn't tell whether he was awed or uncomfortable. "Hey, after a little magical finessing at the permit office and double pay for the construction company, everyone was happy to lend a hand."

The corner of his mouth quirked up at my breezy tone. Okay, that seemed like a step in the right direction.

"I took a lot of inspiration from Jagger's house," I said. We stepped through the open doorframe. "The roof will be mounted with enough solar panels to keep us off the grid. We're in cell tower range, so no need for a home line anyway. And they've built in a similar trick with the gas fire along the walls. I had a tank installed to supply those pipes so we're not dependent on an external line."

We'd learned last time around that the dark rabble would dig right down to interfere with electricity and gas if they needed to.

The interior walls were finished. The first room we stepped into was an open concept living space, kitchen at one end and a big living room at the other. My hands twisted where I'd clasped them in front of me. "There'll be lots of room to have people over. I mean, anyone you feel comfortable inviting. Keevan and Izzy, at least, will understand."

Darton nodded. "It's a lot more space than the dorm room, that's for sure."

I still couldn't quite read his tone. He'd never have expected to end up moving a half hour outside of town into some crazy anti-fae house.

"I know it's not the most convenient change ever," I said. "But whenever you're here, you'll at least be able to relax. No gloom is going to get close enough to this place to sense your presence here, so they won't start being drawn into the area like they might be if you keep staying in the dorm. I can recast the dampening spell every morning before you head out."

"What's this?" Darton motioned to an interior door that already had a deadbolt mounted on it. A strong one.

"That's our dark rabble trap," I said. "If any of them *do* come calling and make it past the other protections, there's an opening that'll look like an easy way to slip in. But they'll end up dropping right into a little enclosure in there, where I've got solar-powered lights and lenses set up to blast them from all sides with concentrated sunlight."

He chuckled. "Whoever you got to draw up the plans for this place must have thought you were insane."

"I... might have used a little magical persuasion to get past that problem too." I nudged him on down the hall with my gloved hand. "This door leads to the garage, where we'll have the van ready to go in case things get dire. I'll make sure it's fully outfitted and gassed up at all times, so you'll have those protections on hand whenever we're on campus too. And these are the bedrooms."

I nudged open an interior door. Sunlight filtered through the translucent tarp that covered the spot where the far, exterior wall would be. The room was at least twice as big as the one Darton currently shared with Keevan. "Three of them, so you'll have space that's totally your own, and we'll have extra in case we have guests who need to stay over. They each have their own en suite bathroom."

"You didn't want to have to argue about who gets the first shower?" Darton suggested with a wry smile.

I elbowed him. "I figured you'd want some breathing room. Obviously it all looks pretty dull right now while it's empty. You can pick out whatever furniture you want. I'm happy to give you final say with the common areas too—I don't care much as long as there's something comfortable to sit on. And—"

"Em." Darton turned toward me, so close that all at once I couldn't breathe. It was just me and him in the hall, the wall at my back and him in front of me. The scent of him, citrus and earthy musk combined, washed away the chalky smell and the pinewood tang of the freshly cut wood. He touched my waist. The heat of his hand traveled through my sweater.

"You've gotten all this set up for me," he said. "Because I said you weren't doing enough to keep back the glooms?"

A lump rose in my throat. I clamped down on the urge to shift closer to him, to feel that warmth all through my body. "I should have made more changes earlier. I should have started working on something like this the moment we got back. There are other possibilities to protect you here, or when you're away from here, that I need to do more research on, but— We got a second chance. I'm not going to screw that up."

He bowed his head. His nose nearly brushed my forehead. My pulse hitched. "Darton."

"I wasn't really angry with you the other day. You know that, right?" He swallowed audibly. "I didn't mean to make you feel you weren't trying hard enough. I wouldn't be *alive* if it wasn't for you. I was just wound up—having Audrey there right after those things were raging all over campus—"

"It's okay," I said. "You were right. I don't want to ruin your life... but I've got to do everything I can to make sure you have one in the first place. And my old strategies only got us so far. I've got to use everything I can."

"Em." His voice dipped. "What about *your* life?"

A strained laugh tumbled out of me. "I can worry about that when I've fixed the mess *I* made."

"The mess you made that also kept me alive."

"In about the least practical way possible."

"I'm pretty sure it still counts." His thumb traced an arcing line across my side. An eager shiver ran over my skin in its wake. I clenched my fingers to stop them from reaching for him. He wanted Emma. He wanted the woman he saw when he looked at me right now. And he might not even have wanted her without the magical bond between our souls twining through his feelings.

He hadn't wanted Merlin, not like that. He didn't want *me*.

"Any way I can help," he said. "Anything I can do that lets *you* worry less, you have to tell me. I should be protecting myself at least as much as you are."

"That's not how this works, Art."

He caught my head as I started to shake it, his hand carefully touching only my hair. The gentle caress was still enough to send a flood of longing through me.

"The hardest thing," he said, "is going to be spending all those nights out here with you, and not even being able to kiss you."

"We talked about this," I said, trying to sound firm even though my will on this subject at this moment felt about as wobbly as Jell-O. "The more you wake up, the harder it'll be to mask who you are. Killing the mercenary bought us some time, but we've still got to be careful."

"The memories that came back to me before ended up helping us."

"Yeah, well, we can't assume we'd get that lucky again. And you'll keep remembering more on your own. There's just no good in speeding up the process."

He lowered his head until his breath tickled hot past my ear. "It's only if we literally touch, skin to skin, that it stirs up the memories, isn't it? There's no reason... that we couldn't..."

His thumb stroked higher, skimming the swell of my

breast through the fabric. My breath hitched. For a second I was caught up in the thought of all the things it was possible to do, possible to feel, without ever touching skin directly.

Then the image flashed through my mind of Darton in the hotel room, his incredulous expression when I'd asked if he liked being reminded of my original body.

I scooted to the side, away from him and his warmth. Darton's gaze followed me, his smile falling.

"I don't think that's a good idea," I said quickly. "It's too easy to get caught up in the moment, to forget what we're not supposed to be doing."

He inclined his head, accepting. But when he met my eyes again, his were searching.

"Are you sure that's all it is? If something else is wrong—if I've done something—"

But he hadn't. It wasn't wrong for him not to want all of me. Telling him how I felt... That would only lead to more pain for me and guilt for him. Neither of us needed that.

"No. It's just being careful." I forced a smile. Sod it. I should never have let us mess around as much as we already had, and then we wouldn't have even been having this conversation. "If I can finally get all that old magic sorted out, then we'll have no restrictions at all."

I meant to walk back to the open ground, where I'd be much less tempted to sway in my resolve. But I took all of three steps, and my vision fractured. My knees gave.

"Emma!" Darton shouted. That was the last thing I knew before my mind blinked away from him and the partly constructed house.

Streaks of shadows shot past my awareness. I

couldn't tell whether I was looking forward or up or down, only that I was tumbling in that direction with no way of stopping. The shadows parted around a dark pool surrounded by jagged gray-brown rock. Its surface churned with thicker shadows. My stomach lurched, and then I was plunging through it.

After the first shock of chilly rushing water, I fell away into an open space beneath. A space where a person could breathe, but I could sense with every fiber of my being that each breath would feel suffocating. As if the darkness gusting around me would fill my lungs if they'd been there with me, clog my throat. The edges of the shadows twisted into figures, faces, bits of scenery. They flicked out at me as my vision carried me onward.

A sense of recognition settled over me. I'd heard of this place. Hadn't ever been there—hadn't ever *wanted* to be—but the details matched. The question was, why had my clairvoyant impulses decided to take me on this little tour of dark spaces?

The question had barely flitted through my mind when I arrived at my answer. The vision spun me around. I felt as if I stumbled, although I had no limbs to stumble with. Then I was staring at a gleaming length of metal twined with fingers of shadow.

The vibrations of magic woven into the sword's core tingled over me. I'd have recognized it from that even if the binding on the grip, the touch of filigree on the hilt, hadn't jolted my memory. My awareness reached for it instinctively—

—and I jerked awake on the newly sanded floorboards in the unfinished house. My head was resting on Darton's knee. He exhaled in a shaky rush as I pushed upright. I stopped, one hand braced against the floor, the other pressed to my forehead. The wave of dizziness rose and ebbed.

"Are you okay?" Darton said. "You weren't even—at least, it didn't look like you were doing any magic, and out of nowhere you just... collapsed."

I rubbed my eyes. The image of the sword was still dancing behind them. "I had a vision. They come like that sometimes. No hello and how are you first. Not much of a good-bye either."

"Like the vision that told you to switch colleges so you'd bump into me."

I nodded.

He studied me. "What did you see this time? Do we need to be worried?"

I must have looked bad. I closed my eyes and opened them again, and managed to get to my feet. "No," I said. "Actually, in some ways it's good. I know where your sword is now."

"My sword... Excalibur?" He leapt up after me. "We can go get it then. It'll be one more way to defend ourselves."

"Ah, well, it's a little more complicated than that. The place where I saw it, as far as I know it's back in Britain. And I'm not exactly sure where in Britain it is. What I do know is it's not any place a person generally wants to go. It's..." I hesitated. "Imagine that all the nightmares you ever dreamt decided to start a club where they shared tips on the best ways to torment you. That's not really a place you'd want to hang out for any amount of time."

"Oh." Darton couldn't disguise the disappointment in his voice. "Then we're just going to leave it there?"

"I don't know." I grimaced. "When I get a vision, it's usually telling me something I need to know."

What the hell was coming for us now, that we'd need Arthur's soul-bound sword to get us through it?

7

I stopped by the door to the dorm room I'd taken over and cast a quick distraction spell on myself. Tweaking the school records bought me a lot of wiggle room, but I wasn't going to get away with squatting up here for very long if students started noticing me coming and going. I rolled the stiffness out of my shoulders, grimacing at the air mattress I'd been sleeping on.

Just a couple more days, and the new house would be finished. Then I could sleep on a proper bed—in a room that didn't have a half-a-foot-deep hole in the wall from some party boy on a bender.

The bag of salt I was carrying hadn't alerted me to any dark rabble entering the building during the night. Still, the back of my neck prickled as I headed down the residence building's stairs to Darton's floor. I had enough protections on and around this place that I should have known minutes before anything with malicious intentions got close to him... but it was hard to feel completely certain of his safety before I had him in my sight.

No one gave me a second glance as I emerged from the stairwell. Exactly as I liked it. The distraction spell itched at my skin, but I left it on. I didn't want anyone noticing me following Darton either. *He* knew I'd be keeping an eye on him, but none of the other students would realize my stalking was sanctioned.

Bodies jostled around me, dodging me without taking note of me on any conscious level. The hall smelled like clashing perfumes and laundry someone *really* needed to take home to their parents' washing machine. My nose wrinkled. I wasn't going to miss this aspect of dorm life either.

Down the hall, Darton emerged from his room. Keevan stepped out behind him. The rakish guy made a sweeping gesture with his hand, teeth flashing bright on his dark brown face, and Darton started laughing. He gave his friend's shoulder a playful shove.

A twinge of fondness ran through me, watching the two of them. Watching Darton looking like a regular college guy. Then my stomach twisted. There wasn't going to be any more early morning teasing once we moved into the new house, at least not between him and Keevan.

Well, they'd have lots of other time to horse around. And it wasn't as if Darton had a problem with my company. His gaze slid past his friend and found mine amid the dorm hall chaos. Even with the spell, his soul knew mine well enough to spot me. He smiled, and the ache in my stomach dissolved.

They headed for the main doors, and I ambled after them, leaving plenty of distance. Darton's morning Law and Political Theory seminar was at the same time as my Developmental Biology lecture, so after I'd seen him into that building safely, I might actually continue my own studies today.

I wasn't the only person who knew Darton's schedule by heart. Izzy was standing near the bike rack just outside, a wool jacket buttoned over her typical airy cotton dress and her pale auburn hair drifting with the breeze. She waved to the guys, but to my surprise, her gaze slipped past them, searching.

For me? I muttered under my breath to disperse the distraction spell, and her eyes brightened. She moved to fall into step with me as the boys continued across campus.

"Hi, Emma." Her brow knit. "It is okay to keep calling you that name, right?"

"After twenty years of hearing it, it feels just as much mine as the original one. Don't worry about it." I glanced sideways at her. The furrow between her thin eyebrows hadn't left. "What's wrong?"

"I..." She rubbed her mouth, her head dipping down. "I'm probably just being silly. But after everything this weekend..."

"It's fine," I said. "Whatever it is, I want to know. And even if it's silly, I promise not to tell you I think so."

Her lips twitched with a faint smile. "Okay. It's just that I saw this guy last night. There wasn't anything *obviously* strange about him. He was, like, normal height, normal build, normal brown hair, normal clothes, you know. But when I looked at him, I got this uncomfortable feeling. A lot like the feeling when my eyes catch on one of those glooms."

A chill traced down my spine. "You saw him *here*? Around the college?"

"No." She shook her head firmly. "I was out at a restaurant on the other side of town with some friends. I saw him standing across the street when we were waiting for the taxi to get home. And that was all he was doing—just standing. I might just be extra jumpy. It was late. Lots of regular shadows." A nervous giggle slipped out of her.

"Did he do anything at all while you were there?"

"No. Nothing weird. He stood there for a minute like he'd stopped to think about something, and then he walked off. I tried to act like I hadn't even noticed him—no one else did—but I don't know if he realized he'd bothered me." She looked up. "Do you think he's someone we'd need to worry about?"

"From what you've said, the only thing I'm concerned about is the vibe you got from him. But I'd have to see him myself to know for sure." I sucked in a breath. "If he gave you that feeling, it *could* have been a dark fae. And obviously we don't want another one of those lurking around here. I'll see what I can find out. Thank you for telling me."

"I thought you should know." She brushed her hair back from her face. "I've got to get to class. If I see anything else—"

"Let me know, right away," I said with a nod. "Text me if you're not sure where I am."

She meandered off down one of the side paths. I continued trailing after Darton, who'd parted ways with Keevan while I'd talked to Izzy.

My hand dropped to the salt pouch in my pocket. The lines I'd laid down across and around campus should have alerted me if even a gloom had passed over them, let alone a full dark fae. I closed my fingers around the pouch. My awareness drifted into the tendrils of magic between the salt there and the crushed crystals of it scattered along the ground in every direction.

The lines lit up in my mind—a circle around the residence building, an extra sprinkling along the border of Darton's room, wider circles around the core of the campus, the outer buildings, the farthest edges of the college grounds. They all shone with power, unbroken. No, nothing had passed this way without my knowing.

Maybe it really was just Izzy's nerves getting the best of her. But I didn't feel comfortable counting on that.

Darton disappeared into his seminar room. I hesitated outside. Then I turned and headed in the direction of the science buildings—but not to go to my lecture.

I'd spent some time examining the physics course offerings in the last few days. There was a class on electromagnetics right now I'd been considering sitting in on. With Izzy's news, that course of action suddenly felt a lot more urgent than keeping my grades up.

Thankfully, it was a big class. I slipped in just as the professor moved to the lectern and nabbed a seat right at the back. As her staccato voice pealed through the room, I dug out a notebook and pen.

Jagger and his internet buddies had come up with strategies for tackling the dark rabble that had never occurred to me. For all I knew, they hadn't taken things far enough. Simply combining my magic with sunlight and lenses had allowed us to overcome the fae mercenary. If learning a little physics would give me more options— better options—I'd switch majors in a heartbeat.

Maybe I should have started with a more beginner level course. I hadn't studied physics since high school, and some of the professor's talk about voltages and directionality went over my head. Still, I dutifully jotted down every term and idea that sounded like it might pack a punch. I could look up simpler explanations later.

A manmade current shouldn't affect the dark rabble directly, but if I could figure out how to turn it into natural energy without draining my own power converting it... I really should have paid more attention to this side of science before.

Machines and electronics with their orderly circuitry had always given the light fae side of me a vague discomfort. They seemed much more to the tastes of the dark realm. But it was hard to picture a sizzling current of electricity and not see an element of chaos there. My fault for letting those old prejudices divert me.

By the time the lecture finished, my head felt heavy with unfamiliar concepts. I'd filled five pages with my messy scrawl. Well, that was plenty of homework for the day.

I ducked out ahead of the main rush of students, hurried for the entrance—and almost ran right into my Organic Chemistry professor coming out of an office.

Professor Kapoor stepped back with an automatic apology. Then his gaze focused on my face. His eyebrows drew together as he realized he knew me. "Emma."

"Professor." I bobbed my head, wondering if I could get away with making a run for the doors. I had the feeling that would cause more problems than it fixed.

"I haven't seen you in a couple weeks now," he said. "I have to admit I've been concerned. We're getting into the core material for finals—you've missed a key lab—"

"I know," I said quickly. "I'm really sorry. I just— Things have come up. Ah, family things." That was almost true. At this point my king was more my family than anyone else. "I had to take some time away."

"I can make some allowances for extenuating circumstances, but only if I'm aware of them. Do you have a moment to talk now? I may be able to arrange a repeat of the lab, and there are readings you'll want to get to as soon as possible."

He motioned for me to follow him, but my legs locked in place. Dread squeezed around my gut.

Who was I kidding? Sure, I could go along with him and pretend my absence had been a temporary anomaly. But I'd be wasting his time and mine, wouldn't I?

I knew my priorities had shifted. I couldn't be attending labs and doing course readings when I had an entirely new field of study to master, glooms to fend off, a possible dark fae to watch out for... And those priorities weren't ever going to shift back, not unless I failed and started over in a whole new life, waiting for the moment I encountered my king again.

Darton might be able to hold onto most of his normal life for a while longer, but my "normal" life—it was over. It had been over, really, the instant I'd set eyes on him in fencing club. There was no use in denying that fact.

I swallowed hard. "I really enjoyed your class, Dr. Kapoor," I said. "But I'm actually—I'm just here tying up some loose ends. Unfortunately I won't be attending any classes anymore."

Professor Kapoor's eyes widened. "It's okay, really," I said before he could start in on any questioning. "I'll pick up my studies again when I have the chance." *Most likely, in a whole new life and body, but let's not get into that.* Then I turned heel and took off. As long as I kept my gaze forward, nothing I lost could bother me too much.

8

The paved yard around the new house might not have been pretty, but it made a decent training ground.

"You want to keep your body behind the dagger as much as possible." I moved into a defensive stance for Darton to model, my sneakers rasping over the concrete. The pose wasn't that different from one I might have used while sparring in fencing club—other than my current weapon was a chopstick. "To make it as difficult as possible for them to get close to anything except the blade. One or two glooms on their own won't be able to do you much damage, if they even try to. But if they get a taste of your presence, we'll have them calling a whole new horde down on us in no time."

"Right," Darton said. "No getting touchy-feely with the shadow creatures."

I rolled my eyes at him, and he grinned. With a gloved hand, I pushed his arm so he bent his elbow. I was keeping as much of *my* body covered as possible to avoid any "touchy-feely" between us. Not that every inch of my skin wasn't fully aware of exactly how close we were standing.

"Don't extend your arm all the way," I said. "You want to have the flexibility to jab a little farther if you need to."

Darton took a few experimental swipes with the light fae dagger. It flicked through the air, the silver blade gleaming in the late afternoon sunlight. He lowered his hand. "A dagger doesn't let you keep your enemy at much of a distance, does it? Is there any way you could enchant one of those fencing swords for me?"

"Oh, yeah, because you wouldn't draw *any* attention at all walking around campus brandishing an epee or a sabre."

He grimaced. "Point taken. I have gotten a few weird looks just from people noticing the dagger. It's hard to keep it totally out of sight."

"You shouldn't have fighting so much on your mind anyway," I said. "You're not equipped to really tackle any kind of fae creature. This practice is just to make sure you're as prepared as possible in an absolute emergency. Those things are magic, and it takes magic to really defend against them."

"Hence the request for magical weaponry. But I get it, I get it." Darton tucked the dagger back into his pocket. "I do feel better knowing I have *some* way of at least slowing those things down if I need to. I seem to remember I did a fair bit of fighting on my own, no magic involved, way back when, though—and I was pretty good at it too."

"Yeah, you were, I'll give you that. But those battles weren't against fae."

And in the later battles, he *had* had magic on his side, at least in his blade. Sometimes in other ways as well. A memory trickled up from one of those early skirmishes of

Arthur's rule, before the extended conflict had really weighed down on any of us. I let it wash over me.

I was hanging back from the main force of the fighting, as usual, next to my sack of freshly snapped sticks. Dragging the life energy from them one by one and letting them crumble into dust, I blinded that soldier with a flash of redirected sunlight, tangled this one's feet with a sudden eruption of grass, and set a group of them off balance with a gust of wind. My lungs strained with the effort, but I didn't hesitate for a second.

If I'd tried to outright kill any of the men, the energy that bent to my will would have recoiled. Setting them up for our soldiers to land their blows didn't offend my fae nature, though.

In the midst of a fray, I could always track exactly where my king was fighting. Excalibur gleamed with an unearthly light, brighter with the determination in Arthur's soul powering its swing. Man and weapon moved together as one being. He swung, sliced, and parried as if it weighed half what the huge broadsword truly did.

Shouts and clangs echoed across the field. Our men fell back, shields raised to fend off a shower of arrows. I grabbed a handful of sticks and whipped the projectiles aside with a cutting breeze.

Our enemies on the ground surged forward. One lunged with his spear at a solder who'd stumbled in his momentary retreat. The young man whipped up his arm, but his grasp on his short sword was wobbly. It fell from his hand when he blocked the first blow. The enemy soldier raised his weapon to strike again.

And Arthur was there. The spearhead glanced off Excalibur. The enemy soldier growled and spun around, thrusting his weapon toward my king's side. Arthur neatly batted the spear away, sidestepping—and opening his back to another soldier who'd just whirled toward him.

His name caught in my throat. I didn't have time to grasp more than the few remaining sticks still in my hands. 'Shove them, gone, away," I gasped out, and shoved my hands forward with all the energy in those sticks, wrenching more from within me.

A blast of air rammed into both of the soldiers swinging at Arthur. It propelled them right off their feet with a jerk. They hurtled through the air, disappearing among the trees where the archers were hiding.

The effort yanked at my soul. I teetered and almost fell, my vision hazing. Someone caught my arm. The medic who helped me tend to the injured after each battle had come up beside me.

"Merlin?" he said.

I shook my head, as much to clear it as to say I didn't need help. My legs steadied. I heaved a breath and snatched up another handful of sticks.

When we'd finally sent what remained of the enemy force running, I'd all but forgotten that moment of over-extending myself. My king hadn't.

"Merlin." Arthur grasped my narrow shoulder and spun me around. His tawny hair stuck up in sweaty tufts and dirt smudged his sunburned face, but even so, there wasn't much I'd rather have looked upon. Until I realized those bright blue eyes were narrowed with anger. And that the anger was aimed at me.

"I heard you almost fainted from a casting," he said, still holding me in place. "Right after the last volley of arrows."

"I'm fine," I said quickly. "I was fine."

"You nearly burned yourself out tossing the men I was fighting into the woods."

"I was fine," I repeated. "And I was saving your life, Your Highness. You're welcome."

His jaw clenched. "I didn't need saving, Merlin. I can handle myself. You're supposed to be looking out for everyone, not focusing your energy on me."

"And I was doing that almost the entire time. Forgive me from *preventing your imminent skewering when I had the chance."*

"I wouldn't have been skewered. I've already got a bloody enchanted sword, Merlin. What was the point of all the effort you put into that if you're not even going to let me use it when I need to? I can't lead these men if you're stepping in the way."

Ah. There was the heart of the matter. I should have known. Any inclination I'd had left to banter fled me. I touched Arthur's arm.

"I overreacted," I said. "I didn't have much time to think, and I used a lot more punch than the situation required. I apologize for that. But you've been getting plenty of use out of that sword of yours all the same, and having it doesn't mean you can be outright careless. You can't lead anyone if you're dead. It doesn't make you invincible."

His expression softened slightly. He sighed. "I know that, Merlin."

But I'd wondered if he really did. And now, watching Darton rest his palm against the hilt of the dagger, testing how quickly he could draw it, I was almost glad that damned sword was far away in the last place I'd ever want to pay a visit. It had been a great weapon, sure, but I didn't need my king getting ahead of himself in the confidence department. A tool was only as effective as the person wielding it.

An engine's growl carried across the fields. It was almost dinnertime.

A taxi turned up our drive and deposited Priya in the yard. She hustled over, hefting a grocery bag bulging with supplies for the meal we'd made plans to cook. Her eyes widened as she took in the house. The big white block of a building seemed to glow a bit even in the fading daylight.

I motioned her to the front door, Darton following us. "Come on in."

She stepped inside, gawking at everything. "Wow. You really decked the place out nice, Emmaline."

"I figured there were some ways I didn't want to imitate Jagger," I said. "If we could potentially end up holed up in here for a while, there's something to be said for comfort."

Darton and I had squabbled—mostly playfully—until we'd settled on a pair of plum leather sofas, an assortment of dark-stained wooden tables and cupboards, and wool rugs thick enough to dig one's toes into. The old-fashioned styling of the furniture didn't entirely match the house's modern design, but given that the people living here were two old souls in modern bodies, I couldn't say it wasn't fitting.

The aspect I enjoyed the least was the lack of windows—but light willing we wouldn't be in here much during daytime hours anyway. Priya peered up at the broad electric fixtures, which beamed thanks to our stored solar energy. "You copied his approach to lighting."

"Yeah, well, windows make for too easy an entry point for anything really determined. And the solar energy is fresh enough that these lights would put off any gloom, at least."

"Only glooms?"

I smiled. "We've got other methods for anything bigger. This place is both technologically and magically enhanced."

"You've got one up on Jagger there, then," Priya said. Her expression turned more serious. "It's too bad he didn't have any wizards around to make his place extra secure."

My chest tightened, thinking of the smoking ruin of

his house. "Yeah."

Darton leaned against the kitchen island, his pose casual but his gaze intent. "You said you need magic to really take on the dark fae. Couldn't you teach other people to cast spells and all that?"

He wasn't ready to let the idea of taking on the dark fae himself go yet, clearly. Could I teach people like him, he meant.

"What, open a wizarding school?" I teased. "No. It doesn't work that way. I can only work magic because I'm half fae. I was *born*—the first time—with the ability to bend the energy of life and light. Less ability, because of the human half. That's not something you can teach. At least not in any reasonable length of time. I think there have been people who've managed to reach some level of connection... but only after decades of concentrated study."

"Oh." His tone did only a passable job of hiding his disappointment.

"That's not completely true," Priya put in. "Anything living can use its *own* life energy, right? If it gets worked up enough or whatever. My fae guardians had stories about people or even animals pulling off some great magical feat by sacrificing their lives."

I looked at her balefully. "Yes. Technically, under the right circumstances and with the right mindset, you can turn your life into power if you get yourself killed. But since our main goal here is making sure Darton *doesn't* get killed, that's not really a strategy of much use to him."

She shrugged. "I was just being thorough."

I didn't think Darton needed any *more* self-sacrificing ideas getting into his head. He was frowning now, his gaze distant. "It's not a big deal," I told him. "You don't need to do magic. You've got me. That's the whole reason I'm here."

"It's not that." He rubbed his mouth. "I feel like I already knew that, about the sacrificing and the magic. But not from you—this you, anyway. I can't remember who told me, or when."

"It could have come up in some conversation in our first go-around. Don't worry about it. It doesn't help us anyway."

To my relief, Priya redirected the conversation. She took one more look around the room with a happy sigh. "Well, I'm definitely going to have to start visiting on a regular basis. Shall we get cooking?"

She dumped her bag on the kitchen island. I ambled over to join her, bringing up the recipe on my phone.

Darton peered at the bag's contents. "Need any help with dinner?"

I shooed him off. "I learned a very long time ago that kings and kitchens don't produce the greatest results. Or at least not this king." At his mock wounded look, I gave him a gentle shove. "Go relax. That's another skill you could use some practice at."

Darton pretended to huff, but a minute later he was sprawled on one of the sofas, channel surfing on the TV mounted over the fireplace. Priya and I got down to work, washing and peeling and dicing. As the frying pan sizzled and the smell of frying garlic and onion filled the air, I started to relax. I liked the house, but for the first time, it really felt like a home.

Maybe this new normal, one I could share with people who knew what I was and who I could trust with that knowledge, would be pretty good after all.

I got to float on that feeling for maybe five minutes. Then the pouch of salt in my pocket shuddered.

I froze with the spatula poised over the pan. Priya's head jerked around. "What?"

At her voice, Darton turned off the TV and sat up. I rested my hand over my pocket. The vibrations of the warning spell tickled through my palm.

It was the boundary around the edge of our property that had been tripped.

"Something's come into the yard," I said, my heart thudding. "Chances are it's just a wandering gloom. The outside lights should put it off."

"What should we do?" Darton asked.

"*You* don't do anything." The last thing I wanted was him charging out there hoping to play hero.

I waited, fingers still pressed to the pouch. The boundary would trigger again when whatever it was left. Or if it crossed the line I'd laid down just a few feet from the walls. The line it *shouldn't* be able to cross if it was only one of the dark rabble. But then, the rabble that had come at Jagger's house shouldn't have been able to hit him as hard as they had either.

The salt didn't stir. The hiss of the frying vegetables filled the room, no other sound breaking it. My hand tightened around the spatula. I offered the utensil to Priya.

"I think I'll take a quick look, send it on its—"

The salt all but jumped from its pouch, and a *clang* cut off my voice, reverberating through the walls. My pulse hiccupped. I spun around, my hand flying to the wand I'd stuffed in my back pocket. Darton sprang up, tensed.

"The sun trap," I said. "We caught something." I

strode to the hall. The way the trap worked, whatever it'd caught had probably already been burned away. But my stomach still knotted as I grasped the door handle.

Darton and Priya had followed me. "Stay back," I told Darton. "Let me take a look first."

He nodded, but he'd already drawn the fae dagger. I put my hand out to emphasis my request and tugged open the door.

My fingers slipped from the handle. I sucked in a breath, my jaw going slack.

The interior walls of the sun trap were completely reflective, to bounce the solar-cell light at any intruder that triggered it. But the material I'd picked worked like a one-way mirror—from the outside, I could see in. And what I saw standing in that octagonal case wasn't a gloom or a shadow creature but a man.

No, not a man. A dark fae. Light blazed at him from all sides, making him twitch and shiver. His thin lips had drawn back in a grimace. His dun brown hair stood on end, and his knobby fingers dug into his arms where he'd hugged them over his chest. And clots of shadow churned in his hooded eyes.

Those eyes looked straight at me, even though he shouldn't have been able to see me through his side of the wall. They tracked me as I pushed myself to step inside. My heart battered my ribs. The trap hadn't killed him yet, but it was clearly torturing him. The thought darted through my mind to set him free, send him off with this as a warning.

But I couldn't shut off the trap without giving him full freedom to use his power. And if his intention had been honorable, presumably he'd have knocked on the door rather than trying to sneak his way in.

His face contorted further. The wand wavered in my hand.

He opened his mouth, and a snarl of a voice carried through the wall. "Merlin. I knew it was you."

"What the hell?" Darton said. He and Priya had edged through the door I'd left open in my shock. The dark fae cut himself off with a low muttering I couldn't make out. A casting. *No.* My arm jerked up. "*Blaze, burn, sear him clean,*" I shouted.

My will and the wand wrenched at the energy in the solar cells. I caught a glimpse of the dark fae grinning a twisted grin at me. Then light flared inside the trap, so brilliant I was blinded. My vision stuttered. The wand crumbled. My legs wobbled as I gave over a fragment of my own life to the spell.

The light faded, the panels on the trap walls cutting out. Only the regular fixture on the ceiling kept glowing.

Nothing remained in the trap except a mound of sunken flesh and fabric.

9

The lights in the house's common room beamed over me just as brightly as before, but the warmth didn't penetrate my skin. The smell of our unfinished dinner only made my stomach ache. I paced from the kitchen island to the nearer sofa and back, passing the spare wand I'd retrieved the second I'd stumbled out of the sun-trap room from hand to hand. The smooth, firm oak wood in my grasp was just grounding enough to stop me from spiraling into utter panic.

"*Two* full dark fae in the space of a month," I said. "This shouldn't be happening. It's *never* happened. Nothing worse than the dark rabble has ever bothered with our past incarnations."

"That you remember," Darton said tentatively.

"I would have left notes if a full fae had come calling before." Unless it'd turned up and immediately slaughtered us before I'd had the chance to write down a record. Which I supposed was possible. But I *did* still have at least vague memories of our last several deaths, and none of them had come about that way.

I pinched the bridge of my nose. "There might even

be three. Izzy said she saw a man who gave her a strange vibe. He could have been the fae we just burned up—she said he had brown hair—but we don't know that."

Darton had stiffened. "What? Izzy never mentioned that to me. *You* never mentioned that to me."

I waved off his implied complaint. "You didn't need to know. She wasn't sure, and I had no reason to be—and there wasn't anything you could have done about it anyway. We were already set to move in here."

"How do you think he found us? I thought that spell you cast would stop the dark fae from noticing me?"

"The lesser dark creatures," I said. "The ones we usually have to worry about. I'm only half fae, and not even in that body anymore—if a dark fae comes looking, I can't completely hide you, only divert them for a bit. They've just never come looking before. Maybe this one was a friend of our mercenary. Maybe he mentioned what he was hunting." He just hadn't seemed like the type to have close friends—or to want to share his prize.

"Well, he's gone, right?" Priya said, her voice halting. She'd looked a bit shell-shocked since I'd ushered them back out here. She shifted on her feet as if testing how well each could hold her weight. "You took care of the problem. Nothing to worry about."

Without her usual cheer, the reassurance fell flat. I got the impression she was hoping I'd pick up the thread and reassure *her*. "Other than disposing of the mess in the trap? For now. After this, we can't assume there aren't other dark fae who know about Darton too. But how long is it going to be before another one comes? Before one comes sometime we *don't* have a handy way of overcoming them?"

"We stopped the mercenary without needing any special traps," Darton said.

"With a plan that required the coordination of five people and you nearly bleeding to death. That's not something I can whip up in the spur of the moment. As of now, there's nowhere you're really safe except for in this building."

And I wasn't even completely sure of the house. The sun trap had needed my assistance to overcome the dark fae's defenses. I hadn't gotten much of a chance to evaluate my opponent.

The mercenary we'd fought before had been a young fae, strong and determined, but without the resilience and wisdom of age. If a fae much older than him heard of Arthur's presence and took a mind to come after him—if more than one of them came at the building at once—if they found a way in that wouldn't shunt them into the trap—

Darton crossed his arms over his chest. "Well, I can't stay in here forever."

"You can't go wandering around out there when we don't even know what we're facing." I swept my hand to vaguely indicate the vast world of dangerous unknowns outside.

"That wasn't how this was supposed to work. I've got classes, I've got football practice and games. I'm not giving up my entire *life*."

Priya had ducked her head, but at that she raised it a little. "It'd be better than not having a life at all, wouldn't it?"

The overhead lights gleamed off her eyes, and she winced. I paused, momentarily distracted from my other looming concerns.

"Are you okay?"

"Yeah, I just—" She rubbed her temple. "This headache hit me out of nowhere. Must be all the excitement." She managed a weak smile. "Sorry I'm not more help."

"No, it's okay," I said. "Why don't you go lie down in the guest room? You can grab painkillers from the bathroom cabinet in my bedroom if you want them."

She nodded and shuffled off in the direction I indicated. I waited until she'd disappeared behind one of the doors before I turned back to Darton. I drew in a breath to steady myself.

"She had a point, you know. 'Having a life' is only relevant if you're actually alive."

Darton grimaced. "And being alive is only relevant if I get to have an actual life."

"I know. You're right too." I stepped closer and touched his elbow. "We did take care of the mercenary before, and the trap did stop tonight's fae before he could do... whatever it was he wanted to do. So I won't ask you to never set foot outside these walls again. I just want a little time to get my bearings. There's obviously even more going on than I'm aware of."

My thoughts slipped back to the mercenary's death nearly two weeks ago. *I am for my master*, he'd called out as the sunlight burned him away. *I am for the greatest one*. The Darkest One, he had to have meant. With Priya's comments about sacrificial magic lingering in my mind, I had to wonder if he'd meant those words as more than just a final statement of defiance. Had he managed to lend her power? Or passed his power on to others he knew were on the way?

Darton's stance had loosened slightly, opening to me. His voice was still hesitant. "And what does 'a little time' mean, exactly?"

"You take a few days off," I said. "I can conjure you up a doctor's note or whatever you need. I'll work on some new ideas I think might bear fruit and watch to see what else comes our way. And then we'll talk again about what makes sense. I promise I'll do everything in my power to make sure you can leave here again without taking your life in your hands."

* * *

"Come on out, Shirley," I said, shaking the sack. The glooms didn't actually have names, as far as I'd ever heard, so I figured there wasn't any harm in me giving the ones I dealt with one of my own choosing. And this one struck me as a Shirley through and through.

The scrap of darkness I'd collected on campus several days ago crept from the mouth of the bag and hesitated. We were stationed in a patch of shadow cast by a patio umbrella I'd placed in the middle of the concrete yard. Bright morning sunlight beamed all around it. The nearest neighboring shadows were hidden in the short grass several yards away. There was nowhere for the gloom to escape to.

It wriggled along the edge of the shadow unhappily. I pawed through the tools I'd brought out for my experiments. My fingers closed around the handle of the taser.

"This is going to hurt me more than it's going to hurt you," I informed the gloom, although I was pretty sure it wasn't going to hurt either of us. Mechanically generated electricity seemed unlikely to have any more effect than mechanically generated light: unpleasant but not actively destructive.

I muttered at my finger to open a split in the skin. A little blood would lubricate the magic. I mashed the bead of red liquid into the sage leaves on the ground. Then I whipped them in a circle around the gloom, flicking on the taser as I did.

"Bind it, hold it still."

The electricity crackled. The gloom twitched. With a quiver in the air, the magical barrier I'd cast solidified around it. The dark vermin bumped up against the invisible wall and retreated.

I touched the barrier and frowned. No, mechanical electricity hadn't added any oomph to my casting at all. It felt the same as if I'd cast it normally. And the electric surge obviously hadn't bothered the gloom all that much either. I murmured to dismiss the spell. Okay, on to the next option.

I picked up the piece of amber, big enough to fit solidly in my palm, and the rabbit skin with fur intact. After several swipes of the stone across the fur, the space between them crackled faintly with static. Not a lot—I didn't enjoy the thought of just how much fur and stone I'd need to generate the kind of power I was probably going to need to take on a full fae—but enough for me to test it out.

"Bind it, hold it still," I cast again in the old tongue. I pressed my bloody finger into the sage leaves just before tossing them around the gloom again. My other hand scraped the amber over the fur and raised it to smack into the sage.

An electric sizzle shivered into my hand. The air popped.

The gloom spasmed and wisped away.

Cattle sod. I stared at the spot where it had been for a moment and then lowered the stone. Well, I could obviously say *naturally* generated electricity and the dark kind did not get along.

The new magical barrier had still snapped into place, even though there was nothing left for it to contain. It had a sturdy feel to it the first one had lacked. But I'd lost my test subject in my zeal. Oops.

I shoved my supplies into the bag that wasn't much use to me until I found another gloom, and stood up. I could lay bait that would draw glooms this way, but the thought of encouraging the dark rabble to investigate our little shelter here made me cringe.

Drive out a ways, set the trap, and gather a few—that's what I'd need to do. While I was waiting, I could figure out how to amplify the effect I'd just generated. A barrier that would hold a gloom in place wasn't going to do sod all against the Darkest One.

Maybe I'd gather enough dark vermin to experiment more with the destructive aspect too. If more full dark fae *were* headed our way... we'd need all the defensive options we could get.

I lowered the patio umbrella and reached for the post to heft it under my arm. A prickle ran over my skin. I paused, my head jerking up.

The fae sensitivity I'd inherited from my father—the first one, long ago—drew my gaze to exactly the right spot. The spot where a tan figure with a mane of blond hair crouched in the distance, where the field beyond our yard met a stretch of forest.

My body tensed, but I'd already recognized he wasn't an enemy. At least not the typical sort. The sunlight beamed off him, setting off a shimmer in the air around him. I could almost see the fence posts through the edges of his form.

He was fae, but not dark. My kind—the light. Not that I'd been getting along all that well with their sort recently either. The last time I'd gone to the nearest light fae enclave, I'd ended up bringing a hoard of dark rabble to their doorstep. They hadn't been especially pleased about that.

And, being fair, I'd *never* gotten along with the flighty, erratic extended family my father had brought me into. The *flighty* and *erratic* parts are plenty of reason right there.

This one's wits clearly weren't any brighter than most of his kind. Even though it must have been obvious I'd spotted him, he was still hunched down as if he figured I might forget I'd noticed him if he simply didn't move. I mentally rolled my eyes.

"Hey!" I called, heading toward the field. "This property belongs to me, the daughter of Eóghan. If you have business here, you should speak to me about it."

The fae man flinched. Then he blinked away into the sunlight as if he'd never been there. I stopped in my tracks, watching, but he didn't reappear.

He'd flitted off to wherever he'd come from, I had to guess. My fingers clenched around the neck of my sack.

Were the light fae spying on me directly, now that Priya was no longer reporting back to them? Or was he watching this area for some other, darker reason?

I wasn't sure which was worse.

IO

"I come bringing coursework and takeout," Keevan announced as he sauntered into the house. "You don't have to thank me for the first part." He handed Darton the assignments he'd gone around to pick up and waggled a plastic bag crinkling with containers of Thai food. The tangy smells of curry and lemongrass wafted from it.

"And here's the stuff you asked for, Emma." Izzy held up the padded case she'd carried in. "Keevan's sister helped us out. Lenses, copper wire of different sizes, assorted batteries." She looked at me a little curiously. I motioned for her to set the case on the floor.

Priya edged inside behind the others. Her gaze lingered over the main room as if she hadn't already seen it, but she didn't move from the door.

Had the drive up been awkward? Priya didn't know Keevan and Izzy other than from our bizarre road trip fleeing the mercenary's dark rabble army last month. But when I'd mentioned to her in a text that Darton's best friends were dropping by, she'd immediately jumped at the chance to tag along. Maybe she was still feeling nervous after our encounter with the dark fae the last time she was here.

Darton moved to help Keevan lay out the cartons of food on the table. I grabbed plates from the cupboard. "How's the new car working out?" I asked Keevan.

His old one had been ruined beyond repair when Jagger had, well, blown up his own house. A fair bit of the blast had hit the car. Since I was the one who'd gotten Keevan dragged into that mess, I'd given him the money to replace it.

"It's great!" he said. "Runs better than the old one. I should get you to destroy my things more often." He gave me an easy grin to show he really did mean the joke in good humor.

Izzy had wandered into the living room area. She studied the walls and the ceiling. "Is this place rigged to explode like Jagger's was? Darton said you modeled it after his place. But I've got to say it looks a lot cozier in here."

"It's got a few tricks," I said. "Hopefully none we'll have to use."

"Come on," Keevan said. "Better eat while the food is all hot."

Izzy headed over to the kitchen, but Priya was still standing in the narrow space of the front hall. I went to meet her.

"Hey, Priya."

Her head twitched and turned toward me as if I'd startled her. She blinked with a jitter of her eyelids. "Hey."

I frowned. "What's up?"

"Nothing. Nothing." She flexed her shoulders and fixed her eyes on my face. "I was just thinking. What's new with you since I was last here?"

That was a remarkably casual question considering

what she'd seen that last time.

I shrugged. "Not much. I think some of my experiments might be heading in a productive direction, but I've got a lot more work to get through before I'll have satisfied any of my real goals." I started walking to the table, and Priya followed me. "I did want to ask you—I saw a light fae hanging around the property yesterday morning. Have you had any contact from your enclave— anything mentioning one of them coming out this way?"

Her gaze had wandered to the sofas. I waited a moment, but it was as if she hadn't heard me. I cleared my throat. "Priya?"

Her head jerked around with the same stiff movement as before. "Oh. Sorry. No, I haven't heard anything from back home. I can try to get in touch and see if they're up to something. I do still have a bit of sway with them."

"I'd appreciate that. Even if it isn't one from your enclave, if they know anything, I'd like to know it too."

I tugged out a chair for her to sit beside me. Keevan and Izzy had already settled in on either side of Darton. Priya hesitated for a second and then lowered herself into the seat.

She wasn't acting like herself, that was for sure. Something had to be wrong. I didn't think she'd appreciate me interrogating her in front of the others, though. Maybe I could get her apart for a little one-on-one talk after dinner.

We all dug in. I stuck to the vegetarian dishes, since my stomach was already tight with tension. Meat didn't always sit well with my digestive system, another lovely feature of my light fae heritage.

Within a minute, Keevan had Darton laughing. My liege relaxed in his chair even more as Izzy related a story about her unpredictably wacky Post Modern Literature professor. Watching them, I let out my breath, releasing some of the tension with it.

Darton had survived being stuck in here for the last two days. He could still enjoy himself. With the new supplies, I could hope that I'd be able to come up with a protection spell I'd feel happy—or at least, happy enough—with tomorrow. I'd promised him I'd get him back to his regular life as soon as I could.

Priya spooned just a little of the pad thai and green curry chicken onto her plate, and what was there, she only picked at. I couldn't actually say for sure she'd eaten more than a couple bites when Keevan leaned back with a groan. He patted his belly. "Okay. One more bite and *I'll* explode."

Izzy giggled, and he flashed a brighter smile her way.

I started gathering the empty cartons. Darton stood to help me clear the table. Priya stiffened and then leapt to her feet.

"I'll help!" she said brightly.

She grabbed her plate and mine, and darted around the table to set them in the sink. As Darton followed suit, she spun around toward him. I paused, my gaze fixed on her, a creeping sensation running up my back.

There was nothing to worry about. It was just *Priya*, for light's sake. But every instinct was telling me that something here was very, very wrong.

"Darton," I said, not knowing what I was trying to warn him against, only that I needed his attention on me. That impulse might have been the only thing that saved him. Because just as he swiveled to look at me, Priya jabbed her hand toward him.

Her hand that was suddenly clasped around a thin, glinting blade.

Darton's sudden movement threw off her aim. The knife sliced across Darton's side rather than plunging straight in. Darton made a choked sound and stumbled to the side.

"What—whoa!" Keevan said, grabbing his friend. Priya lunged forward, blade swinging. Before she'd made it even a full step, I was already spitting out words. My intent wrapped tight around the life energy inside me.

"*Up and over, bring me there.*"

A surge of air propelled me over the table. I flung myself at Priya, catching her just as she slashed at Darton's chest again. My arm smacked into hers. I wrenched her down toward the floor, grasping one wrist and groping for the other. A whine wavered from her throat as I wrestled to keep her down. She stabbed and kicked, faster than I could keep up with.

The thin blade severed my shirt sleeve and cut into the flesh beneath. Pain lanced through my forearm. I sucked in a sharp breath and fumbled with my free hand for the twigs in my pocket.

My fingers closed around them. "*Still and steady, hold her,*" I gasped out. Priya's body froze beneath me. She stared up at me, wide eyed, her lips parted around her panting breaths.

"What— What the *hell?*" Keevan said.

I pried the knife from Priya's hand. It was plain steel, but sharp enough that I nearly nicked my finger at the slightest graze. Not one of ours. She'd brought it with her.

To do *this*? To try to gut Darton right here in our kitchen?

My gaze shot to him. Darton had sagged against the kitchen island, his hand pressed to his side. Red was streaking across the fabric of his shirt.

"Get something on his wound," I said quickly. "Stop the bleeding."

Izzy sprang into motion. She grabbed the nearest hand towel. I wanted to leap to his side, to seal the cut with my magic, but I didn't dare let go of Priya. I had no idea what she might be capable of right now.

"Priya?" I said. Her eyelids fluttered and her expression stuttered. Then her lips twisted into a mocking grin.

My stomach lurched. I'd seen that grin before. On the face of the dark fae in our trap, in the moment before the light had destroyed him.

The moment before I'd *thought* the light had destroyed him. He'd been casting. And Priya had been in the room with me, despite my warnings. I should have been more firm about them, clearly.

I gave an hour or two of my life into a brief muttering of a spell. "*Light, come.*" A glow sparked between my thumb and forefinger. I lowered them to Priya's face. The grin jerked away. She flinched, recoiling as much as my hasty binding spell allowed.

"What's wrong with her?" Izzy said. She was hovering near Darton, who'd taken the hand towel from her and jammed it against his side. I didn't see any blood seeping through it yet. The cut mustn't be dangerously deep. But I was hardly happy about him doing any bleeding at all.

"It isn't Priya," I said. "Not really. She's being sight-ridden." I'd done the same myself, with animals and occasionally people—casting my soul from my body into another when I needed to take action in disguise.

When *I* had, though, I'd always had my own body to come back to. The dark fae man had made a more permanent leap. The signs had been so subtle I'd missed them, but thinking back, the clues fell into place: Priya's sudden if mild aversion to the lights, her stiffness with her body as if finding it unfamiliar, her general distraction.

He must have hidden, partly dormant in the back of her mind, over the last few days. Slowly gathering control for when he'd get his chance at Darton.

I narrowed my eyes. "How did you get here, Dark One? Who sent you?" I didn't need to ask *why* he'd been sent. The same reason the mercenary had come after us, obviously: to kill Darton, to steal Arthur's soul, in the hopes they could free the Darkest One.

The spirit inhabiting Priya's body lay stubbornly silent beneath me. I brought my conjured light close to her again, right up to her eyes. She grimaced, a hiss of pain escaping her.

"How did you know to come here?" I demanded.

"That's no business of yours," she bit out.

"I can put you back in the light box, you know," I said. "The cells have been charging all day. Lots of fresh sun-powered light for you to bask in."

Tension trembled through Priya's body, but I didn't see the slightest waver of the fae's resolve in her face. I wasn't likely to get answers by tormenting him. He could have tried to bargain for his life the first time he'd been in the sun trap, but he'd focused on fulfilling his mission instead. He mustn't have expected to make it much farther than this alive.

There were other sensitivities I could press on. Dark fae were known for their pride.

I eased back a little. "Well, seeing how you've reacted to my magic gives me enough of an answer. You clearly don't have enough power for any higher fae to consider enlisting your services. A lone wanderer who happened on a lucky scrap of information, desperate to get some attention, huh? It's pathetic, really."

Keevan made a choked sound, half amused and half disbelieving.

The fae twitched in Priya's body. "You know nothing."

"I know what I'm looking at," I said calmly. "A helpless soul trapped in a human body. How degrading. You lowered yourself to this state only to be captured by a wizard who's barely half-fae at this point. If any other dark ones do hear about this, they'll be laughing in your memory."

"*I'm* laughing," the fae snapped. "To think of how swiftly you'll fall, Merlin. I see no greatness in *you*. And the only fate awaiting you is dire. Rhedyn won't rest until your body and soul are ground to dust."

I froze. *Rhedyn.* I hadn't heard that name in anything but my memories in centuries.

Before I'd recovered from my shock, the fae spat out a few hasty words in his own tongue. My binding spell cracked. Priya's arm lashed out—but not at me. It rammed her hand into her mouth, as if the fae meant to choke her on her own fingers. As if all that mattered now was taking *one* of us down with him, regardless of who.

My pulse lurched. "No!" I smacked the glow I was

still holding against Priya's face. She flinched, her muscles going just slack enough that I could wrench her arm away from her mouth. Her lips started to move, and I slapped my own hand across them.

"*Seal them, tight and true.*"

She struggled under me, shoving her knees at my stomach, swinging her free fist. Keevan sprang in, grabbing her other arm. I pinned her legs under mine, crossing my ankles. "*Still and steady.*"

Her body stiffened once more. Her mouth stayed pressed shut as she glared up at me, my spell holding it closed and shutting off the dark fae's primary route to magic. The time for talking was done. Out here in the open, at least.

I sat back on my heels, my breath rough in my throat. "All right," I said. "To the light box it is."

II

Darton was waiting in the hall, leaning against his bedroom's doorframe, when I emerged from the sun-trap room. He straightened up and came to meet me as I shoved the deadbolt back over.

"How is she?"

I swiped my hand past my aching eyes. My head was muggy, and my mouth felt as if I'd been licking ashes. I wasn't sure what hour of the morning it was, but it was definitely way past the time this body would have preferred to be sleeping. This brain, too.

"I think the fae's spirit is burned out of her now," I said. "But I'm having her sleep in the trap until I can test immediate sunlight on her tomorrow, just to be sure." After all, I'd thought I'd destroyed that dark fae once before and been wrong then. My gaze dipped to his side, to the spot where I'd healed his wound a few hours ago before I'd started the more intensive rounds of my interrogation. "How are you?"

Darton's arm dipped closer to his abdomen. "There's nothing left except a twinge." Then he attempted to smother a yawn.

"I assume Izzy and Keevan went home?"

He nodded wearily. "They would have stayed if I'd let them, but I told them the company would make it harder for you to concentrate."

"You didn't have to wait up either. Come on. You should be in bed." I nudged him back down the hall toward the bedrooms.

He went, but slowly so that I'd walk beside him. "I wanted to know right away if the fae said anything else—about how he found us. About what they want."

"They want what they've always wanted," I said. "For whatever reason, their queen has a special interest in you, Your Highness. And it seems her influence is seeping out of her prison more than it ever has since I sealed her away."

"Is that what he said?"

I grimaced. "No. I had to infer. I tried questioning more, adding some... pressure, with the lights, but after a point I just wanted him out of Priya. Before he could try to hurt her, or any of us, again. The dark fae have a high tolerance for pain and a deep dedication to those they recognize as their superiors. I was lucky I got anything at all out of him."

Darton stopped at the end of the hall and turned to face me. "You seemed upset when she—he—mentioned that one name. Raydin?"

"Rhedyn," I said, knowing he might not even be able to pick up the subtle difference in pronunciation. My chest tightened. "Yeah."

"Who's he?"

I pushed my hair back from my face. "She. She was one of the Darkest One's oldest and most trusted underlings. We clashed a few times, back in my first life. And it's partly her fault you and I are in this whole mess. I was busy fighting her off when the Darkest One attacked you, or I'd have been able to intervene faster." Maybe stopped the fatal stabbing completely. At very least had a handful more seconds to figure out what sodding spell I was casting.

"She *was*. Past tense?"

"I— " I sighed. "I thought she was dead. Or sealed away with the Darkest One. By the time I was living to an old enough age to start asking around in the enclaves back 'home,' no one had seen or heard word of her in decades. But apparently this particular life is full of unpleasant surprises."

My head drooped. Hogs balls, I was tired. And not just of tonight. If Rhedyn was still alive, if *she'd* sent this dark fae after us... how many more were on their way? How much worse were our lives about to get? Because I couldn't for a second believe they'd get any better, not if she was on our trail.

And who else would her minions hurt? My thoughts went to Priya, curled up on the floor of the sun trap with the pillow and blanket I'd brought her, her face tight with exhaustion. I swallowed hard.

"Hey." Darton touched the side of my head tentatively. I let him draw me to him. Let myself breathe in the familiar citrusy-earthy smell of him, soak up the warmth in the rise and fall of his chest. Ignored the skip of my heartbeat. I could take comfort from him. There was nothing more than friendly in that. And light knew I needed it right now.

"You're doing everything you can," Darton said. He

stroked my hair, sending a shiver I should not have enjoyed so much down my back. But it didn't loosen the clenching in my chest.

"I knew Priya was acting strangely. I knew the dark fae had been trying to cast something when I destroyed his body. I should have considered, checked, made sure..."

"You've had kind of a lot on your mind, Em."

My hands balled against his shirt. "That's no excuse. Protecting you from the dark fae—that's my *one* job. If I can't manage even that—"

"You did." Darton's arm tightened around me. "I'm okay. Priya's going to be okay. You kept all of us safe."

"But you almost weren't. And I don't even know for sure that she is. He could have done anything to her after she walked out of here with him inside. I have no idea what she's been through that she hasn't been able to tell me yet. If he'd managed to kill her, I'd never have known. And she didn't even need to *be* here. She only wanted to help me."

My throat constricted around those last few words. I'd learned a lot from Jagger in the very short time I'd become acquainted with him, but there was one piece of advice he'd pressed on me that I hadn't listened to: Keep my friends and Darton's out of this mess. He'd said the right thing was to take care of anything to do with the dark fae kind myself.

I knew that wasn't entirely true. I'd only managed to stop the mercenary because I'd trusted Priya and the others to stand beside me. But maybe Jagger hadn't been entirely wrong either.

Darton bowed his head next to mine. "I'm sorry," he said hoarsely.

I frowned. "What have you got to apologize for?"

He drew in a breath. A quiver ran through his body, so quickly I probably wouldn't have noticed it if I hadn't been leaning against him. "Maybe you would have noticed what had happened to Priya sooner if I hadn't been griping about missing a few football practices. You were trying to protect me from a guy who wanted to *kill* me, and I acted like you were the problem."

"No. No." I pulled back to look at him. The anguish on his face wrenched at me. "I get it. It was a totally normal reaction. You've hardly had time for the situation to sink in. You've only *known* who you are, what we're up against, for a few weeks. You wouldn't be you if you accepted everything I said without ever questioning it."

His gaze slid away from mine. "I could have picked a better time to be questioning. Maybe this is new to me, I've seen what the dark fae can do. I remember... enough. You've been doing everything you can to keep me and everyone else safe, like you always do. I *know* that. So the last thing I should be doing is making it harder for you. Whatever you think we have to do from here on, whatever measures we need to take—"

"Art," I interrupted. My fingers curled into his shirt. I waited until he met my eyes. "I don't want to ruin the life you have here, if I can help it. I've never wanted to. We'll figure out the best balance we can. If you don't like the sound of any strategy I propose, I want you to tell me."

"And get in your way? We've seen how well that works out. Your best friend possessed, me getting knifed in our kitchen..."

Another brief tremble passed through him beneath my hands, and the clouds in my head parted with a sudden understanding. Darton was feeling guilty about what had happened to Priya, yes, and worried about me overextending myself, like always, and he had to be nearly as exhausted as I was. But it was more than that. He'd also been a hair's breadth from dying this evening.

Even a few weeks ago in the forest when he'd asked me to split open his arm, we'd still been the ones in control. Tonight, if I'd been a second later with my warning, if Priya had moved a smidgeon faster, the evening might have had a very different ending. And of course Darton was even more aware of that than I was. He was the one who'd been bleeding against the kitchen counter.

His former memories weren't solid enough for the idea of death to feel like more an inconvenience than a true *end*.

"That wasn't your fault," I said. "And we survived it."

"This time."

"Art."

His expression had gone terse, his eyes almost dazed, not quite meeting mine. "What am I really contributing here? You've got all your magic. I have no soldiers to command, no lords I hold sway with, not even a goddamned sword."

"*Art.*"

"Why exactly am I still worth all this trouble—"

I couldn't think of a single thing to say that would break him out of the downward spiral of emotion. But there were other things I could do with my mouth, and other ways of shutting a person up.

I yanked him toward me at the same time as I raised my head to press my lips to his.

Somewhere inside me, I'd had intentions of

moderation. One quick kiss to startle him away from those uncertain thoughts. There was no need for more than that.

But the second my mouth caught his, a raw, needy sound escaped him. His fingers slid into my hair, tracing sparks over my scalp. He kissed me back, hard, and just like that, I was lost.

One of his hands traveled down my side to grasp my waist and pull me tighter against him. His lips coaxed mine apart, his tongue tangling with mine. For an instant, his hold started to slacken. A memory taking hold. But he must have managed to keep some awareness, because the next instant he was spinning me to brace me against the wall, his body hot against me from mouth to thighs.

I teased my fingertips up the back of his neck and received an eager hum as my reward. A memory of my own tickled up in the back of my mind: coming across a pond after a long day on the road with the then-prince, Arthur deciding a swim was just the thing to cool off and pulling me in too. Bright sun, chilly water, laughter bouncing through the air. I held the images at a distance as Darton tilted his head to kiss me even more deeply.

The faint remembered sensation of lapping water mingled with the slide of his palm up my torso to cup my breast. A whimper broke from my throat. By the light, how I'd missed this. How I'd missed *him*. Even if it wasn't everything I'd ever wanted, it was a hell of a lot.

Did it really matter, waking him up more, if we knew now the mercenary hadn't been a fluke? The second dark fae had found us despite my best efforts. And my king wanted this, wanted me. Right now I didn't care how or why.

His lips left mine to press a scorching kiss to my jaw,

my neck. A gasp of encouragement slipped out of me. He touched the wide collar of my sweater, easing it down over my shoulder by torturous increments as his mouth followed the same path. When another memory surfaced, I was too caught up to resist it. The sensations it carried bled over the brush of Darton's fingers, the gentle nip of his teeth.

This corner of the king's private audience room was dusty. Someone should really have a chat with the cleaning staff about that. I tugged my nose as I leaned against the cool, whitewashed plaster, warding off a sneeze.

I wasn't even really supposed to be here. I'd tagged along with Arthur to answer his father's summons for lack of anything better to do, but the king had given me one brief narrow-eyed look and told Arthur they had matters to discuss alone. The prince had twitched his eyebrow upward at me before he'd turned to follow.

He was the one I took my orders from, so I'd cast a quick distraction spell over myself and followed. But the spell and the dust combined in a rather uncomfortable itch, and if I did sneeze, I could forget about blending into the shadows.

King and son had sat down on the rather stiff-looking chairs with their brocaded cushions near the room's large window. The heavy curtains had been tied to the sides, so sunlight washed over them. It gleamed off Arthur's hair and the matching gold of the king's crown. If he was wearing that for a private talk with Arthur, he meant business.

"I noticed you spent a great deal of time with Lady Lorena during the visit last week," he said.

"She makes excellent conversation," Arthur replied.

The king smiled. "Is that your only interest? I'd say she's also fine to gaze upon."

Arthur shrugged, with a careless air I could see through even at a distance. I wondered if his father knew him as well as I did. My prince had given me little sense of his childhood family experiences, but these days the two of them barely saw each other outside of official functions and occasional chats like these.

"She's pretty enough," he allowed.

"I bring up the subject only because you must remember that now that you're of marriageable age, any young woman you single out, even briefly, will be subject to speculation."

Oh. So that was the purpose of this conversation. I resisted the urge to fidget. If I could have turned off my ears, I would have.

"I know better than to be compromised in any way, father," Arthur said.

"That's not all I mean." The king shifted in his chair. His smile faded. "You must also be conscious of the impression it gives others. You will want to make a suitable match before long, and the appearance of interest in a... less than suitable lady may discourage your better prospects."

"I suppose you have a list of those you'd consider suitable."

Arthur had kept his voice light, but his father gave him a sharp look. Apparently he had a better read on his son than I'd have guessed.

"You'll want a wife. You'll want heirs. And you'll want to make your choices to offer them the most advantages you can."

"I know," Arthur said. "Have I ever failed to meet my duties yet?"

Despite his casual tone, his back had stiffened slightly. An ache crept through my chest. For him, for whatever he might have wished for himself that he couldn't allow himself to have. And there might have been a deeper pinching too, at the thought of a partner in marriage coming to stand by Arthur's side. Being there to hear his worries and celebrate his triumphs, while I— Where would I be then?

I squashed that worry. I could serve Arthur all the same either way. That was what I was here to do. It was ridiculous to fret about the inevitable future. Even if—

I careened back into the present. The pinching sensation still radiated through my gut, reminding me of all the things I'd known I could never have, even if back then I hadn't yet admitted to myself I even wanted them.

Gods, would I never learn my lesson?

Darton's fingers dipped to the border of my bra. My hand shot up to catch his. I scooted out of his embrace with a shaky breath.

"Emma?" Darton said, peering at me. He gripped my hand as if unwilling to release that one last point of contact. My name of this life from his lips solidified my resolve. Yes. Emma. That was who he was seeing. That was why this could never work.

"It's been a long night," I said. "I don't think... we can make the clearest decisions right now. And I need to be ready to look after Priya in the morning."

The first point, I think he might have argued. At the second, he inclined his head. His gaze, when he lifted it to mine again, still looked hungry. So hungry it sent a tingle through me even as my discomfort jabbed deeper.

"We'll talk tomorrow," he said. He kissed my knuckles and turned to his bedroom.

I wandered into mine with my pulse still thumping, wondering what I could possibly say to him tomorrow that would satisfy us both.

12

Maybe because I was a throwback in a nearly literal sense, attempting to navigate the internet always gave me a headache. I squinted at the computer screen as if I could persuade it to accomplish want I wanted simply through the power of my will. So far that technique wasn't paying off so well, but I wasn't sure anything else I'd tried had been all that productive either.

Give me a clear path, a database with boundaries to navigate or a specific fact to track down, and I could magic my way there. What I was attempting to ferret out today was a lot more vague.

I adjusted my position on the smooth leather cushions of the sofa. This forum I'd stumbled on seemed like a halfway decent possibility. I signed up so I could post the message I'd been leaving all across the World Wide Web.

My concentration didn't stop my ears from picking up the faint squeak of Darton's bedroom door opening. My shoulders tensed. I'd woken up a couple hours before him, but I didn't feel any more ready to try to follow up last night's encounter. I hit the post button and navigated onward, trying to pretend I had nothing else on my mind as he padded down the hall toward the common room.

He leaned onto the top of the sofa, nothing but a thin white undershirt covering his upper half. I was definitely not thinking about how covered—or not—his lower half might be. The flex of his muscular arms against the wooden frame provided plenty of distraction already. Especially when my mind far too easily tripped back to those arms pulling me to him less than ten hours ago.

"What's this?" he said.

"A somewhat half-assed plan." I made a face. "If Rhedyn is assembling any sort of dark fae force, I was thinking people like Jagger—the other hunters he said he stayed in contact with around the world and traded information with—might have noticed. And they might know something we could use to come up with a less half-assed plan."

"You know how to get in touch with them?"

"Well, no, that's what makes this part half-assed. He said he talked to them through private channels, but they've got to spend some time on the regular internet too, right? So I'm posting a plea for help here and there, in the hopes that one of them happens on it and takes it seriously." I motioned toward the screen. "I've mentioned a couple things no one who's never encountered a real fae should know. That should give me a little cred."

"Sounds reasonable." He glanced back toward the hall. "Have you checked on Priya?"

"Yeah. She was okay this morning. Definitely no more dark fae hanging on in her head." My stomach knotted, remembering the way she'd thrown her arms around me when I'd opened the sun trap and pronounced her free. The shakiness of that relieved embrace. The choked apologies.

I'm so sorry, Emmaline. I was there and then I wasn't, he just shoved me down, stole my thoughts away... I knew he was going to try to hurt someone. I knew and I couldn't do anything.

As if her inability to fight off a foe so much more powerful than her was somehow to blame, instead of my carelessness. When I'd tried to reassure her, she'd shaken her head and refused to listen.

"We had breakfast together, and then I called her a cab to get her home," I added. "I think she was more than ready to get out of here."

"Who wouldn't be?" he said with a short laugh.

When I glanced up at him, his smile was more wry than bitter. I still couldn't stop myself from saying, "What I said last night, about making sure you don't give up the life you've had—I meant that. It's still possible that the dark fae was lying to unsettle me, or that even if more are coming we can put them off..."

I couldn't say I believed either of those possibilities to any large degree, and probably Darton guessed as much. He reached over to tuck a strand of my dark brown hair that had escaped its habitual ponytail behind my ear. His fingertips barely grazed my cheek, but every nerve in my body sparked all the same.

"I meant what I said last night too. You do whatever you need to do. I'm not going to fight with you about it. I trust you."

I met his dark blue eyes, all the parts of last night I'd been trying to avoid thinking about leaping back into the front of my mind.

He trusted me. And I was about to lie to him—again,

about the same thing I'd been lying to him about for fifteen hundred years.

At least I could say it was the only thing I'd ever outright lied to him about, omissions notwithstanding. The contents of my heart weren't *really* in his rights to know anyway.

"Everything... after that conversation," I said. "That was my mistake. I didn't mean—"

Darton swallowed audibly. "I get it," he broke in. "Emotions were running high. Neither of us was thinking completely straight. I mean, not that I minded, but..."

"But until we know exactly what we're dealing with, it's still safer the less woken you are," I filled in. *Yes, that is absolutely the main and only reason I'm going to be avoiding kissing you again.*

"Then I guess there's nothing more to say about it for now."

"No," I agreed. Not for ever, either.

He straightened up and ambled to the kitchen, but I was left with the uneasy sense that we hadn't resolved anything at all.

* * *

The early November chill had left the grass all along the edge of our massive paved yard in a sorry state, wilted and yellowing. The wind whispered over the limp blades as I circled the grounds. Nothing moved on the field between the concrete and the forest and farmhouses on the other side.

No light fae had shown themselves since I'd spotted that one man a few days ago, but they might have simply been keeping more distance. Or using magic to disguise themselves that was subtler than my half-human senses could detect.

Of course, it wasn't the *light* fae I was particularly worried about.

I was just coming around the back of the house when my gaze caught on a darker splotch amid the yellow-green. My legs locked. I scanned the field, but there was still nothing in view except me and the ripples of the wind.

I stepped tentatively onto the grass. Several paces from the concrete, a swath of blades lay dead, brown with rot. And not just a random swath. The grass had been withered in the shape of a rune.

The void. The blankness of death that to the dark fae was the most perfect sort of order.

A chill deeper than the bite in the looming winter ran down my back. With the noon sun shining brightly overhead, I didn't feel an immediate danger. I'd waited until the morning's clouds had cleared precisely so that I'd know I had the sun's energy to defend me if it came to that.

But another dark fae had been lurking around our home. Leaving his or her mark for me to find. Taunting me with the death he wished for me and my king.

I rubbed my arms and swiveled back toward the house. We'd had enough of games. If Rhedyn was out there, I wasn't going to wait to see what else she might have in store for us. There had to be a way to bring the battle to her.

Darton was in his bedroom, probably keeping up on his assignments, so I didn't have to explain myself when I strode straight through the common room to mine. I ducked into the expansive closet I'd included in the house's building plans.

I hadn't moved all of my materials out of my storage locker. I needed to know the essentials—my old journals, basic magical materials—would be there for me to recover in my next life, if I got that far. But since the possibility of even a next life was starting to seem thin, I'd brought several crates of supplies back here to stash them closer at hand.

The lid of one and then another creaked as I shoved them open. My fingers closed around baggies and bundles of dried herbs. Lavender, feverfew, anise. I couldn't compel a vision to come, but with the right combination of ingredients, I could encourage one.

Of course, I didn't want just any vision. I'd have to give it some direction.

I set the herbs burning in a bowl on the floor and sat down beside it. Leaning against the footboard of my bed, I closed my eyes and reached back into my memories of my first life to my first encounter with Rhedyn. The images surged up, drowning out my awareness of the room around me.

The pine smell of the woods tickled my nose, but that wasn't what had set the rest of my nerves prickling. Heavy branches blocked most of the dwindling sun, leaving the forest beyond our clearing hazed with an early evening.

I couldn't see anything lurking between the trees. Couldn't hear anything over the stomping of the horses' hooves and the clatter of cooking pots being arranged by the fire. But I knew, with a sensation that wriggled right through my bones, that our camp of soldiers was not alone.

My king came up beside me and set a hand on my shoulder. "You look disturbed, Merlin. More so than usual, I mean."

I shot him a narrow look, and he smiled at me, but with a

certain amount of weariness. We'd been on the road, clashing with forays of hostile forces, for over a month. And we didn't have any idea when that battling might end.

"Ha ha, sire. There's nothing for you to worry about. But I think I might take a walk."

"I'd suggest you take a sword with you if I didn't know you're as like to cut your own arm off."

I would have prodded Arthur with my elbow if that hadn't seemed too familiar a gesture with the men he commanded all around us. "Good thing I have more efficient ways of defending myself then. Why don't you go polish that sword I charmed for you?"

Before he could come up with a retort to that, I set off through the woods. I didn't know exactly where I was going, but the prickling under my skin amplified as I moved farther north. So I kept walking that way.

The sounds of the camp faded. Shadows drifted around me. One flickered, and my head jerked toward it.

A woman stood in the deeper shade beside the broad trunk of an elderly pine. The edges of her ash-blond hair and tan skin blurred into the shadows. She was a dark fae, and from the depth of those shadows, one who'd spent a long time on this earth. My hand leapt to the wand tucked into my belt.

She smirked at me, her eyes glinting like polished obsidian. "What do you think you're going to do to me, halfling?" Her voice was low and smoky.

"Whatever I need to," I said. "Although if you move off of your own accord, I won't have to do anything at all."

She shrugged. "I'll do your pet king no harm tonight. He's far too important for trifling with, isn't he?"

There was something mocking in the words, but I didn't understand what she was implying. The dark fae didn't see any true importance in human rulers. But they had shown a periodic and odd fascination with Arthur's family, my father had told me.

"What's so special about him to you, that you're following him around just to gape at him?" I asked.

She tossed her hair dismissively, but then her body stilled. Her eyes had focused on something beyond me. I turned.

The movements of the camp were just barely visible between the trees. On the side of the clearing nearest us, Arthur was demonstrating an effective angle with which to swing a blade to one of the novice soldiers.

Excalibur gleamed in his hands even in the waning light, charged as much by the strength of his soul as the sun. Ah.

"You appreciate my handiwork," I said.

The dark fae's eyes twitched back to me. She smirked again, but this time it was more of a grimace. No, she did not like the look of that sword at all, as much as she was trying to hide her reaction from me.

That was good to know. All the months I'd spent working over that blade suddenly seemed more than worth it.

"Don't think too much of yourself," she said coolly, and sliced her hand through the air with a few muttered words. Pain cut across my side like a frigid razor. It dug into my lungs. I—

—opened my eyes with a gasp for breath in my bedroom fifteen hundred years later.

Yes, thank you, I would prefer to skip the part of that memory where I rolled around on the forest floor in agony for an hour. I *had* managed to cast a hasty counter-spell, but it'd still taken that long before my efforts had dulled Rhedyn's assault enough to allow me to stand. She'd been—she *was*—a powerful dark fae indeed.

The smoke from the sizzling herbs had coated my mouth and throat. My thoughts seemed to slosh in my head. Good. I had to chase that woozy feeling.

I leaned over the plate and inhaled even more smoke, until my lungs burned with it. Then I slumped backward.

"*Sight beyond sight, sight beyond sight, show me what I wish,*" I murmured in the old tongue. Over and over, keeping my mind focused on Rhedyn's smirking face, on the tang of pine, on the creeping forest shadows. The words and the memory blurred together. My tongue thickened. The back of my head opened up into spiraling darkness.

I fell away from the room and down, and down, until I felt as if I'd flipped feet over head. I blinked, but the darkness didn't clear.

My plummet slowed. Sounds reached my ears: the sharp *plink* of drips hitting a metal surface. A rumble like a distant passing train. And a voice, unfamiliar and yet with a cadence that sent a shiver of unpleasant recollection through me, muttering too low for me to make out the words. The same few phrases, chanting. Like I had been, just a minute ago.

Magic.

A damp chill seeped through me. The water dripped on. I tried to turn, to orient myself toward the voice, to move close enough to see the speaker. My mind-sight hitched, and the vision shattered.

I jerked back into the awareness of my body. The sensation of dampness crawled over my skin, even though the air in the room around me was crisp and dry. I rubbed my hands over my arms to dispel the goose bumps.

I was home. Home and as safe as I could be anywhere. But all at once I couldn't shake the impression that doom loomed over us as closely as a thundercloud on the verge of bursting.

13

"He *promised* he'd come," Priya said, shifting her weight from one foot to the other. "But then the light fae don't exactly have the best sense of time, do they?"

"That would be the understatement of the century." I swiped my hand across my mouth and glanced around us.

We'd been standing a few paces from the front door of my and Darton's house, waiting, for nearly half an hour. It should have been a day worth enjoying—clear sky, birdsong in the air, that air a tad warmer than the past week—but everything seemed to rest on our overdue visitor. "Do you know *how* he'd be coming, or from which way?"

She sighed. "Beats me. He insisted he'd meet us here."

"Should we go inside and find something else to do until he shows up?"

"I don't know if he'll bother knocking on the door if he doesn't see me. You never know how weird they're going to be about human stuff." She glanced sideways at me. "Or sort-of human stuff. However we'd classify you. Hey, have there been any other signs of the dark fae around since we talked yesterday?"

"Other than the rune markings they've been leaving every night for me to find in the morning?" I said. "Well, they haven't tried to confront me or to get into the house. I guess what happened with the first one scared them off." Or else they were preparing for a larger assault than I'd anticipated. "You've been okay, since... since all that, haven't you?"

"Never better," Priya said cheerfully, but her smile looked a little stiff. Of course it would take more than a few days to get over being possessed.

"If you ever need to talk, or anything," I said, and trailed off uncertainly. I had centuries of practice at keeping my distance from everyone other than my king, because there'd never been anyone I could be myself around. Practice at being a good friend, not so much. And most regular friendships never included a problem quite like this.

"It's fine, Emmaline. Really, it is."

I still didn't totally believe her, but Priya's tone was gentle enough that I let the subject drop. And then there wasn't any more time for conversation, because a slender young man with gleaming bronze skin blinked into view on the drive.

"Ohanko!" Priya said, and bounded over to meet him. I trailed a little beyond. The light fae smiled at Priya, but his stance was wary. When his gaze shifted to me, he went still, staring as if in disbelief and awe.

Wonderful.

"Yes, it's really me," I said dryly. "The great Merlin in the flesh, if not the stuff I was originally born with."

The fae had the awareness to look chagrined, which

put him ahead of about ninety percent of those of his kind I'd talked to in the last several centuries. "I didn't mean— I've heard a lot of stories, but I never thought I would meet you," he said in a melodic tenor. "It's remarkable what your magic has accomplished."

Okay, give the guy another point. The last light fae I'd had an extended conversation with had used words more like "unnatural."

"This is Ohanko." Priya wrapped her hand around his elbow. "He was basically my brother, when I was growing up in the enclave. Ohanko, Emmaline. Or Merlin, I guess."

Ohanko dropped into a deep bow—full respect for my soul's accumulated age. I bobbed my head in return. "It's a pleasure to meet you. Do you want to come inside?"

He glanced down at the pavement, which he didn't look entirely comfortable standing on. "I'd rather not close myself off, if that's all right."

"Sure, sure, no problem. Here, we can sit in the field if you'd like that better."

We ambled over to the grass. Even though it was still just as wilted as a couple days ago, Ohanko sank down onto it with apparent relief.

"Priya says you know something about the light fae guy I saw spying on us last week," I said.

He nodded. "He was one from my enclave to the north. We did not mean to... 'spy.' We were merely concerned and wanting to monitor the situation as well as we could."

"And what situation is that, exactly? Me and my king hanging out here."

"Oh, no. Your business is your own. Our concern lay

with those who might not see it that way. About a week ago, we became aware that a large number of dark fae had arrived from across the large salt water." Ohanko motioned vaguely to the east.

To the Atlantic? I tensed. "How many is a large number?"

He cocked his head, considering. "Perhaps a dozen. And they all immediately made their way in this direction."

An uncomfortable prickle raced down my back. A dozen full dark fae coming after us from across the sea— from my and Arthur's homeland, I had to assume—was more than I'd ever imagined I'd have to deal with.

It wasn't just our homeland. It was Rhedyn's too. I doubted that was a coincidence.

"Have you gotten any sense of a leader among them? Or of whom they might be directed by?" Had she herself made the journey?

"No," Ohanko said. "Their actions have made little sense to us. Our scout observed them arriving in the forest nearby. Then, one was swallowed by your home. And all but one of the others drifted away in a sun's span."

Even the most with-it of light fae leaned toward metaphor. I suppressed my impatience. "So there's one still here." The one who was decorating our field so enthusiastically. "And the others left at least a few days ago, after we caught the first guy in our sun trap? Where did they go?"

"The one that has lingered has a purpose we have not seen. The others left so quickly our scout did not track them. They are not all together, at least. When so many come together, we were able to feel their arrival. One or two dark fae on their own, at a distance, may as well be shadows."

So they could be anywhere. I supposed I should be relieved they weren't still scheming altogether, but my stomach was churning. They had to be up to something. Something inspired by what they'd observed of our little fortress here? There was nothing good that could come of that.

Ohanko had lifted his gaze toward the house again. "Where is the king?" he asked. "He *is* here, with you?"

"And safer inside rather than out." Especially with one of those dark fae still lurking around, leaving us vaguely threatening runic messages. I grimaced. How the hell could I give Darton any piece of his regular life back when there could be more full fae lurking around any corner? "Is that all you can tell me about the dark fae?"

"I wish I could be more helpful," Ohanko said. "But because Priya has asked, I will join the scout in surveying the area. If I hear or see anything new, I will bring it to you."

"Thank you. I appreciate that." I got up, my mind already spinning off in other directions. I couldn't count on the light fae just happening upon crucial information. Maybe it was time for a little vision-riding of my own—in a less permanent, non-destructive way, of course. "I think I need to look into this further in my own ways."

Ohanko inclined his head and then dipped into another low bow. I returned it with a brief bob and headed for the house. Priya paused for a moment to say a few last words to her foster brother. She jogged after me and caught up just as I was pushing open the front door.

"What do you think they're up to?"

"I don't know," I admitted as we walked into the hall.

"But there are ways I can try to find out."

Darton came out of his room at our voices. "Did Priya's... friend come? What did he say?"

"Nothing that's of a whole lot of use to us yet." I waved Darton aside, striding down the hall. "I'll let you know when I can—"

My phone jangled. I stopped and pulled it out of my pocket. It was Dad's number—his cell phone, not the home line.

If it had been Mom, I might have let her go through to voice mail and caught up with her later. But Dad hardly ever called me. *You can't have a proper conversation unless you're face to face*, he'd said more times than I could count. Usually our only direct communication between visits was him texting me the occasional gif or meme he found particularly amusing.

I raised it to my ear. "Hello?"

Dad's soft, dry voice carried into my ear. "Oh, hi, Emma. I just needed to... Your mom's had a bit of an accident."

I'd already started to brace myself at the fumbling hesitation in his words. At his last statement, my stomach dropped. He wouldn't be calling me about it if it were just a *bit* of a concern. "What? What happened?"

"Well, she— She's okay now, or at least the doctors say she will be."

"Dad. What. Happened?"

He made an uncomfortable sound. "You know how steep our driveway is. She was backing out to make a client call, and it seems the brakes lost power. The car rushed right down and hit the tree on the other side of the road."

Sodding hell. "But you said she's okay? The doctors

have really looked her over?"

"Yes. Yes, don't worry about that. There wasn't enough time for the car to get going all that fast. She jarred her neck some, and they're getting her to lie still for a bit to make sure there's no major damage, but they haven't seen any reason to believe there is. I wouldn't be calling you if that's all it was."

My fingers tightened around the phone. "What do you mean? What else is there?"

"Well, ah... This is going to sound strange. But maybe you can make some sense of it." He paused. "When I heard the crash, I came running out of the house. There was a man standing at the end of the drive, looking at your mom in the car. I don't believe I've ever seen him before. He rubbed me the wrong way to begin with, just standing there looking and not doing a thing to try to help. And then as I ran by, he said..."

Dad's voice faded out. My heart had caught in my throat. "What, Dad?"

"He said, 'Tell Emmaline to watch where she walks.' I don't— It was so bizarre, and I had to help your mom, so I didn't stop to question him, of course. And then when I thought of him again, he was gone. It sounded almost like... like some kind of threat, but you've never been mixed up in anything to account for that."

He said it as a fact, but the question was implied. "No," I lied. "I have no idea what that could have been about. Do you think—did he mess with the car? Is that why—"

"It doesn't seem like it. The brake lines weren't cut or anything that suggests conscious tampering. The inspector said they should work just fine now, that it was some kind of momentary power failure."

As if something had sucked the energy out of them. No creature in the world could do that more easily than a dark fae.

I bit my lip. "Well, I'm really glad Mom's okay. You tell her to call me as soon as they're letting her move around more. And—do you remember what the man looked like? In case he comes around here or something."

"It's all a bit of a blur now, I'm afraid, but he was big, dark hair, probably around my age? If anything more comes of it, I'll let you know right away. And you take care, all right?"

"Of course, Dad," I said.

I lowered the phone to my side. It took a moment before I could breathe past the clenching in my chest. Darton and Priya were both staring at me.

"My mom," I said. "One of the dark fae got my mom in a car accident. Nothing serious, but it seems to be that they wanted to send me a warning."

Darton's eyes widened.

"A warning about what?" Priya said.

That was a good question. I frowned. "I don't know." After all, we were already holed up in here, effectively hiding from them. What kind of 'walking' had he meant to discourage me from doing? "Maybe he just wanted me to know that they know about my parents. That they can hurt them if they want to."

"Not a warning. A threat." Darton's hands balled. "They have to be trying to convince you to stop protecting me. That's the message, isn't it? Hand me over or they'll do worse?"

"The one that talked to my dad didn't say anything

that specific. But a demand like that could be the next step."

I dragged in a breath. Sod it, I didn't even want to think about this. My first loyalty was to my king, always, but my parents of this life were still my parents. I didn't want them tormented by fae.

"You should go," Darton said. "Make sure they're safe. Deal with whatever dark fae is hanging around up there. I can handle a few days on my own here in the house."

I shook my head. He didn't even know the full story Ohanko had told us yet. "No. There are too many of them. The light fae said a dozen or so were hanging around here just a few days ago. Separating us could play right into Rhedyn's plans." And I didn't know if I could take on even one full dark fae on my own, without the tricks I'd built into the house. I was hardly prepared to go mobile.

"I could try to persuade the light fae to watch over your parents, to some degree," Priya said. "I don't know how willing they'd be to get involved, but—"

The buzz of an alert interrupted her. Darton made a face and dug out his phone. He clicked through to whatever message he'd gotten—and froze.

"What?" I said, my stomach lurching all over again.

Darton's mouth pressed into a tight, flat line as he stared at the screen. After a moment, he turned the phone to show me.

Someone had sent him a text with a video file. The written part of the message said only, *WE HAVE EYES*. Darton clicked to start the video playing, and I immediately stiffened too.

On the screen, Darton's sister ambled across the lawn outside what must have been her high school with a couple of friends. The camera tracked them down the street. Audrey and the other girls laughed and chattered, jostling each other playfully. They clearly had no idea they were being followed. At the corner, they ducked into a coffee shop, and the video cut out. But the message, and the threat held in it, remained.

14

"If they hurt Audrey, I'll—I'll—" Darton's jaw locked with emotion. He flicked through his contacts list to bring up his sister's number, gripping the phone so tightly his knuckles were whitening.

"Is that... normal fae behavior?" Priya murmured beside me as Darton raised the phone to his ear. "Using human tech like that?"

"Not exactly," I said. My insides felt as if they'd tangled into one huge knot. "But it doesn't surprise me that the dark fae could adapt if they found a use for it. Machines and electronics appeal to their love of order."

"Audrey, when you get this, give me a call right away, okay?" Darton said into the phone. So she hadn't answered. He started to pace, tapping at the screen again. His second call went through. "Hi, Mom. Yeah, good, I, um— Is Audrey around? Oh, okay. Yeah, I know how much she loves window shopping. Right. Of course. I've actually— There was just something I wanted to ask her quickly. I've got to go, but I'll call again soon."

His hand fell to his side. He swiveled again, heading for the front door. "She's out at the mall with some friends. At least, as far as my mom knows. If we drive fast enough, we can get up there in less than two hours. There's got to be something—"

I hurried after him. "Darton, we can't go. It's *you* they want, and you'd be giving yourself right to them."

"So what? We can't just leave Audrey there to... to whatever they're going to do to her. They already hurt your mom."

He grabbed his bomber jacket. Before he could start pulling it on, I grasped his wrist and tugged him to face me. His eyes were wild, barely seeing me.

"Darton. Art. *Arthur.*"

He made to pull away. I yanked off my gloves and caught his face between my bare hands.

At the contact, he went still. I held his frantic gaze, my heart thumping. "Arthur," I said again, and the panic in his expression retreated, just slightly.

"Merlin." His head dipped until his forehead brushed mine. I heard him swallow. "It's my little sister. She's only seventeen. She has no idea..."

"I know," I said, keeping my voice steady. "I don't want them to hurt her either. We won't let them. We're going to figure this out. But if we're going to do that, we need to stop and take a breath and think it through. You racing over there unprepared is *exactly* what the dark fae would want. We don't have to play into their hands."

"What else is there to do?"

"I don't know, but there's got to be something." I traced my thumb gently over his cheekbone. "You told me a couple days ago that you trusted me. You still do, don't you?"

He dragged in a rough breath. "Yes. Yes, of course I

do."

"Then stay here with me now, and we'll come up with a plan together."

He nodded slowly. Then he tipped his head so his lips grazed mine. My pulse stuttered, but I let him have the kiss and whatever reassurance it gave him. When I didn't pull away, he pressed his mouth to mine a little harder. Hard enough that the stutter turned into a full out fluttering. Then he stepped back, leaving my skin flushed from head to toe.

Priya cleared her throat, her gaze trained purposefully away from our little embrace, and the blush in my cheeks deepened. But before we could move on from comfort to planning, she stepped closer to the door.

"I think I hear a car. Were you expecting anyone else?"

"No." I froze, listening. The growl of an engine reached my own ears, faint but growing. It must have already been coming up the drive.

Darton reached for the door, but I nudged him backward. "You're still staying in here for now," I told him. "Let me find out what's going on, and then we'll deal with everything else, as quickly as we can. I promise."

Wand in hand, I eased open the door and stepped outside. A dented burgundy Volvo was just pulling into the concrete yard. It parked about twenty feet away, which seemed a safe enough distance. The driver side door swung open, and my tension fell away.

"Hello there," said a familiar gruff voice as a familiar grizzled face appeared over the door. "I've been told a woman lives here who knows how to kill dark fae."

"Jagger!" Priya squealed, and dashed across the

pavement to wrap the older guy in a hug he returned somewhat awkwardly.

I ambled over, a smile stretching across my face. "We didn't know if you'd made it out of the building."

The fae hunter waved his hand dismissively. "It'd take more than an exploding house to do me in. I had a hideout under the place—only big enough for one, or I'd have gotten you all in there too. It took a little effort getting back out of it, I've got to admit, but here I am."

A twinkle glinted in his eyes, but I thought I saw a new, thicker scar or two amid the spider web of pale lines that crisscrossed his face. Jagger had gone through a lot, and given up a lot, to help us.

"We still have your van, if you need it," I started, but he cut me off with a shake of his head.

"It seems like you've got more need of it now than I ever did." He peered past me toward the house. "And you've been busy in the last month. Is that a roof full of solar panels I see?"

My smile twitched higher. "I took a lot of inspiration from your handiwork. Here, come in. It's safer inside. There's at least one dark fae that's been lurking around the property. What are you doing here?"

"I joined up with a buddy a couple states over," Jagger started as we went in. He bobbed his head to Darton, who blinked at him in surprise. "I've been making the usual rounds with him, keeping an eye on things like usual, but I've kept a particular eye out for any situation that sounded like you might be involved. Couple days ago someone in the network pointed out a posting they'd seen that sounded possibly legit, asking for our help. I took one look at it and knew it was you. Wasn't hard to track you down after that."

He leaned against the back of one of the sofas and folded his arms over his broad chest. "So you've had some more dark fae dealings. Is this the same one as was chasing you before?"

"No," I said. My excitement at seeing Jagger alive began to wane. We were in so much more trouble this time compared to the last. "That one we dealt with. It's a long story," I added when he opened his mouth to ask. "What's really important is a whole group of dark fae have come with the intention of getting at us now. I think they've been brought together by... a particularly powerful fae who I had some difficult encounters with in the past."

Jagger hummed thoughtfully. "And you think my network might be able to help?"

"Maybe not. But I thought at least you might have information we don't. It seems that these fae came across from Europe. Probably Britain, from what I know about their leader. I'm guessing you have connections all over the world?"

"I know a few folks in the UK." Jagger studied me. "What connections have *you* got over there that their dark fae would be crossing an ocean to get at you?"

I'd never told him the full story of who I was, or who Darton was either. It would only have complicated matters, and there hadn't really been time. There wasn't now either, as much as I owed the truth to him. "Another long story that I hope I'll be around to tell you about properly someday. But that's where I tangled with that one powerful fae, and from what we've gathered, she's the one who sent the others. Their methods of attack have been a little... unusual, though."

As quickly as I could, I laid out what we'd seen so far and what we'd learned from Priya's fae foster brother. Jagger nodded and asked a few brief questions, but mostly listened. When I got to the part about my mom's accident and the video of Audrey, Darton started pacing again. He didn't say anything, but his tension radiated off of him.

"It seems obvious they're making threats," I finished. "But they haven't given any clear indication what it is they want from us. It's all strangely vague for dark fae. There's got to be more to the picture that we just haven't caught on to yet."

"The kind of behavior you're describing does sound odd to me," Jagger agreed. "Unfortunately I'm not sure there's anything I can tell you that would shed more light on their intentions. That bunch has been keeping their heads down enough that I haven't heard any word about their activities through the wire. But a couple of my British colleagues have reported some unusual movement over on their side of the pond. Could be that's connected?"

My chest clenched. What were the chances it *wasn't?* "I wouldn't be surprised. What kind of 'movement' exactly?"

He took a small tablet out of one of his military coat's large pockets. "It wasn't anything striking enough that the details stuck in my memory. Let me look up what they've mentioned."

As Jagger brought up his sources, I sidled over to Darton.

"Whatever's happening in England, it isn't going to help us here," he said quietly. "We still have to make sure Audrey's safe. And your parents. And mine. And—" He froze. "What if they go after Keevan and Izzy too? The dark fae have more reason to want to target them than our families—they helped us kill the mercenary."

"The dark fae don't have quite the same concept of revenge we do," I said. "They'd probably see the mercenary's death as a fair reflection of his abilities. But that doesn't mean they'd leave our friends alone." They'd already used Priya, after all. "Why don't you check in with them? Let them know to be extra cautious of strangers hanging around them. If they get really worried, they can always hide out up here."

At least they'd understand the danger. I had no idea how we could properly warn our families.

"Here we go," Jagger said. "Significantly heightened dark fae and vermin activity noted around the north end of Somerset, particularly in the vicinity of the Camroth Interchange. Sightings of dark creatures by passersby, unusual dying off of vegetation, human-like figures spotted walking beneath the freeway and then 'disappearing.' Taken altogether, they're sure some dark fae is expending a lot of power there."

"What have they done to stop it?" Priya asked.

Jagger grimaced. "Nothing so far. They're keeping up observation. Dispatched a few dark vermin that were getting particularly restless. No one's actually been hurt, and there's been no indication the dark fae plan to hurt anyone. When there are full fae involved, it's more likely to stay that way if we don't interfere. *We've* never found any way to outright challenge one." He raised his eyes to look at me.

My mind was still stuck on the location he'd mentioned. "Where exactly in Somerset is this interchange?"

"I can show you a map." His fingers skimmed across the screen. He turned it for me to see. "Not the most exciting locale."

I took the tablet from him and zoomed out so I could see the full lay of the land. My breath caught in my chest. My mouth opened, but in that first moment I couldn't force the words out.

I should have known. I'd suspected something close. But it was still a shock seeing it confirmed so blatantly.

"Em?" Darton said.

I forced the words out. "The Darkest One. That's where she's sealed. There are caves, under the ground there..." The images from my vision, when I'd tried to provoke one of Rhedyn, came back to me—the chill and the dark and the dripping water. The distant rumble. Cars on the interchange. "Rhedyn is down there. She's working to free her master. Right now."

His mouth snapped shut. Jagger looked between the two of us. "I don't know anything about a 'Darkest One,' but I'm guessing from the sounds of it this is pretty bad."

"I can't let it happen. If she gets out—"

"Your spell has held for hundreds of years," Darton broke in. "This one fae isn't going to be able to break it just like that. Right? Or she would have already. The others could be grabbing Audrey while we're talking about this. Our families—they're the people already in danger. We have to deal with them first."

I paused as his words wriggled into my head. The timing and method of the dark fae's "threats" had confused me from the start, but now the pieces were starting to draw together into an almost coherent picture.

"Maybe we don't," I said. "Maybe trying to deal with

them will only encourage them to do worse. Think about how this all played out. I got that call from my dad, and less than ten minutes later you got the text about Audrey, and right after that Jagger showed up. The dark fae have been lurking around for *days*. That video of your sister— she was at school, so it must have been yesterday or earlier. But they waited until now to send it."

Priya's brow knit. "That is weird. What do you think it means?"

"I don't know for sure. But it's almost as if they knew we were going to get information from Jagger they didn't want us to have, or to respond to. They realized who he was and that he was heading here when there wasn't much time left, and threw everything they could at us. Like they were trying to get us to leave here before he arrived or to dismiss what he told us."

"How could they have known he was coming when we didn't?" Darton said.

Jagger's expression tensed. "About an hour ago, when I crossed the state line, I put your location into the GPS for the first time. Don't like those systems, but I knew I was going to need a little help finding the place. If the fae can send you texts, they could have some way of monitoring pings to this location. The account is registered to the car—they might have dug up some info on my friend that made them wary."

Darton swept his arm through the air. "So what are you saying? The car accident, filming my sister, those things don't mean anything? What's *stopping* them from hurting someone else?"

"We can," I said. "But not by running over there and giving them the chance to grab you, which I'm sure they'd love too. It's a game of distraction. There's no reason for them to play if we're not."

"What does *that* mean?"

"They've got two goals: Get you out in the open, or at least keep us distracted from what Rhedyn's doing. There's no point in trying for either of those if we've left the country." At his noise of protest, I barreled on faster. "You know I had that vision. Of your sword. It must have been telling me we're meant to go find it. Rhedyn was afraid of it. I remembered that. If we can manage to retrieve it, it must be able to stop her."

Darton's voice shook. "There are dark fae stalking my sister, and you want me to just abandon her to go on some hunt across the ocean?"

"It sounds like she'll be safer that way," Jagger put in.

"Yes," I said. "Darton, I can't promise anything, but the dark fae thrive on logic and order. Making chaos just for the sake of it is totally against their nature. If they don't think they can control us by hurting her, or anyone else, they won't do it. They'd get nothing out of it, not even satisfaction. And frankly, if we leave, they'll probably be too busy chasing after us to even consider it."

"I still don't—"

I grasped his hand with my still bare one. "Art. Remember what we talked about. We need a plan, and we need to be smart about it, or we're never going to get ahead of them. This is the best thing we can do. It protects our people here, *and* so many more. The Darkest One wants nothing more than oblivion for all living things. And she's had fifteen hundred years to stew over her defeat. She's not going to hold back when she gets out, and the light fae are out of practice defending against a force that strong. It's not just your sister and my parents. It's *everyone* in danger if we don't act."

Darton dragged in a breath. His fingers tightened around mine. His mouth twisted, and for a second I thought he was going to keep arguing. But when he spoke, his tone was resigned.

"All right. Then let's get out of here as fast as we can."

15

A knock sounded on the front door, and Priya sprang off the sofa. She joined the three of us already standing by the hall as I let our company in.

"The rescue squad is here!" Keevan announced, striding in with Izzy behind him. He took in our combined expressions, and his own darkened. "Ah, okay. No cause for celebration yet."

"We *are* here, anyway." Izzy looked to me. "What exactly do you need us to do? Are we smuggling you out of here or something?"

"No, we just want to confuse the trail." I handed her an opaque plastic bag containing Darton's "lucky" football jersey—smeared with his blood. He hadn't seemed happy about picking out two objects of great personal meaning to him or the blood part, but he'd followed my instructions without complaint. Even now, he was shifting his weight, just eager to get going. "You and Keevan will bring this in the van and head south. Jagger and Priya are going to take off to the north. And Darton and I will borrow Keevan's car to get to the airport west of here."

I held out my hand, and Keevan placed his spare key

in it. "Seems like you're making a habit of commandeering my car in one way or another," he said with a half smile.

"Well, this time you should get it back. I'll leave it in the airport parking lot and text you the exact location. The fae are just more likely to have taken note of the van and Jagger's car by now. You haven't been here since things got really bad." I turned to Priya. "How long should we give Ohanko?"

She checked the time on her phone. "I think we're good. He didn't think it'd take too long to lead the one dark fae here on a bit of a chase. We shouldn't have to worry about that one seeing us leaving now." She raised her head to meet my eyes. "I'll do everything I can to get the enclave on board making sure the others don't touch either of your families."

"And my colleagues have already confirmed they're on their way," Jagger put in.

"Okay," I said. "Then we're ready to go. Everyone, into the cars and out of here, and make it quick."

"Wait!" Keevan said. He grabbed Darton in a brief hug. "Look after yourself, man."

Izzy embraced Darton in turn. "Let us know when you're over there safely."

We wouldn't be safe over in Britain until Rhedyn was dead or locked away and the Darkest One secure once more, but I didn't see any point in rubbing that fact in their faces. They stepped back. Izzy's hand groped after Keevan's and squeezed it. He glanced at her, a hint of a flush shading his dark brown cheeks.

He really should just tell her how he felt already. But I didn't have time to impart that advice right now.

"Out, out," I said, hefting my bag and shooing

everyone to the door.

We spilled onto the yard and dashed for the vehicles. Doors whined open and thumped shut. I dropped into the warm leather seat of Keevan's new Toyota and jammed the key into the ignition. The second the engine rumbled, I hit the gas.

Darton yanked on his seatbelt. He set his hand on the door for balance as we swung sharply around toward the drive. "Do you really think the trick with the shirt and the book is going to work?"

"Between your emotional investment and the physical essence in your blood, they'll give an impression of your presence. Enough that any dark fae sensing it will assume you're in that vehicle. In a few minutes, we'll be too far apart for them to compare."

I pushed the gas pedal harder as we reached the highway. Behind us, Jagger swerved in the opposite direction. The van roared up behind it. I raised my hand, not sure if any of them could see my farewell through the windows. Then we left them behind in the dust.

"All we have to do is get on that plane," I said. "Then there's nothing the fae can do."

"What if they follow us on?"

I shook my head. "A dark fae would never take that risk. Being that high up—that close to the sun—with no control over most of the windows? They couldn't tolerate it. They'll have arrived by boat, and that's how they'll have to get back. It'll give us a few days head start."

Not that Rhedyn wouldn't have a contingent of dark fae at her beck and call on the other side of the ocean, of course. But a dozen fewer was still good in my books.

* * *

The airport parking lot was a mass of cars, honking horns, and blinking lights. With the help of a twig and a few muttered words, a spot opened up for us not far from the shuttle stop. We grabbed our things and ran, catching the shuttle just as it pulled in.

As the shuttle carried us off toward the Departures terminal, I took a swift inventory of my things. Several wands, twigs, and bundles of herbs and salt filled my expansive carry-on purse. The additional supplies in my suitcase, tucked in with toiletries and a few changes of clothes, I hoped would be enough to see us through the entire trip. However long—or tragically brief—it might be.

Darton had a shoulder bag and a small duffel. He'd been so distracted while he was packing I think he would have forgotten to bring socks if I hadn't popped in and looked things over. He pulled out his phone, checked his messages even though he hadn't gotten any alerts, and returned it to his pocket.

Audrey still hadn't called him back.

All at once he went rigid. "Passport," he murmured to me, leaning away from the other shuttle riders. "I don't have my passport."

I waved his concern off. "That's an easy fix." I fumbled through my things for a scrap of paper and folded it. "Lick your thumb," I told him, turning to face him so no one else could see what I was up to. He did, and then swiped it over the paper at my gesture. I grasped one of the wands, closed my eyes, and murmured two verses under my breath.

When I looked again, I was holding a perfect replica of an American passport, complete with Darton's photo. He blinked at it and let out a hoarse chuckle.

"I don't know if I'm ever going to get completely used to how amazing you are."

"That's fine with me," I said with a teasing tug of his jacket's fur-trimmed hood. Just for a second, the tension looming over us seemed to recede.

The shuttle spat us out at the far end of the terminal. We hustled over to the baggage check. We'd just dropped off our suitcases and started toward the Security lines when Darton's ringtone blared.

His hand jerked to his pocket. He yanked out the phone and whipped it to his ear.

"Audrey," he said, so choked up I'd have been surprised if she couldn't hear his relief over the phone line. "Thanks for getting back to me. No, no, everything's okay over here. I'm sorry if I made you worry."

She must have started talking, because he fell silent. His face darkened. I watched him, my heart sinking.

"Uh-huh. Yeah, I can see why that would make you nervous. Why don't you— Why don't you stick around at home for the rest of the weekend, just to be safe? Have your friends over there if you want to hang out. Exactly. And if you see her around on Monday... Yeah. That's right. But let me know too, okay? Either way. I want to know."

He stopped just before the beginning of the line as he hung up, and lowered his head.

"What?" I said, as gently as I could. My nerves were jumping.

"It's nothing big," he said. "But, at the mall, she saw this woman watching her. Not for very long, but over and over again, all around the place, over a whole two hours. She says it felt like the woman *wanted* her to notice—like she'd keep looking just long enough for Audrey to glance over, and then the next time Audrey checked she'd have disappeared. Until ten or fifteen minutes later."

An uncomfortable itch nibbled over my skin. "Like maybe she was hoping Audrey would get nervous to tell someone about, so it'd get back to you?"

"That's what I'm thinking." Darton ran his hand through his gold-blond hair. "You figure it was one of the dark fae."

It wasn't a question, but I answered anyway. "That seems like by far the most likely explanation."

He looked to the Security lines and back toward the exits. His jaw worked. "They're there right now, *stalking* her..."

I touched his arm. "We already knew that. And I hate that they're scaring her. But you gave her good advice. And they haven't done anything but watch. As soon as you're too far away to intervene, they'll stop trying to provoke you."

His gaze slid to me. "You're sure? Absolutely, one hundred percent sure of that, Em?"

"Absolutely one hundred percent." I squeezed his elbow. "I promise, Art: What we're doing right now is the *best* way to protect everyone. We leave now, and Audrey's never going to see that woman again."

He swallowed thickly and nodded. "Right. Then this is still what we've got to do."

He hefted his bag onto one of the conveyer belts. I followed suit, a weight settling in my gut.

I didn't offer promises lightly. So I sure as hell hoped I hadn't just made one I couldn't keep.

16

Car retrieved. No burn marks or shattered glass. Definite improvement over last time!

The corners of my mouth twitched up as I covertly typed in a response to Keevan's text. *Glad you two returned safe. Any fae sightings?*

One of the flight attendants walked by with a rattling drink cart. I tucked my hand closer to the hard plastic armrest.

Keevan was the last to get in touch. A couple hours ago, Jagger had confirmed he'd split up from Priya and joined a couple of colleagues heading east to my parents' hometown, and Priya had been in touch about an hour after that to say she was about to go into her enclave's territory to make her petition.

I'd also talked to my mom just before the flight had taken off. Hearing her warm voice, upbeat despite her minor injuries, had left my nerves a little more settled.

Keevan's response popped up on the screen. *Nothing definite. A couple came into the diner where we grabbed lunch and seemed to give us odd looks, but maybe they just thought we looked odd.*

I rolled my eyes. *Keep your eyes open and stay safe. This is the perfect excuse for you two to stick together in the next few days, you know. Maybe you could make a date of it.*

Shut up, Merlin, Keevan replied, with an emoji that was grinning as it stuck out its tongue.

I shot back one with a broad smirk and turned off the phone.

Darton shifted beside me. He'd managed to drift off after the attendants had brought dinner around, and now his head was slumped against the padded seat. His hair had fallen forward to shade his closed eyes. Typical Arthur, able to conk out anywhere if he took a mind to it.

I scooted a little down in my own seat and tried to relax into the stiff padding. After a moment, I let my head tilt sideways to rest against Darton's. The faint rasp of his sleeping breath tugged at my heart.

Right now, for these few hours, *we* were safe. No dark fae could touch us up here in the sky. But it wasn't long before we'd be coming to earth again.

If the Darkest One broke free, we'd be the first she'd want to destroy. It was by my will that she'd been trapped all those centuries, and she'd always wanted Arthur, for reasons she'd never bothered to share with me.

This could be the last time I spent with my king. I hadn't wanted to think it that plainly before, hadn't dared to even start to speak it to him, but I knew it was true with an ache that pierced right through the center of me. We'd barely had a month knowing each other again, Darton had hardly recovered a fraction of the memories inside him...

It wasn't fair. Our lives in tandem had always been cut so short. I wanted to see the Arthur of middle age, the Arthur turned elderly, the full life he would have built on that kingly foundation.

Well, maybe we would get that this time, just this once. This trip would be the first time I'd come close to confronting the Darkest One since I'd cast my spell and doomed us all to our bizarre, recycling fate. And I was arriving with ideas I'd never considered before.

I just wished I'd had more time to test those ideas, to experiment. Was I *ready* to face her? To cut her off from the world of the living for good?

I didn't know the answer to that question. I might not until I was standing there in her cave, with her and Rhedyn before me.

My eyes slid closed. I didn't sleep, but for a short while in the hazy airplane lights, I dozed. When Darton stirred against me, I jerked back into full alertness.

He tipped his face closer to mine, his nose briefly brushing my cheek in a sort of caress. Then he straightened up in his seat. He reached across the armrest for my hand.

I'd put my gloves back on, but the warmth of his skin still seeped through the fabric. I squeezed his hand back, a sudden lump filling my throat.

"Do you remember," he said quietly, looking at the back of the seat in front of him, "when we talked about why I would be king? Whether it was my choice?"

He'd been dreaming memories again. The description he'd given wasn't the most detailed, but I knew immediately what conversation he meant. The words penetrated my own store of memories and dredged one up to the surface. I let it slip into my consciousness.

The fire crackled. The skinned rabbit carcass sizzled over it on the makeshift spit, filling the air with a savory, smoky smell. I leaned back on my hands on my bedroll in the only position I'd found that didn't aggravate the dozen or so muscles protesting from a day spent on horseback. My prince poked at the fire with a stick and sat down beside me.

I might have minded the riding, but I didn't mind this part of traveling. When it was just the two of us, no need to mind my words or restrain my powers. When Arthur could let out his breath here and there too.

Back at the castle, his responsibilities piled up the second he passed through the gates, as if his arrival had triggered an avalanche. His father was shifting more and more kingly duties onto Arthur's shoulders.

Apparently the prince's thoughts had traveled along similar lines. "If we make good time, we should be home tomorrow evening."

I made a noncommittal sound. "Maybe we should find some very urgent matters to divert us along the way, then."

He shook his head at me, but he smiled too. "I need to be there when I can. If you don't like the court, you picked the wrong fellow to offer your services to."

"Humph." I lay back with hands behind my head. "Let me give that some thought."

"I'm only going to be busier once I'm king. I've been heading toward that role since I was born."

I peered up through the bowed branches of the oaks around us. The sky was purple with the deepening evening. "That's just the way it is, isn't it? You were born to the king, therefore you will also be king."

"Well, yes. Isn't that how it's always worked?"

"Around here, in recent times, I suppose. Do you ever wonder why? Why should it be set in stone like that? I don't see why simply being born should oblige a person to take on a position like that automatically. You still have choices."

Arthur gave a bark of a laugh. "Do I now?"

"Of course. You have some. You could run away into the woods if you wanted to. What is anyone else going to do about it? I'll cast some magic—they'll never find you."

He really laughed then. "I suppose you'd like that."

Part of me would. But another part of me knew he wasn't meant for a life as some sort of forest-bound hermit. My father wouldn't have prepared me for this mission otherwise. Whatever Arthur was meant for, it was big enough that it worried the fae.

"I have no preferences," I said blithely despite the knot that had formed in my stomach. "I will follow wherever you go."

The prince was silent for a moment. Then he said, "How many choices have you had, Merlin?"

The knot tightened. I made a dismissive face. "Some. Enough."

"Hmmm. Well, whatever choices I have, taking on the crown will be one of them. I want to be king, even with all the work that comes with it. I can do at least as much good as my father has. I have to try to, in any case. For the people. They need me more than the woods do."

The impressions faded back into the interior of the plane. I swiped my hand across my mouth. My prince had done so much *more* good than his father had. How much farther could he have gotten, if not for our dark enemy and that one bloody moment?

"Yeah," I said to Darton. "I remember."

He paused, still not looking at me. "Why—why did you argue against it? I thought you were all for my being king."

"What?" I pushed myself upright. Funny how our memories could cast such different lights on the same discussion. "That wasn't what I meant at all. I knew you would be great. It just bothered me that you never got a real chance to make that decision for yourself. As your friend, I'd have liked you to have the opportunity to do whatever you wished to, without feeling bound to any specific direction."

"Oh. Okay. I'm sorry." His mouth twisted wryly. He traced his thumb over the back of my hand. "I guess I haven't ever had a whole lot of control over my life, huh."

The lump in my throat rose higher. "No," I said. "But I'm still doing whatever I can to change that."

"I know." He drew in a breath. "And, in case you ever wonder, based on the pieces that have come back to me so far, I think I would have decided to follow in my father's footsteps either way. Even if there hadn't been any pressure to at all. It felt... right. I don't know how to explain it."

"You don't need to," I said. "I don't doubt it. It was who you were—inside, even when no one else was around to have a say."

We stayed like that, our hands clasped, until the attendants brought around a quick breakfast. I'd barely wolfed down the miniature muffin and rather sad looking omelet when the captain announced the plane was beginning its descent. A prickle of anticipation ran over my skin.

Jagger had arranged for one of his UK contacts, a mother and son duo who lived on the outskirts of London, to meet us at the airport. I guessed I'd find out from them what the most recent developments in Somerset were and what resources they could offer, and then I'd get to work hunting down that sword of Arthur's. Although I was more worried about what would happen *after* I located the pool of nightmares I'd seen in my vision.

A different sort of tingle passed through me as we shuffled with the rest of the passengers off the plane. A flicker of energy, with an almost probing sensation to it, sent my nerves twitching. My head jerked up. I scanned the plane, peering through the windows, opening my deeper awareness at the same time. Nothing fae-like caught my attention anywhere nearby.

My anxiety must be getting the better of me.

We made it through passport control and hustled to the baggage claim area. Our suitcases seemed to take forever coming out. I was just starting to curse myself for not finding some way to pack more lightly—but it was so hard to know what tools I might need here, and I had to be prepared for Rhedyn—when the first of them finally tumbled onto the conveyer belt. We hefted them off and jogged over to customs.

Thankfully we looked innocent enough that the officer decided against digging through my suitcase, sparing me the energy of diverting her from its contents. In the hall beyond, a line of people waited for friends or family to arrive. My gaze darted over the signs and stopped on one simply printed with *Emma & Darton.*

The woman holding it was middle-aged, with a bird-like face—big eyes framed by round glasses, a pointy nose and small chin—and a chin-length bob of straight, mahogany-brown hair. She was flanked by a young man I assumed was the son Jagger had mentioned. He'd inherited her hair, which he wore short and casually mussed, but high cheekbones and a strong jaw he must have thanked his father for.

"Emma and Darton," I said as we came to a stop in

front of them. I offered my hand to the woman.

"I'm Mavis," she said with a brisk voice and a firm shake. "Glad to see you made it here unharmed. This is my son, Eric."

Eric gave us a little salute and a warm flash of a grin that quickly faded. "Let's get you out of here. There's been more trouble brewing just in the last hour."

17

"Trouble?" I repeated as Mavis and Eric ushered us toward the airport parking area. My body had already tensed. Not that I'd been expecting we'd arrive to a relaxing holiday, but I'd thought I was going to have at least a minute or two to get my bearings before we were launched into the fray. "What's happened?"

"We have a colleague who monitors certain types of energy via satellite data," Eric said. "Starting just under an hour ago, he's been reporting some strange—*big*—surges that we know are usually associated with fae magic. It isn't close to our site of concern in Somerset, maybe four hours north, but that doesn't mean it isn't connected."

"It's bigger than anything we've seen 'round the interchange," Mavis added. "We've caught some reports on the 'net of odd lights and other visual phenomena in the area as well."

"Odd *lights*?" I frowned. "That wouldn't be dark fae, then."

"We actually wondered if there's some sort of conflict going on." Eric stopped at the back of a big green SUV. Like the two vehicles I'd seen in Jagger's use, solar panels covered its roof and lamps dotted the sides of its frame. He pushed the hatch open and swung my suitcase inside. "Maybe light and dark at odds—fighting with each other."

Darton heaved his bag in beside mine. "The light fae I've met haven't been very eager to fight."

"No," I agreed. They generally preferred to just stay out of any affairs that didn't immediately involve them. "But if the dark fae set on a bunch for some reason, they'd defend themselves. As well as they can." The light fae I'd seen recently had let many of their more forceful magical skills lapse from lack of practice. I hoped those here were better equipped.

Mavis opened the driver's side door. "I know your main concern was the goings-on at the interchange, but we feel this situation is more urgent. And like Eric said, the two situations could be connected. Unless you have a major objection, we'd prefer to take a look around the area up north first."

"I can understand that." I paused by the SUV's back door, sucking in my lower lip. I *definitely* wasn't ready to confront Rhedyn without Excalibur on our side anyway. And there was no reason I couldn't get to work on that part of our problem in a moving vehicle. "All right. We should get the full picture before we decide what to do next."

The inside of the SUV smelled like worn leather laced with a hint of herbal smoke. I took a deeper sniff. Chamomile and rose. They must burn a little in here regularly for the protective energies. I'd give these hunters points for knowing how to do that much. So many people in this day and age had completely forgotten all the wisdom of the past, even though some of it was totally sound.

I settled into the comfortable seat and tugged open my purse. The last time I'd been able to gather fresh twigs was during a brief detour just before we'd reached the airport. The life energy in those would be half faded by now, but there'd be at least enough left for a basic finding spell. I could collect some more at our next destination. Before we got too close to the possible fighting, preferably.

As Mavis drove the van out onto the highway, rain tapped against the windshield and roof. The sky overhead was a mass of thick gray clouds that blotted out all but the faintest glimmer of sunlight. I couldn't help grimacing.

Eric had turned in his seat to look back at me. He must have caught my dismayed expression.

"It's been like this three straight days now," he said. "The cloud cover hasn't let a single beam of sunlight in, all across the whole south of the country. I know we've got a reputation for the wet on this side of the pond, but honestly, it's pretty unusual for the weather to be this bad. It's hard not to wonder if there's a supernatural component."

I nodded, my hands clenching at the thought. "The dark fae could be directing the weather. Cutting off the sun will make it harder for the light fae—or me—to interfere with their plans. Less immediate power we can draw on."

"So they could do that then? Just conjure up a sky full of clouds."

"If they wanted to enough to give it the necessary focus and energy." If the fae wanted to, they could do a lot worse. "I guess like Jagger you two have mostly dealt with

150

glooms and other dark vermin?"

Eric gave me a crooked smile. "There hasn't been much call for anything else. This is the first time I've ever seen the full fae make a big enough commotion to worry us. Mostly they leave us to us and them to them." He cocked his head. "So how does a lovely lady like yourself end up tangled up in all this fae drama?"

My own lips twitched, but more in amusement than appreciation of the compliment. I wasn't here to be *lovely* and I didn't care a great deal about being a *lady* either, for that matter. "Call it a birthright," I said. "It's probably best we leave it at that."

"Hmm. Jagger did say you're a mysterious one. But I do like a woman of mystery." He waggled his eyebrows playfully. "As you can see, I'm very charming. That's got to earn me at least a clue."

"Eric," Mavis said, sounding fondly exasperated. Darton coughed into his hand.

I resisted the urge to roll my eyes. "It doesn't really make a difference. All you need to know is that I'm very familiar with the fae, and what they're up to in Somerset is going to be very bad for all of us if we don't stop them."

He held up his hands. "Okay, okay, keep your secrets. But you never know. This charm might sneak up on you."

Darton reached over to rest his hand on my shoulder. His fingers pressed my skin tightly. I glanced at him, but his gaze was fixed on the back of Eric's seat. Well, really it was more of a glare.

"Don't you have energies to be monitoring or something like that?" he said, his voice tight.

Eric twisted a little farther to meet Darton's eyes. His own tone stayed friendly. "We've got a bit of a drive. No harm in passing at least part of the time enjoyably."

If we didn't shift the conversation, I had a feeling no one was going to be enjoying it shortly. I cleared my throat before Darton could reply. "*I* do have other responsibilities to take care of. I don't suppose you have a paper map of the country—or at least part of it—that I could use?"

"Of course," Mavis said. She motioned Eric to the glove compartment and smiled at me in the rearview mirror. "It doesn't take long in this line of work to realize you shouldn't rely on satellite reception for your directions."

Eric pulled out a stack of folded maps, some rattier than others. "You'd prefer the full spread of the country?" he asked.

"For now," I said. "I might need to narrow it down later."

He handed one of the more worn ones back to me. "What exactly are you going to do with that?"

"There's something we need to find before we take on the dark fae who's leading the activity by the interchange," I said. "And I need a better idea of where we should be looking. Think of it as a sort of dowsing."

I gave Darton's hand a squeeze. He dropped it without my having to ask. I took a deep breath and willed a calm to spread through my muscles while I expelled the air. The map crinkled as I spread it out on my lap.

I grasped one of the twigs I'd taken from my purse and murmured at it. Then I drew it across my palm. A thin red line split open in my skin, blood beading along it. The sting shot through my nerves. The twig crumbled. Eric inhaled sharply.

"I'm fine," I said. "I've done this hundreds of times."

"She has." Darton didn't sound as if he exactly approved of that fact, but I wasn't asking for his permission. Life blood gave every act of magic twice as much punch.

I gripped another twig between my fingers and closed my eyes. My arm swayed as I held it out over the map. "*On paper as real, show me the place I seek,*" I murmured in the old tongue.

Part of me was braced for questions from my spectators, but Darton knew well enough by now to keep quiet, and Eric appeared to be a fast learner. As I let go of those concerns, my mind raced back to my vision from more than a week ago. The sensation of plunging into sticky, churning shadows. The gleaming sword I'd spotted in their midst. *Excalibur.*

"*On paper as real, show me the place I seek,*" I repeated. My hand bobbed as the sense of that pool of darkness washed through me. A slight tug, to the left. Away. A little to the right again.

The marshy flavor of algae and rotted reeds coated my tongue, but a shiver of energy came with it. A sense of all the power in that blade, burning in the pool's midst, just not brightly enough to penetrate it completely. The sword needed Arthur's soul to reach its full potential.

A chill flowed up my drifting arm and bit into my chest. The sensation of darkness deepened. For a split-second, my mind fell away into the memory of my vision. My companions and the interior of the car spiraled away. I reached and reached and—

—slammed to a halt. The impact smacked me as if I'd hit a concrete wall. A wave of pain and fear crashed through my mind, tossing me back so hard my eyes flew open and my hand jerked. The twig cracked and disintegrated as it hit the map.

I held myself still, breathing hard, my thoughts still rattled. I'd never been put off quite like that before.

"Em?" Darton said tentatively. He was staring at me, his face clouded with worry. Eric was staring too, his eyes wide and awed.

"It's okay," I said quickly, although it wasn't. The place in my vision, that pond of shadows and nightmares, *really* didn't want me coming there. But I had to anyway. It was the only chance we had.

The map had crumpled in my lap. I tugged it straight with my good hand as my fingers curled against the cut on my other palm.

My search hadn't been completely in vain. When the repelling force had struck me, my hand had jerked down— and smeared blood across a county in the northeast, near Scarborough. The spot it had been hovering over when the supernatural forces I'd been seeking had responded.

Thank the light for my reflexes. At least I had a general area to focus on now. When we were done here, I could head out that way. Closer, I could get a better lock on the pool's exact location. And I'd be prepared for its defenses next time.

"I've never seen anything quite like that," Eric said. "Are you some kind of magician, Emma?" His tone was still jaunty, but a thread of wonder ran through it.

"You could say that." I grasped a handful of twigs and murmured a few words to seal the cut on my hand. Then I folded up the map. "I don't think you'll want this back now that I've bled all over it."

"Nah, nah, we've got plenty." He was still watching me. "I have the feeling I'm really going to enjoy getting to know you."

"I don't suppose with your magical ways you can figure out what the fae are up to?" Mavis said from the driver's seat.

I grimaced. "Unfortunately no. I can sometimes glean pieces of information about distant events that are useful to me, but I don't have much control over how or when that happens. But the old-fashioned method of going and having a look still works just fine."

My gaze slid to the windows as I spoke. We'd left behind the London suburbs sometime while I'd been tracking my nightmare-ish pond. I wasn't sure how much time had passed in my reverie. It didn't feel like long, but sorcery stretched the mind in strange ways. All I could see beyond the road were grassy dells and a couple of farmhouses in the distance.

A sense of deja vu tickled over me. I sat with it, examining the feeling, as Mavis took one turn, and then another, the second onto a two-lane dirt road that sent pebbles rattling against the underside of the SUV. Forestland sprouted up on either side of the road. The tickle wriggled deeper into my chest.

I knew where we were going. Because I'd come this way many, many times in the past fifteen centuries, if not more than once in the last hundred years. The energies of this place were etched into my very soul.

Why wouldn't they be, when it was the place of my first birth? My original enclave—well, my father's enclave, more like—was the source of the disturbance the fae hunters had noticed.

Had Rhedyn ordered an attack on them for reasons only she could know? If she'd thought attempting to harm them would affect me anywhere near as deeply as going after my parents of this life, she'd been pretty impressively mistaken. For one, the light fae could defend themselves as need be on their own. And for another, I hadn't felt close to any of the fae living here by even the end of my first life. Well, except for my father, but he was long faded into the greater light.

That didn't mean I wouldn't intervene on their behalf if I could, of course. The enclave might not be my home anymore, but its inhabitants were far more my people than any of Rhedyn's were.

Several minutes later, Mavis pulled the car to a stop at the edge of a ditch. "This is as close as we can get in the car. I suppose we should watch from here before attempting closer observation. Our computer-savvy friend is still monitoring the emissions and so on. He says they're still fluctuating oddly, but no more than they were earlier."

I undid my seatbelt. "The rest of you are best off staying here anyway. I know the folk in these woods. I can go talk to them directly."

18

"You *know* these fae?" Eric said. If his eyes got any larger I wasn't sure his head would contain them. "Have you ever even been to England before?"

"A while back." I pulled a few of my wands from my purse. Light willing, I wouldn't need them. "Part of that long story."

Darton released his seatbelt as well. "Do you want me to come with you?"

I hesitated, meeting his gaze. He looked back at me mildly. I didn't think he had any great desire to chat with the fae kind—at the only other enclave he'd visited, he'd been either ignored or gawked at depending mostly on the maturity of the fae—but we'd developed an unspoken understanding around certain topics in the last few weeks. One of which being that I didn't generally like to leave him out of my sight when fae trouble was afoot.

I still didn't. But part of me balked at bringing him along to my father's enclave nearly as much.

He wouldn't be just a curiosity to them. Thanks to my father, Arthur and his rule had become entwined with the enclave's history—and not, from what I remembered from those return visits in my first life, in a positive way. The light fae preferred to keep themselves separate from humankind. They hadn't approved of my birth, and they absolutely hadn't approved of my father's coaching me to insert myself into the world of "lesser" people.

I had no idea what was transpiring around the enclave right now, though. If the light fae were under attack by the dark, Rhedyn's forces could easily stumble on the hunters' car and recognize Darton for what he was. It wasn't as if Mavis and Eric were prepared to deal with an onslaught.

No, as always my king was safer at my side.

"Let's go," I said with a jerk of my head. To Mavis and Eric, I added, "I'll try not to be long. Wait here unless it gets dangerous. If you have to take off, we'll get in touch to meet up as soon as we can." Jagger had given me Mavis's phone number.

"Now, just a—" Mavis started, but I'd already hopped out and shut the door. Darton followed suit.

It was still drizzling, but at least not outright pouring. I tugged my jacket's hood over my head and motioned for Darton to join me. Wand in hand, I leapt the ditch and tramped into the woods. Damp autumn leaves squished under my sneakers.

"Is there anything in particular I should be watching for?" Darton asked as the trees closed in around us.

My gaze darted over the landscape. The interlacing branches overhead held off all but a faint misting of rain, and a loamy smell filled my nose. None of the shadows pooled that around the tree trunks and shrubs looked more alert than the usual variety. Which was how they should be. In usual circumstances, glooms wouldn't come drifting this close to a light fae enclave even by accident.

"If you see something dark that's moving, shout," I said. "But I'll probably notice first anyway."

"Right." He squinted in the gloomy daylight. "How *do* you know this place?"

"It's my father's enclave." I clambered over a log. "My original father. I lived here up until a few days shy of when I first met up with you."

"Oh." Darton blinked, looking started. "I knew— I mean, you said you were half— Somehow I never thought about you spending all that time growing up with just the fae."

I shrugged. "I didn't know anything different back then. I'm lucky my father was as worldly as he was. Although I suppose I drove him to it, to some extent. You can't expect a half-human child to behave the same way and accept the same rules as a full fae. And he always believed in doing his research."

"So... is he still here? Do you have family waiting?"

"No. He was getting on toward elderly when I was born. He passed into the greater light a long time ago. And fae don't really have *family* the same way humans do. The light sort kind of... grow, rather than being born, and then they end up raised by the whole enclave. It's only when they mix with humans you get actual parents and so on."

Darton seemed to take a few minutes absorbing that idea, walking in silence. Then he said, "I'm not sure about these hunters Jagger set us up with."

"Mavis and Eric? What's wrong with them?" Nothing about them had struck me as particularly concerning. They'd put up with my weirdness calmly enough. I always appreciated people who could hold their questions in check.

Darton rubbed his mouth. "Eric comes across kind of pushy, don't you think?"

I glanced over at him, my own mouth twitching to contain a laugh. "Please tell me you're not jealous over a little half-hearted flirting."

He scowled at me. "It didn't sound that half-hearted to me."

"Ah, that guy strikes me as the type who turns on the charm at anyone who appears female and within the acceptable age range." I nudged Darton with my elbow. "It's not as if I have any interest in indulging him, Your Highness. I do have rather a lot of more important things on my mind."

"Obviously," Darton said. His shoulders relaxed a bit. He reached over and took my hand. I threaded my fingers through his, enjoying the contact even through my glove more than I really should have. I could be allowed one small indulgence here and there, though, couldn't I?

None of the forestland looked especially familiar, but that was the way of the light and the living—always growing, changing. We skirted a dense clump of saplings and navigated a muddy stretch of ground that sucked at our shoes. I had just a second to appreciate the feel of solid earth beneath my feet again when two glimmering figures appeared in our path.

"Son of Eóghan," the woman said. "Your companion must come no farther."

I halted, breathing deep and opening my senses. I couldn't feel even the faintest shiver of the enclave's boundary yet. Why were they stopping us so early?

"Neither of us is going to cause any trouble," I said. "Surely he can at least wait at the fringes?"

"I promise to be a considerate guest," Darton put in with a tip of his head. That small motion made both of the fae flinch.

I frowned. Before I could comment, the woman spoke again. "This is the ruling of the elders. We will not have him near our home. He may wait here or return to those who brought you."

I hadn't expected them to welcome my king with an embrace, but this reaction was rather extreme. From the set of the woman's mouth, she wasn't open to any negotiation on the subject, though. Light fae didn't have quite the same dedication to strict authority as the dark fae did, but they still carried a deep respect for the elders— those of the deepest roots, as they often put it. I scanned the forest around us again. There'd been no hint of dark fae presence here so far.

"I can't leave him in the middle of danger," I said. "I understand there's been some sort of disturbance here— that's why I've come. Are there dark fae about?"

The light fae man's lips curled into an expression of disgust. "The shadowy ones are all busy elsewhere—past the forests, by the sea, under the earth."

Typical light fae poetic nonsense, but I knew how to interpret that much. They knew what Rhedyn was up to, then. But they hadn't bothered to do anything to stop her. That was typical too.

"He will face no danger here," the woman said.

"Will the two of you stay and make sure that doesn't change?" I asked.

They both looked at Darton warily, but the woman nodded. "We will await your return."

"I don't get it," Darton said. "What's the problem?"

"We'll only waste time trying to argue about it. They're not likely to budge." I squeezed his arm. "I'll be back as soon as I know what's going on. You stay alert. You've got the dagger still, don't you?"

He touched the hilt protruding from his pocket. He'd returned the weapon to that spot as soon as he'd been able to retrieve it from his checked luggage. It wouldn't get him very far if a full dark fae appeared, but it didn't appear likely we'd be facing any here after all. What were all those energy fluctuations about then? Maybe the hunters' colleague's system had simply gone haywire? That wasn't a comforting thought.

I hurried on through the woods, my hand tight around my wand. Even if there weren't dark forces about, the less time I left my king with only the uncertain protection of those two fae, the better. They hadn't looked like they wanted to come within ten feet of him.

As I approached the enclave, the sense of the boundary ahead rippled over my skin. I pushed onward, still scanning the brush—and hesitated. A big, old oak that stood about ten paces to my right triggered an immediate rush of recognition. Could it really be...?

I edged closer to it, my breath tight in my throat. The second I laid my hand on the gnarled bark, I was sure.

It was my father's tree. The one that had contained our home all those years ago. He'd always liked living close to the edge of the enclave, so that he could slip away for his field observations without facing too much judgment. The enclave's boundaries must have been redrawn since that time—perhaps several times—and they'd left this oak behind. No one had taken it over after my father had died.

Childhood memories from that first childhood, so

long past, trickled through my head. Racing around this tree, daring my father to try to catch me. Using the life energy pulsing through its trunk to magically scramble up its towering trunk. Perching on the broad branches overhead and peering through the forest, watching the full fae come and go. Wondering what my life would be like when I was old enough to have responsibilities of my own. Until Father called me down for some new lesson or test.

I'd never given my human mother much thought. I'd never even met her to remember her, after all, and Father had rarely talked about her. As far as I knew, he'd sent her back to her people not long after she'd given birth to me, releasing her from the charm he'd placed on her—a much more potent charm than Eric's human sort.

After so many lives with fully human births, with at least somewhat "normal" families, I felt that empty space in my recollections now. Had *she* even remembered me— that she'd had a baby, that her son had been taken from her? Or had those nine months with my father in the enclave dissolved into a blur like so much of my many lives between then and now?

The breeze shifted with a wisp of wisteria scent, and an elder fae stepped forward through the enclave's boundary. His black hair fell in several long braids about his smooth but nearly translucent face. He studied me with pale blue eyes.

"Merlin," he said in a dry crackle of a voice. Apparently he was old enough or skeptical enough—or both—that he felt he could dispense with formalities.

He struck me as vaguely familiar, but not in a way I could pin down. I gave him a slight tip of my head out of politeness. "Indeed. If we've met before, you'll have to remind me. I don't keep good memories of my past lives beyond the first."

"Cormag," he said. "I was a friend of your father's—but your birth was before my time."

I made myself step back from the oak. "Well met. I suppose I should go speak with all the elders. I understand there's been quite a commotion here. You've drawn the notice of the humans, you know. At least the more alert among them."

No concern touched his placid expression. He held out his hand to motion me still. "I'm aware. It was our intention to draw mortal eyes this way. We knew they would draw you with them, like a current. Your light echoed across the land the moment you arrived here."

Oh, light save me. The light fae tendency toward flowery vagueness never got less annoying over time. "You were trying to summon me?" I said.

"As quickly as possible. To tell you to return to the place from which you came."

I blinked at him. Well, he wasn't beating around the bush now, even if he was still weirdly vague in his directness. "Technically," I said, patting the oak, "I came from right here."

Cormag frowned. "But you have no roots here now. And you will not set them down. You and your king must make passage across the ocean once more."

"Okay, yeah, no can do," I replied. "If that's all you wanted to say to me, I might as well get back to my king and take care of more important business."

I started to turn. Cormag cleared his throat sharply. "Merlin," he said. "Do you know why your father prepared you to follow the one named Arthur?"

I paused, glancing back at him. "I got the gist. The dark fae had been interested in his family line. Father was afraid they'd been meddling somehow, or that they would. He wanted me to be on hand in case they... escalated the situation."

"Surely you were aware the troubles ran deeper than that?"

I swiveled to face him again and folded my arms over my chest. "I only know what my father bothered to tell me, which honestly didn't include much detail. I'm pretty sure the Darkest One's attack took him as much by surprise as it did me. Which, by the way, is why we're here at all—to make sure she doesn't bring down even more death and destruction. It'd be nice if you showed a little more concern about that possibility."

Cormag's lips pursed. "If she does go free, your king will be the soul she's most eager to destroy. And we'd rather the aftershock play out on lands as far from here as possible."

"Or how about I just stop her from getting free in the first place? That sounds like a solution that works better for everyone."

"You don't appear to have had the greatest success at stopping her in the past."

My mouth twisted. "I have to *try*. I at least contained her for an awfully long time. It isn't just Arthur. Do you have any idea how many people she might—"

"Your father believed," Cormag broke in, "that the greatest disaster that might befall us *and* humankind was not the Darkest One's existence but what she might do if she claimed your king. The best for all would be if he passed from this world far from her, never to return. But failing that, we want neither of them nearby."

His bland selfishness sparked the frustration I'd been trying to suppress. It flared into outright anger. "Great," I said. "That sounds like the perfect plan. Make vague predictions of doom and expect everyone to fall in line. To protect you. Because obviously nothing matters other than making sure this particular enclave isn't disturbed."

Cormag gazed back at me steadily. "You are only distressed because you do not understand what your magic has been harboring. I can clear that mist. Wait here."

He made a gesture over the oak's trunk and stepped through the bark. Apparently the magic that had formed my father's house inside hadn't completely dispersed.

I stayed where I was, shifting my weight from foot to foot, half tempted to stalk off while Cormag was gone. But whatever he had to show me, it might be of some use. I was already working from an immense shortage of information. If he knew something about the Darkest One I didn't, it didn't matter how self-centered he and the rest of his kind were being.

Cormag reappeared in front of the tree with a whisper of a rustle. He was holding six leather-bound books, each not much taller than his hand. He offered them to me.

"Your father's journals, as relate to the family line of your king. It was only recently, while I tended to this old tree, that I came across them. He had tucked them away, all but hidden them. Perhaps he was embarrassed of anyone seeing how much he'd indulged his obsession. I expect he meant to pass them on to you once the spiraling of your unnatural spell allowed it, but he never had the opportunity."

I accepted the journals into my arms. Tipping most of them into the cradle of my elbow, I opened the first. My father's cramped handwriting stretched across the crisp pages in faded lines—but not so faded I couldn't read them. The year and the names noted near the top of the first page told a long story on their own. My eyebrows rose.

"This was Arthur's grandfather's grandfather," I said. "Father was worried about his family for *that* long?"

"Longer still, as you'll see," Cormag said. "That time was only when he first began to commit his observations to paper."

"Okay." My lungs tightened. I'd known Father had been concerned, but I hadn't realized his interest in Arthur's lineage had run that deep for so long. "I don't suppose you could sum up the key points. It'll take me a while to read through all of these."

Cormag lifted his chin with a haughtiness he hadn't shown before. "I hope you will glean more from them than I could, with all of your mixing with humankind. But it was clear to me that your father was sure the dark fae's interest and intertwining in the strands of that ruling family would be catastrophic. And your king stood as the pinnacle of that catastrophe."

19

I saw Darton before he saw me. He was leaning against a younger beech tree, gazing pensively into the forest in front of him. The misting of rain had darkened his hair, so it gleamed more bronze than gold. His handsome face was pale in the dim light.

There wasn't a hint of a threat about him, unless you were the type of creature that ought to be frightened by the fae dagger in his pocket. He looked, in that moment, vulnerable and alone.

Alone. Where had the light fae sentries wandered off to? They'd given me their word.

I strode forward, and Darton's head jerked around at the snap of a twig underfoot. Two streaks of light flitted past me. Ah, so his unwilling protectors had stuck around, they'd just disguised themselves. What, did they think this "catastrophe" lurking in Darton would somehow rub off on them if they offered a little polite conversation?

I wiped at the moisture that had beaded on my face as I reached him. I had nothing left to say to any of the fae of this enclave anyway. I tipped my head toward the road. "All right, let's get out of here."

He straightened up and matched my pace, tramping back through the brush. "What happened? Are the light fae in some kind of trouble?"

"No. Well, no more trouble than they've stirred up in their own heads. The dark fae haven't done anything to them."

His gaze fell to the journals I was still clutching. "What are those?"

My gut knotted. I couldn't tell him about Cormag's insinuations, not when I hadn't had a chance to come to my own conclusions. Especially not when it would also require admitting that I'd lied to him all those years ago about why I'd come to him in the first place. I had his trust now—I needed to keep it.

"One of my father's friends passed on some of his old journals to me," I settled on. "There might be information about the Darkest One in them. I'm hoping I can find out more that'll help us take her on."

"So they're going to help us against the dark fae after all?"

I let out a choked laugh. "Oh, no. Not a chance. They don't seem to think there's any point in bothering with the attempt. They just want to make sure she keeps clear of them. What happens to the rest of the world—who cares?"

"They—what? Wow." He shook his head, seeming lost for words. Then he hesitated. "You don't think they're right, do they? That there's no point in trying to stop her?"

"Of course not. It's my spell that Rhedyn thinks she's going to break. You can forget it if I'm going to sit around and let that happen. I stopped the Darkest One once, if imperfectly. I can do it again—I've just got to figure out

169

how. We didn't cross an entire ocean to lie down and give up now that we're here."

Darton nodded. "So it's just us again."

"Well, just us and whatever help the hunters can give us."

I watched him from the corner of my eye as we walked on, but nothing in his features or his gait gave me the slightest reason to worry. He was still Darton; he was my king reborn. My liege had been a lot of things, had shown all the mercurial emotions any human did during our times together, but the one thing I'd always known with bone-deep certainty was that he was *good*.

Did it even matter whether he contained some pending disaster I couldn't sense? If Cormag was right, if the Darkest One could create a catastrophe by getting her hands on Arthur's soul, then it would be catastrophic regardless of where it happened. We had a hell of a lot better chance of making sure it *didn't* happen if we stuck around and got in Rhedyn's way before she freed her master in the first place.

Giving in to the enclave's demands would just be signing a death sentence for a whole bunch of different people, which I cared about even if they didn't. No, we had to stay.

Stay and fight.

The SUV came into view through the trees ahead. I picked up my pace.

Darton glanced over at me. "You're looking very serious. Where are we headed next?"

I gave him a tight smile. "I'm thinking it's time we get that damned sword."

* * *

A hand shook my shoulder. I blinked and jerked awake, finding myself slumped in the back of the SUV. Eric was standing over me by the open door. The rain had picked up again, now drumming against the roof and the umbrella he was holding. The landscape beyond him was a blur of misty green. The damp trickled in past him and dappled my skin.

He cocked his head at me. "We're at the place you said to stop. It looks like you were able to get a little sleep?"

"Yeah." I pushed fully upright and checked on Darton. He stirred against the far window, where he'd propped his head to catch a few Zs of his own. A quick glance at the dashboard clock told me it was early afternoon. Still a few hours left of what amounted for daylight in this weather.

My father's journals lay in a heap at my feet. I hadn't wanted to set them on the seat between us in case Darton decided to flip through one and realized what they were really about. He might not have recovered enough of his former self to understand the archaic language—the fae had no written alphabet of their own, so my father had used human writing—but I wasn't going to count on that.

Not that my earlier skimming perusal of the journals had turned up any information that was much more specific than what Cormag had told me.

The dark fae had been interested in Arthur's family for several generations. My father had observed the Darkest One's minions venturing onto their grounds on various occasions. He'd noticed the visits increasing in frequency around each pregnancy in the family. He'd felt a sense of shadow growing around them. He'd watched the

Darkest One assembling creatures and fae around her after Arthur's birth, as if she were preparing for some imminent event.

But he'd never uncovered any details. He'd hoped that I would, with my ability to blend into human society. He'd just never bothered to tell me that.

I'd known from our conversations back then that he'd been disappointed I wasn't reporting more, but he'd never told me what sort of *more* he was expecting, never given me any guidelines other than to watch for the dark fae in general. Maybe I would have come up with something more useful if he'd been clearer about his concerns. I might have some sensitivity to dark powers, but not on the same level as a full fae like him.

But he hadn't wanted to bias me. That much had been clear from the most recent journal. He'd been afraid if he said exactly what he thought the dark fae might be up to, I'd interpret signs that way even if they truly meant something else. He hadn't even written his ideas down for his own records. In every note that touched vaguely on his "suspicions," his discomfort with even continuing to entertain theories he hadn't been able to confirm bled through.

The scientist in my father, such a strange characteristic for a light fae, had caused us more trouble than good in the end.

After a couple hours of paging through those ancient volumes, I'd decided a more valuable use of my time would be catching up on some rest. Light knew I was going to need all my wits when we went for the sword.

"So, what exactly are we doing here?" Eric peered over his shoulder. "This place isn't much to look at."

"This is just a stopping point," I said. I rubbed my eyes, wiping the last remnants of sleep away, and grabbed the dried flowers I'd set aside in preparation. "We're close enough to our actual destination now that we can get a guide to show us the rest of the way there."

This spot, where I'd told the fae hunters to stop and wake me, lay in the middle of my bloody smear on the map from my earlier search. But I wasn't going to bother with the map this time. There was a simpler conjuring that should work, and that didn't require me extending my mind to that wretched place directly. I wasn't keen to experience the backlash again.

I cupped my hands around the marigold petals and leaned my face close. As I inhaled their fragile perfume, I reached back in my mind, searching for the emotion I needed. Something fraught and tangled, painful and yet poignant.

It wasn't hard to find the right image. My memory of my king's first near-death swam up. The courtyard crowded with revelers, the platform where Arthur had given his speech, the gaunt yet elegant figure of the Darkest One looming over him, cloaked in shadow. The metallic taste in my mouth as I'd run, heart thumping, knowing I couldn't move fast enough. The words sputtering up my throat. The crackle of energy, charred and electric, flaring around me.

The agony at the thought that I might lose him. That it would be my fault if I did.

My throat tightened. I exhaled that emotion into the space between my hands with a whisper. "*Like to like. Float and follow the roads home.*"

Holding the pained feelings in my chest, I breathed in

and out with the same incantation until the energy tingled against my palms. I motioned Eric away from the door. He backed up a step, watching me avidly. I scooted to the open air and opened my hands.

A shimmering ball, whirling with pale blues, deep indigo, and a streak here and there of crimson, drifted away from my palms.

Mavis's eyebrows leapt up where she'd turned to watch from the driver's seat. "Well, then, that's something, all right."

"What *is* it?" Eric asked.

"Our guide," I said. The ball floated onward, a few feet off the ground. The raindrops passed through it without making it so much as quiver. To my relief, it stayed over the road—I hadn't been entirely sure that part of the spell would stick. As it gusted farther away, it started to pick up speed.

I reached to close the door. "Now we follow it. Let's go, before we lose sight."

The ball's faint glow stood out against the dim landscape. At the first crossroad we reached, it veered left. Mavis shook her head with a disbelieving chuckle, but she turned the wheel to stay on its trail.

The ball traveled faster and faster as it honed in on its target. Thankfully in this obscure corner of the country, with the inclement weather, no one else was on the road to see our bizarre procession.

Darton leaned forward in his seat as Mavis increased the gas. He frowned at the windshield. "Is it going to take us right to the sword?"

"Well, yes and no. It's going to take us to the place where the sword is hidden." Where the dark fae must have chucked it once it had been out of Arthur's hands. Presumably hoping no one would ever find their way back to it.

"Which is the place full of nightmares that you talked about before," Darton said.

"That description was... not entirely accurate. I was trying to make a point when I said that." I paused, my skin prickling with the awareness that we had an audience this conversation. There were some things I didn't want to have to explain to the fae hunters on this short an acquaintance. But I could cover the basics without getting into trouble.

"I've mentioned to you before that the dark fae love order. They encourage death, and they enjoy the sharp, simple emotions that can lead up to it, like anger and fear. But when people are dying, a whole lot of other feelings can come into play that hover somewhere between light and dark, love and hate, joy and pain. Regret. Desperation. Longing. Emotions like that are much too chaotic for dark fae comfort. So when they take a life for themselves, they shunt anything like that off into a trash can of sorts."

"A trash bin of sad feels?" Eric said, his mouth twitching with amusement.

I glowered at him. "In practice it's more like a pond. The light fae—when they talk about it, which isn't often—call it the Pool of Turmoil. And you can laugh at the idea, but it's not going to be any fun going into the place. Other people's emotions can affect you even in regular conversation—and the ones in the pool are all packed in and condensed after thousands of years of collecting. Be glad you get to sit on the sidelines."

"I'm totally fine with sticking to spectating for this

one," Mavis put in.

Arthur rubbed his jaw. "So if the dark fae throw all those emotions in this 'pool' because they don't like experiencing them, then can we at least assume we won't run into any dark fae while we're there?"

"Yes," I said. "Thankfully. But there are other sorts of creatures you wouldn't want to meet that enjoy the turmoil. And what's in a person's own head can be the most dangerous threat there is, if it's warped in the wrong ways."

Eric studied my face. "What's so special about this particular sword anyway?"

"It's magic," I said simply, and almost smiled at his consternated look.

"I get it, I get it," he said with an exaggerated sigh. "I haven't earned a spot in the secret club yet. I'll keep working on it."

"Ho!" Mavis exclaimed. "I think we're here."

The SUV eased to a stop. I looked to the windshield just in time to see my conjured ball flit off the overgrown dirt track we'd ended up on. It streaked across a rocky protrusion jutting up from the ground and disappeared over the other side.

I shoved open the car door and scrambled out, tugging my purse with me. "I've got to keep after it. There's no telling how much farther off the pool is. Stay here. And turn on the lamps so I've got light to return to. I might need it."

I dashed around the back of the SUV and clambered up the small, rocky hill. Footsteps thumped behind me. Darton caught up as I reached the crest.

"I think you meant 'we,'" he said. "It's my sword. I

have to come, don't I?"

I wasn't completely sure he did, but I wasn't sure he didn't, either. And my glowing ball was disappearing through a notch between two boulders up ahead, nearly out of view already. "Come on then."

We hurried across the uneven terrain, scattering pebbles and shifting wobbly stones. The ground dipped and rose, and dipped and rose again. The rain pattered against my hood and dripped onto my face. I wrinkled my nose, pressing onward. Darton shrugged his bomber jacket closer around him.

"How much farther do you think— Oh."

We halted on a mossy peak. Below us, a thicker, darker mist than the one that had coated the moors churned within a ring of jagged rocks. A glinting black surface showed through the hazy currents. The ball plummeted down and disappeared into the pond.

"There you have it," I said, my body tensing. "The Pool of Turmoil."

"So we just dive right in?"

I shook my head. "It's not really water. We can walk right down into the hollow. But... it's going to be unpleasant. From what I've heard, the emotions don't just affect you in the present, they stir up awful memories from your own past. And transform them into moments even more awful. It's hard to tell what's real and what isn't. Most who've stumbled into this place never find their way out again."

"Ah." Darton crossed his arms over his chest. "But we've got some special trick to getting through it?"

"Just our smarts. I can't even count on my magic once we're in there. The pool could warp my intentions too. We just have to stay focused on our quest—on Excalibur—no matter what happens. Don't think about anything other than the sword. No matter what we think we're experiencing."

"All right," Darton said. "I'm ready. Let's get this over with."

He started down the rough slope. I had to bite back the words to call him back. To tell him to sit his butt down and let me do this alone after all.

He probably wouldn't listen to me even if I did. And as always, he was safer with me than on his own.

I skidded down the slope after him, catching his arm just before our feet hit the mist. "Darton," I said, and when he turned to face me, "My liege." He went still at the term of respect. I latched onto that opening. "I know the fae who made this place better than you do. I'm better equipped to fend them off. I want you to swear to me you'll let me take the lead, that you won't do *anything* without my go-ahead. Please."

Darton's mouth twisted. He hesitated, but then he inclined his head. "All right. I trust you. I swear."

He held out his hand to me. I curled my fingers around his, and together we stepped down into the mist.

20

The waves of hazy emotion lapped at my feet, my legs, my torso, and then my face as we edged down along the ridged bank of the pond. They seeped straight through my clothing, grazing my skin with chilly tendrils of feeling: a trickle of melancholy, a waft of anguish.

As I'd told Darton to, I schooled my mind carefully blank. Any thought that swam up I dismissed. I trained all my attention on the image of Excalibur I'd seen in my vision. There was nothing to see around us now anyway except shifting currents of energy in hazy shades of gray, from pale cloud-like tufts to shadowy dark streams. They coated my nostrils and throat with a damp, mildewy smell. I wrinkled my nose.

Darton's hand stayed clamped around mine. After several steps, it was the only solid thing I was aware of. The ground beneath us had faded away. Our feet seemed to walk straight on without touching anything beneath them. I dragged in a breath and exhaled sharply as a jab of desperation wrenched at my lungs.

"Are you okay?" I said. My voice came out warbled. I looked toward Darton, but the shifting haze obscured his face.

"So far so good," he said with a squeeze of my fingers and a ragged laugh. "Just think about the sword—and how much I'd like to have it right now, to slice through this stuff. I can handle that."

A silvery billow rushed at us, too fast for us to dodge. It washed over me and raced through my skin into my nerves. A sharp itching sensation broke out through my flesh, as if every muscle had fallen asleep. My pulse stuttered with a burst of adrenalin.

And then the haze parted ahead of us.

Two rows of figures stood around a long wooden table. They were leaning over the polished top, pointing fingers and snapping at each other in a cacophony of voices. At the head of the table, a young man with a crown resting on his gold-blond hair raised his hands.

"Order! Order, my lords!" Arthur's voice rang out. Darton froze beside me. I made out the pale, peaked face of my former self cringing near the doorway. I'd never enjoyed those political meetings. I couldn't even have said which occasion this memory was based on—they all had seemed to go pretty much the same way. Lots of yelling and fists knocking the tabletop and very little actual decision-making.

"That was me," Darton said beside me. Some of the color had drained from his face, but his eyes were wide. I couldn't tell if he was more shocked or impressed. Of course, he'd never seen himself—his original self—from the outside before. The memories he'd experienced had been from behind those bright blue eyes.

"It's still you, in the ways that matter most," I murmured.

The lords had settled down at their king's command, at least for the moment. They sat, frowning. One started to speak, and Arthur raised his hand, his expression firm. He'd always managed to evoke that commanding air when he needed to, even though I knew he didn't take much pleasure from drawing hard lines.

"A compromise should be possible," he said, and pointed to a map spread on the table. "Lord Damblin, your biggest concern appears to be access to the river, and Lord Salloway, yours is maintaining your quarries. We can account for both concerns, if we consider the boundary between your districts to be here." He drew his finger across the map. "Neither of you would lose anything you value. And there will be no more need for argument."

The first lord he'd addressed leaned back in his seat. "All right. I can agree that is fair. But if we run into further troubles, be sure I won't sit quietly about them."

Ha. Fat chance of any of them ever sitting *quietly*.

The other lord was shaking his head. Of course. When did they ever make any discussion easy for my king? I'd often thought he should just toss the lot of them out and rule the entire country directly, but when I'd remarked as much to Arthur, he'd pointed out even he would make a mess of trying to juggle that many concerns. *The lords serve a key purpose in administration, as frustrating as they may be.*

"There is still the matter of the farmlands along the river," the second lord said. "I will not have my realm placed at a disadvantage."

Arthur smiled patiently. "I think you will find my recommendation gives equal agricultural territory to both sides. Although if you have a suggestion you'd consider more fair, by all means, share it with us."

The lord frowned at the map, opened his mouth, shut it again, and grimaced. "I am not convinced, but I acknowledge that I can see no better alternative at the moment."

Darton leaned close to me. "This doesn't *seem* like a nightmare."

"Not yet." I hooked my arm around his. "Come on. We're not here for this, and you can be sure it'll sour soon enough."

I tugged at him, and he moved sluggishly, still staring at the memory playing out before him. And at that moment, the Pool of Turmoil decided to put the proof to my words.

"Excellent," Arthur was saying. "Now on the matter of—"

A lord at the far end of the table sprang to his feet with a shriek of chair legs against the hazy floor. "Why do we all just listen to this man—no, this *boy*?" he demanded. "What does it matter if he wears the crown? We all know he's too young, too untried, to truly understand the concerns we face. He never stood by his father's side here with us."

Well, that was blatantly untrue. My skin prickled. This wasn't just a memory anymore. The pool was skewing it into a nightmare.

"Now, then," Arthur started, holding up both his hands, but more of the lords leapt up before he could get another word out.

"Ruverton is right," spat out the lord who'd been agreeable just a moment ago. "You have no authority over us—none that you've earned."

"What have you ever done for us or this country,

truly?" another sneered.

Okay, Darton *really* didn't need to see this. And I didn't want to find out how far and how fast it was going to spiral.

I hauled on his arm, and he stumbled. His gaze was fixed on the scene before him, his face even paler than before and his expression completely still, as if it held him transfixed. Maybe it did. I had no idea exactly how the pool worked its effects on the mind.

"He's a fool!" a lord shouted, flinging his hand toward Arthur. "He hasn't done a thing to earn that crown."

"We should take it from him. Find one who can carry it properly."

"Yes, yes, let us take the crown."

The hollering voices whirled around us as if lords had popped up on all sides. The ones at the table drew swords and daggers I hadn't seen until just then. "Good men!" Arthur yelled, lifting his arms, but the protest had no effect. The crowd of lords ran at him, their blades poised to strike.

"Come *on*," I hissed, and yanked at Darton again. His feet seemed to have melded to the invisible ground beneath us. I grasped his wrists with both of my hands and heaved, and all he did was list toward me, sidestepping to keep his balance. His eyes didn't shift for a second. Was he even *blinking?*

The figure of his first self vanished in the midst of the onslaught of lords like a gloom caught in the sun. The nobles spun around, weapons in hand, searching for a new target. Their glares caught on us as they noticed our presence for the first time.

Swine crud. We had to get out of here, *now*.

"Darton," I snapped. "Arthur!" I inhaled sharply. Then I drew back my hand and slapped him across the face.

The impact stung my palm, so I can't imagine it felt all that pleasant to his cheek. Darton flinched. His gaze jerked down to me. "Em," he said, with a flush of anger. "What—"

"We have to run." I pulled his arm, and this time his legs moved.

We plowed on into the shifting mists, the thunder of chasing footsteps echoing after us. Swung blades hissed through the air. "Stand and face justice!" someone hollered, but the voice was already fading. I waved aside the thicker currents of fog, squinting in the dimness, and finally drew to a stop.

Darton swiveled around beside me. He stared back the way we'd come. "That was— Did that really happen in our—"

"No," I said before he had to finish. "You were never set upon by a swarm of rabid lords. It's the tumultuous emotions of this place. Like I told you, they infect everything—including our minds if we let them. So let's not?"

"Right. Right." He turned back to me, shamefaced. Then he touched his cheek, which was still decorated with a splash of red in the shape of my hand. "Was assaulting me really necessary?"

I rolled my eyes. "Believe me, if I *assaulted* you, you wouldn't be standing around asking questions about it. And yes, I'm pretty sure a little smack was a better choice than letting you get run through with a dozen swords."

"But... it wasn't real. Would they actually have hurt me?"

"Did what you were seeing feel real in the moment?"

He paused. "Well... Yeah, I guess it did."

"If your mind believes it, then just about anything can do damage. Let's not stick around to test that theory out any further." I peered through the haze. We had a sword of our own to seek.

A glimmer of feeling grazed my chest. Not the strangled, twisted feelings of the pool, but something clean and bright. And sharp. I could almost taste the metal of the blade on my tongue.

"I can sense it. Excalibur. I think..." I turned slowly, reaching out toward that sensation. It was distant, wavering, but—there. "This way. The sooner we find it, the sooner we can get out of this awful place."

21

My fingers twined with Darton's, still clamped around his hand from our run away from the figmentary lords. I hadn't thought anything of it until, after a few strides, he disentangled them and pulled his arm away from me.

He walked on right by my side, but somehow that simple motion opened a distance between us. I glanced at him, searching his expression for a reason. My gut had clenched. I didn't realize how my mind had slipped until the mist fell away around a flash of color.

Cattle sod. I'd forgotten my own advice about keeping my head clear. I bit my lip, dragging the image of the sword ahead of every other concern, but it was too late. A scene had formed, bright and frantic, in front of us. My memory, this time. I knew it well, in part because I'd thought back to it so many times after it had happened, chiding myself for mistakes made then.

Darton jerked to a stop. What seemed like just a few feet away from us, men on horses charged about an oval ring. The horses' thundering hooves tossed up strewn straw and clods of earth. Beyond the white wall on the far side of the ring, men and women cheered and stomped against the wooden stands. The smell of sweat and damp horse hair drifted over me. It was a smell I had never missed one bit.

The men on horseback wheeled their steeds apart and cantered to opposite ends of the ring. The one at our left lifted his metal helm. Darton startled at the sight of his former face. Arthur—just a prince then, no more than a year or two older than Darton was right now—swiped his arm across his brow and tugged his visor back down. An attendant handed him a new weapon: a gilded spear. He spun it for show, letting it catch the sunlight. The cheers rose.

"I don't remember this," Darton said.

My mouth twisted. "That only means it hasn't come back to you yet. So far it's real. It was a tournament your father organized one year: battle games and the like. And you were the star, of course. I'm sure it'll come to you— properly, without the pool's meddling—eventually. We're better not lingering."

"But if this isn't my memory, it must be—" He craned his neck. "There you are." A little smile crossed his face. Despite myself, it sent a flutter through me.

I followed his gaze to my own original self, standing in the shadow of an awning by the lower edge of the ring, a stack of shields and weaponry beside me. My thick brown hair was mussed from all the rushing around before the tourney and, well, truth be told I was pretty sure it'd been messy most of the time. I hadn't bothered much with mirrors.

My thin hand was clenched around several twigs. My eyes tracked my prince as he swung his stallion around to face his opponent. In my present form, my shoulders stiffened. It was coming soon.

"Yes, there's me," I said. "You've seen me before.

Can we—"

I tried to step away, but the memory surged around us. The horses barreled past us from both sides. The tent loomed at our right. Everywhere I turned, the past rose up to meet me.

I reached for Darton's hand again, shoving aside the pinching inside at the thought of how he'd pulled away before, but his expression stopped me. His eyebrows had lifted. Even with the thumping of hooves and the clanging of weapons around us, he was still watching that long ago version of me.

And the long ago version of me was watching Arthur.

The prince urged his horse faster, swinging his spear, and a grin sprang across my—Merlin's—face. Even in the shadow, my eyes lit up as if I were standing in full sun.

I swallowed hard. I'd never seen how I looked when I was focused on him. By the light, please tell me my affection wasn't as obvious as it seemed.

Darton let out a choked sound that might have been meant as a snicker. His jaw had gone tight. "Look at you, Em. You were mooning like a schoolgirl with a crush. If I didn't know better, I'd have thought—"

"Yes, yes. Very funny," I broke in. Now, in the present, my cheeks had flamed and my stomach knotted. "We can laugh about my ridiculous expressions some other time. First we need to find our way out of this mess."

"This time it's *your* mess," Darton pointed out. He started to turn, and hesitated. "What are you doing?"

He meant the me of the past, not me now. Because the figure standing under the awning had just palmed one of those twigs. Merlin tensed as Arthur swung his horse around in a whirl of dust. The prince's opponent jabbed out with a pike. Its tip sped toward a gap beside Arthur's shield. Merlin's lips moved in a silent litany—and the pike tip jumped an inch to the left. It glanced off the edge of the prince's shield.

Darton stiffened. The prince didn't appear to notice. His steed wheeled, and spear and pike clashed again. The massive man on the other horse pressed closer, and Arthur pushed back.

The memory spun. The colors streaked around us, and suddenly Arthur was charging at a different opponent, a slim sinewy fellow on a bay stallion, this time with a sword. His blade clashed against the other man's. They traded blows and broke apart. The other man kicked his horse's sides and urged it toward the prince before Arthur had quite turned around.

The prince's stallion sprang backward at the unexpected approach. Arthur jolted in his saddle. And in the corner of my vision, I knew without looking directly that my former self had snatched up another twig with another murmur.

Just a little nudge. Just enough to be sure the prince wouldn't fall. That's all I'd been thinking when I'd been struck by that jolt of panic. But it was also enough that Arthur had felt it.

In the vision before us, the prince flinched as he jerked himself back into balance. His head twitched toward the awning for just an instant before he kicked his steed forward to meet his opponent.

"Em," Darton started.

I shook my head. "Don't. I've heard it. Come—"

And then I was hearing it again. The memory

189

collapsed, and suddenly all there was before us was me and him, Merlin and Arthur, face to face behind the equipment racks. The prince loomed over his wizard. His voice crackled with anger.

"What were you thinking, Merlin? Did you assume I wouldn't notice? Do you see me as that dim?"

I cringed inside my skin. "Darton..."

"Is this real?" he said quietly. "Everything we've seen so far—it really happened that way?"

"Yes," I said. "And believe me, the parts you're unhappy about I deeply regretted. Do we really need to see this?"

Merlin was stuttering, his face gone sallow. "Sire—my liege—I only— It's my job to help you. To support you. That's all I meant to do."

The prince's hands had balled, but I could see, as I hadn't had the wits to back then, how my obvious distress affected him. He kept his arms at his sides and eased back half a step. He'd been angry, yes, but he hadn't intended to make me feel threatened. Even justifiably furious as he'd been, he'd noticed and cared.

"It's your job to help me *when I need it*," he said. "And I don't need that help in everything I do. Do you really believe I can't handle myself in a simple tournament?"

Merlin winced at that. "Of course I don't believe that. You know how much I respect your skills."

"Then you have to remember that some things I must do on my own. Even if you're capable of assisting me. Riding, fending off a foe, those are areas I can succeed in completely on my own. I *want* to do them myself. To know when I've won, it's fairly—that it was just *me*, not some supernatural helper as well."

The real argument had ended there. I'd bowed my head and said my apologies, and my prince had cuffed my head lightly and told me to never to do it again, and I hadn't. At least, except on the battlefield, where his life mattered more than his pride.

In the Pool of Turmoil, my past face pulled into a grimace. "You're such a fool, Arthur. You can't ever see what's right in front of you."

I did not like the direction that comment seemed to be going in. I grasped Darton by the elbow. "Okay, we're veering into nightmare territory now. I'd rather avoid a repeat of the last encounter with various blades."

"What is that supposed to mean?" the prince snapped, advancing on Merlin. "What other secrets have you been keeping?"

Merlin's shoulders tensed. His chin jerked up. "None that you've earned the right to know."

Dear light, I did not want to see this. I swiveled, queasiness burning in my throat, and to my relief, Darton turned with me.

"Oh, shit," he said.

The ring and the stands I'd thought had faded away had sprung up again. And the spectators were streaming from their seats, waving their arms. With a pained whinny, one of the horses crashed through the thin white wall. A herd of stallions stampeded toward us, the tournament-goers gathering in a screaming mob behind them.

This time, I didn't need to drag Darton. As one body, we ran. I ducked my head, focusing only on the flight of my feet. And the sword. The sword with its distant glimmering that was humming a little louder with every step I took.

The currents of mist wavered and flickered with swaths of shadow and color. They dizzied me. Darton's feet skidded. I nearly fell at the jerk of his arm, but he caught me.

We paused for a moment, catching our breaths. We'd left the stampede—and our nightmarish argument—behind.

"Please tell me we're getting close," he said, a little hoarsely.

"Clos*er*, anyway, I think." I closed my eyes in an effort to pin down my sense of Excalibur even more firmly. The glint of its presence danced against my eyelids and tickled through my breaths. "Just don't think. Don't think."

I set off in what felt like the right direction. Darton hurried along beside me. "Don't think," he murmured to himself, his expression strained. "Don't think. Don't think."

The shadowy ground beneath us dropped out abruptly. We both stumbled, our arms flying out. I jarred my shoulder against a lump I couldn't see. With a grimace, I pushed myself onto my knees.

Darton was getting up too. He steadied himself with his hands pressed flat to the invisible surface. His eyes clouded.

"It's cold," he whispered. "So *cold*."

"Darton!" I said, but he didn't stir. He was already too absorbed.

Darkness take us. I raised my head, bracing myself for whatever awful memory awaited us now.

22

The mists had condensed into stone walls and pillars down the length of a massive, high-ceilinged room. It was empty—so empty the silence rang in my ears. An impression of thin sunlight streaked through the narrow, arched windows. My lungs clenched. I knew what I was going to see before I'd even turned my gaze toward the head of the room.

A large marble coffin sat on the floor, its closed lid carved with vines and figures around a blazing sun in its center. No one was around, but the silence was just the prelude to the funeral about to begin.

Arthur and I had been here in this moment, in our real history, but there was no sign of our past selves now.

Darton took a few hesitant steps toward the coffin. His feet thudded against the tiled floor. His hands balled at his sides and opened again, over and over.

"Father," he said.

I hurried after him. "Nothing good can come out of this. We should keep moving." *You don't need to live through this moment again.*

I remembered the real moment far too well, even after fifteen centuries. Edging along behind my prince as he'd walked up to the coffin. The wrench of my heart as he'd dropped to his knees and pressed his forehead to its side. The stuttered breaths as he'd tried to master his emotions.

The sickness had come on so fast. I still didn't know what had caused it or even what exactly it had been. But in the space of three days, the king had transformed from fit and able to a failing body heaving one final sigh. Leaving his son behind with a crown and a heaping of responsibilities he hadn't expected for years to come.

Arthur's strangled voice back then echoed in my mind. *I thought I'd have more time. There was still so much he wanted me to learn from him. So much I wanted him to see I could do.*

I had knelt beside him, not knowing what to say or do that would help, but feeling the need to show I was at least with him. Because he was revealing his pain to me. Because he trusted me enough that he hadn't hidden it— the way he would have to with every one of his subjects and the lords he ruled over when they poured in to pay their respects.

He'd shifted sideways to lean against me, and I'd raised my hand to squeeze his shoulder. For the first time, I'd felt as though I might be the stronger one, just this once. And he was letting me be. So I'd better do the best job of it I could.

He's gone back to the world that made him, I'd said haltingly. *He'll see everything you want him to. And you have your memories and his example to learn from. He knew that you were ready. I saw it, before he passed. He was more proud of you than anything else he's accomplished.*

Arthur had made a sound like a sob he'd tried to

swallow. He'd rubbed his hand over his face and pulled away from me. But as he'd stood up, he'd grasped my hand in his and let himself meet my eyes even though his were reddened. *Thank you, Merlin.*

Here and now, I didn't for a second believe the Pool of Turmoil planned to show us that painful but poignant exchange. And I *really* didn't want to find out what it did have in store to replace it.

Darton had stopped moving, but he was still staring at the coffin. He must be caught up in his own memories again. I gripped his shoulder as I had then.

"Darton, we can talk about your father and his death another time. Out of here. Soon, if you want. But right now you know all that matters is— "

The lid of the coffin shifted with a grating sound. My voice died in my throat. Darton's back went rigid. We both gaped as the lid slowly, steadily rasped to the side, leaving a dark gap at the top of the coffin.

My heart thudded hard against my ribs, but I couldn't force words from my throat. There was a rustle, and a figure pushed through that gap.

Not just any figure. Arthur's father. It was the king's *corpse* that rose from that cold coffin. And not the body that would have lain there on that early day, but one with ragged rotting skin and hollows for eyes and fingers of bone dotted with only fragments of flesh. His formal robes drooped from his hunched frame, little more than stained rags. A stink of putrid decay wafted off of him.

He shuffled forward and swung a patchy leg over the side of the coffin. Stepping toward us. A low, wounded sound broke from Darton's mouth. His hand leapt out to grasp my arm. The contact startled me out of my daze.

"Let's *go*," I hissed, and jerked the arm he was clutching. Darton turned on swaying legs, but he followed me.

"God," he muttered under his breath. "God."

"You!" the dead king cried out behind us in a broken caw of a voice. "The wizard. I know you. I know what you did—and what you didn't. You couldn't wait to see me pass away so you could stand at the top by my son's side, could you? All that magic and you really couldn't find a way to cure me? You let me die. I know it."

Oh, darkness take me. This wasn't just Arthur's nightmare. It had latched on to my insecurities and regrets too.

"Don't listen to him," I said, urging us on down the long room that was starting to feel as if it had no end. A lump of guilt rose in my throat, but I ignored it.

My guilt had always been for Arthur, for failing him, not for any purposeful wrongdoing. *I* knew that, no matter what that nightmare tried to claim. I put my hand over Darton's. "I tried everything I could. I gave years of my life into all the magic that might have made a difference. I'd have given more if I'd thought of something else that might have worked."

"I know," Darton said. "It's just this place, doing what it does. There's nothing—"

He yelped and jerked around. Somehow the king was right behind us now, his bony hand clamped around Darton's other wrist. He loomed so close the fetid smell of his body clogged my nose. My stomach turned.

"You relied on this boy too much," the corpse rasped. "You let him take on responsibilities that should have been yours, shoulder burdens you should have been strong enough to carry alone. A king needs no one to prop him up. No one to hold his hand."

"Let *go* of me," Darton snapped, yanking at his arm, but the whites of his eyes shone with terror.

The king leaned even closer, his face only inches from this incarnation of his son's. "It's unhealthy. Unnatural. I am ashamed to even think—"

"Enough!" I slammed my fist down on the corpse's wrist. The bones shattered, the hand releasing Darton's wrist to thump onto the floor. The dead king shrieked and lashed out at Darton with his other hand, but we were already staggering away. Darton's mouth was clamped tight as if he were fighting the urge to vomit. I wouldn't have blamed him if he'd given in to it.

"Stop right there!" the king yelled after us. "You must listen. You never listened to me enough, my son. Not when it mattered."

"Just keep running," I said to Darton. Then I raised my head and my own feet skidded to a halt.

"Merlin."

A different figure blocked our way in the other direction. A figure tall and broad-shouldered, with a mane of tawny hair and burnished red-brown skin. I'd have said my father—the father of my first birth—looked as if he were glowing, but that wouldn't be completely accurate. He literally was glowing. Light seeped through his skin and blazed from his eyes. It seared over my face as it touched me. Darton sucked in a breath.

"Who—"

"You," Eóghan boomed at me. "Child. You never listened half as much as you should have. Look at you— tied to him in mind, heart, and soul. It's a disgrace on your kind."

His soul, heart, and mind were long dispersed into the light in reality. But even though my supposed father's words merely echoed the dead kings and I knew it wasn't really him, I couldn't stop the retort from leaping from my lips. "My kind is humans as well as light fae. As you well know. As you arranged to be the case. You *wanted* me this way."

"You were to *watch*." He slashed his hand through the air. "To learn. From a *distance*. You can't fix a disaster if you're so tangled up in it you no longer know where you begin and end."

The dead king was catching up with us again, his legs moving far faster than any body that looked like his had the right to do. "Never were strong enough. Never were smart enough," he was muttering, his hollow eye sockets fixed on Darton.

Darton squeezed his eyes shut. His fingers clutched at mine. "No."

I tugged him with me. We whirled together and ran to the side of the room, away from the ghosts intent on haunting us. Where were the sodding *doors*?

Both of our fathers kept pace, gliding over the stones with a hissing whisper that made all the hairs on my limbs stand on end.

"You ruined everything I'd worked for, centuries and centuries," mine was shouting now. "You'll bring about the downfall of both our peoples."

"Maybe I could have done a better job if you'd told me everything you actually knew," I shot back.

"I don't believe you," Darton was saying to the dead king, but his voice was shaking. "I don't. Shut up."

The ground tilted beneath our feet. I scrambled to keep hustling forward. Darton lurched. Our hands broke apart. I snatched after him, and the floor listed again. Trying to throw us backward to our pursuers.

And what would happen to us if they caught us?

"We're getting overwhelmed," I said to Darton. "We're letting them affect us too much—we're sabotaging ourselves. We have to drown them out."

The last word had barely slipped from my mouth when the room around us fell away. The floor swung up at a sharp angle. The walls crumbled away into dust around us, and shadows poured down from above. Darton and I both fell, jarring against the now-uneven tiles, and slid downward.

"No!" I caught Darton's wrist. In the darkness below us, the dead king reached up and grabbed his ankle. My heart squeezed. I let myself skid a little farther and kicked at the corpse's face with all my might.

The dead king plummeted—but so did we. I threw my arm across Darton's back, groping for some sort of hold with my other hand. We bumped and rolled down and down until wind started to whistle around us.

Darton's voice carried through it. He'd been murmuring, but now the words rose up.

"We're here for the sword. We're here for the sword. We're here for the sword."

Drown them out, I'd said. The words our fathers had said, the emotions latching onto us. I gulped air and joined him.

"We're here for the sword. We're here for the sword. We're here for the sword."

Our voices ringing out together sounded ridiculous,

like a schoolyard chant. But as I shouted out the words again, focusing my mind back on that shining image of Excalibur, my fingers caught on a ridge in the surface beneath us. I clutched it, clinging to Darton at the same time.

"We're here for the sword. We're here for the sword."

My throat already felt hoarse. I didn't dare stop. Darton hefted himself a little farther up by another notch in the slanted floor. We heaved and scrambled, panting between recitations. And then the tiles cracked apart.

We thumped down onto the solid, invisible ground we'd walked on before. The mists had closed in around us. I swayed and caught my balance with Darton's elbow. He laughed for a second before resuming the chant.

"We're here for the sword."

His eyes caught mine with a triumphant gleam that shone past the stress marked across his face. I found myself smiling back, despite everything, as I repeated the words alongside him.

The sword. The sword. The tug inside me pulled harder. I veered right, and then left. The hazy currents parted around us, never letting us see more than a few feet ahead.

Then my toes jarred against something hard. I stopped, bracing myself, and looked up.

A laugh jolted out of me. Of course. How fitting. I was standing at the foot of a boulder nearly as high as my shoulders. And protruding from its bulging head was a broadsword glinting with light fae magic.

The sword in the stone.

I didn't think the dark fae that had sent it here had

done so with any sense of humor, but that only made it funnier to me.

"Is that it?" Darton said, breathless. "Excalibur?"

"The one and only. We made it." I laughed again, with relief this time.

At the same moment, a hulking shape reared up over the hilt of the sword, and I realized we weren't finished here after all.

23

The shadowy creature towered over us. A crackling hiss carried from its mouth. I could barely make out its form through the mists, but what I could see was long and snakelike, with a flicker of a forked tongue.

Darton had tensed beside me. "What the hell is that?"

"Nothing good. But we have the sword now. You can handle anything with that."

I hoped.

The creature's head dipped lower, its hiss becoming more of a snarl. A narrow, scaly face, mottled gray and green like the mossy rocks around the pool, protruded from the haze. A fanned ruff twitched from its jaw up to its eyes, which were glossy black and narrowed at us. It bared an incredible number of jagged teeth in its gaping mouth.

Well, technically we didn't have the sword yet. I'd have felt a lot better facing that thing if Darton had been holding it in his hand instead of looking at it lodged halfway deep in that boulder.

Darton edged to the side, his gaze darting between the snake-dragon and the sword. The creature's head wove back and forth as if it were deciding which of us to lunch on first.

"Hold!" a low, frigid voice called out. The beast stilled. A figure that was little more than a silhouette appeared within the mist.

"Hello, Merlin. It took you long enough to make it this far. I've gotten bored."

My chest tightened. "Rhedyn," I said, not fully needing the confirmation.

I couldn't make out her features, but I heard her smirk in her intake of breath. Her physical form wasn't really here, I could tell now—only a projection of her presence. No doubt her corporeal body was skulking around in the Darkest One's cave still.

"Did you think I wouldn't know you were here from the moment you set foot on my ground?"

"I hardly think this entire country is yours."

"Mmm, we'll see. She's eager to return, you know. Our greatest one. I think she'll take everything she can, and that will be plenty."

The dark fae could be just as irritatingly vague as the light when they took a mind to be. But Rhedyn wasn't my concern right now anyway. We'd come here for the sword, and we'd leave with it, no matter what I had to do. That task felt even more urgent now that I could see she was apparently very keen to stop us from completing it.

"All that power and you're still afraid of one little blade," I remarked, and caught Darton's gaze. I twitched my eyes toward the sword, hoping he'd take my cue. We might as well make a grab for it while Rhedyn's pet was holding back. He backed up a step.

"The dark does not feel *afraid*," Rhedyn muttered.

"Light fades. Darkness remains."

"So your kind is always telling me," I said, sidestepping to give Darton more room for his run at the boulder. "And yet here I remain."

"Not for long." Her voice slithered silky sharp from the mists. "The monster I summoned is eager to play with you. And as you can probably guess, he likes to play rough. I thought he was particularly fitting for this situation, don't you?"

I had no idea what she meant by that, but I didn't much care. We were going to have to kill the thing either way.

"If you say so. It'd have been a lot more interesting if you'd made the trip in person, you know. I've got a few things—"

Darton lunged at the boulder. His football player muscles served him well. He hefted himself up with a few quick jerks and grasped the hilt of the sword.

"Kill them!" Rhedyn snapped. Her shadowy form dissolved into the haze, and the snake-dragon attacked.

"Darton!" I called out in instinctive warning. The creature's head swung toward him, and he heaved at the sword.

It didn't budge from the boulder. I swore under my breath and snatched a twig from my pocket. I didn't know how my magic would react to this place, but I was quite certain of how Darton's vital organs would react to having all those fangs sunk into him.

"*Blast and back*," I shouted. A surge of wind smacked into the snake-dragon's face, but the mists drained away the impact. It barely flinched. I accomplished at least one goal, though. Its neck veered to the side as it focused its attention on me.

"Come on, damn it," Darton muttered. He wrenched at the sword again, and I thought I saw it shift an inch. What was the matter with the sodding thing?

The beast snapped at me. I leapt to the side just in time to avoid losing my head. My purse bumped against my back. I had a wand in my pocket and more in the purse, but after the puny effect my first attempt at a spell had provided, I wasn't in much of a hurry to waste them. If I could just keep the thing distracted until Darton got a handle on the sword...

The creature slithered around the boulder, revealing a tapering body supported in the front by two taloned feet. It swiped one of those sets of enormous claws through the air toward me. I threw myself backward with a wince at the snap of ripped fabric. Shredded jeans had never been one of my favorite fashion choices.

Darton was still struggling with the sword. He swiveled, presumably aiming for a better angle, and the creature's spiked tail whipped toward him.

"Art!" I gasped out, too late. He flinched to the side, but the spikes caught him in the shoulder, hurling him off the boulder. He hit the ground with a thump and just barely tossed his arm up in time to shield his head. Blood bloomed across his shoulder and back where the spikes had dug in.

My pulse stuttered. The snake-dragon reared again, the fans of skin around its face rustling menacingly, and my mind went blank. Before I knew what I planned to do, I was leaping at the boulder myself.

I was no athlete, but I wasn't a total wimp. My fingers latched onto the nooks and crevices. "*Cast me far, cast me up*," I whispered to the air beneath me, and that last shove was all I needed. I scrambled onto the lumpy top of the boulder.

The creature's head jerked toward me. I curled my fingers around Excalibur's hilt. "Em!" Darton called from below, as much a protest as a warning, but this wasn't the best moment for a debate about whose job retrieving the sword was.

The tingling of familiar magic—*my* magic—seeped into my palms from the hilt like a hello. So the sword recognized me too. Light willing, that was a good sign. I dragged in a breath and hauled at it with all my strength.

The blade slid free from the stone with a thin humming like metal scraped over smooth glass. I felt relieved for the instant it took before my body registered the weight of the thing in my hands. A broadsword was no amateur's dagger. Five pounds of hammered steel dragged at my unpracticed arms as I fumbled with it, nearly tipping me right back off the boulder.

It knew me, but the magic that had made it sing in my king's grasp didn't work for me. It was his soul, the link I'd forged, that powered it. So why hadn't it let him retrieve it?

No time for worrying about that now. The snake-dragon chomped at me. I managed to swing the sword in a clumsy arc between the creature and me. At the flash of the blade, it jerked to the side. Then its clawed foot slashed out at me.

I ducked and swiveled, but two of the talons cut across my arm. The sword's weight pulled me off balance. I teetered and half slid, half fell down the side of the boulder.

Darton had shoved himself to his feet. The sleeve of

his jacket was streaked with red from the cuts on his shoulder, but his jaw was set hard. His fingers clutched the hilt of the light fae dagger.

The snake-dragon whipped around the boulder, intent on me. Darton leapt between me and it as I scrambled up. He sliced the dagger at the beast's face. The blade nicked its muzzle—it winced and bobbed its head with an angry hiss.

"The sword!" I shoved Excalibur toward him and fumbled for my purse. I had to have *something* in there that would help.

My hand closed around a clump of twigs. Darton heaved the immense sword off the ground. Even through the padding of his jacket, I could see the bulge of his arms as he took on its weight. He was strong, but his muscles had been built by football skirmishes, not wielding heavy lengths of metal. It would take more training before he handled any large sword smoothly.

And this sword still wasn't responding to him as its master. He jabbed it at the snake-dragon, but the creature just dodged and sprang at us again. I gritted my teeth against the pain stinging through my arm and thrust my handful of twigs toward the beast.

"*Darkness begone!*"

A burst of light flared from the twigs—and shattered against the mist drifting around us. Crackles of it echoed back at us, nicking my skin. The snake-dragon let out a sputter that sounded more like a sneeze than any real discomfort. Then it lunged its jaws toward Darton again.

He managed to smack the flat of Excalibur's blade against its nose hard enough to make it recoil, but he staggered backward a few steps too. Blood was still seeping down his shoulder. Without the magical connection and those years of training his former self had experienced, he wasn't going to have the agility he needed to make a killing blow. And I already knew I couldn't handle the sodding thing any better.

My grasping fingers dug deeper into my purse. Their tips brushed something... fluffy?

The rabbit skin. I'd tucked it and the amber stone in while I was packing, just in case I had the chance to continue my experiments.

Well, I couldn't think of a better time to experiment than now. It was either that or resign ourselves to being dinner.

I dragged out the rabbit skin, shoved it into my weaker hand, and fumbled for the amber. The snake-dragon gnashed its teeth and took another swipe at Darton with its claws. They clanged against the sword he'd raised to block them just in time. Darton's mouth had twisted with determination, but I could see the frustration creeping through his expression all the same.

I pushed myself upright and rammed stone and skin together. Before I'd had the chance to rub them more than once, the snake-dragon's gaze swept toward me. As if recognizing the threat I was about to pose, it smacked a taloned foot toward me.

I flinched backward, but one of its claws snagged on the rabbit skin. A yelp of protest broke from my throat as it wrenched the tool I'd been counting on away. I snatched after it, and the beast swiveled abruptly. The spikes of its tail whipped toward us.

Darton and I scrambled away, Darton panting but still clutching the sword. I glanced at him to check his shoulder, and my eyes caught on the ruff of his hood. My heart leapt.

"The fur on your jacket," I said. "Is it real?"

Darton's gaze jerked to me. "*What?*"

"Never mind. Just hold still. Unless you need to whack that thing." If it wasn't real, then this simply wouldn't work.

I grasped his hood and slammed the amber against it, rubbing furiously. Sparks crackled beneath the stone. A grin split my face.

"We've got this," I said, and turned to glower at the snake-dragon. "Come on, you ugly piece of cattle sod. Give us the best you've got!"

"Um, are you really sure that's a good idea, Em?" Darton said as the creature lunged around.

"Just stab it as hard as you can. The aim doesn't even matter."

He sucked in his breath and hefted Excalibur. The snake-dragon sprang. I whipped the amber against the fur ruff one last time and then snapped it against Darton's hand, just as he thrust the sword forward.

Electricity sizzled from me to him and up the blade. Excalibur lit with a flickering glow, and Darton plunged it into the snake-dragon's muzzle.

The blade sliced clean through the flesh. The sparks burst through the creature's body. It gave a wrenching cry as its limbs shuddered. Then it collapsed in a smoking heap beside the boulder.

Darton stared down at it, his breaths coming raggedly. The light washed out of the sword, burning away the dark blood that had stained the blade as it went. In an instant, it looked as if it held no magic at all.

24

"There they are!" Eric hollered. I raised my head as I pulled myself over the last ridge of the rocky hills, and saw him and Mavis running over from the pool of solar light around the van. A sigh stuttered out of me. I wanted to sink down right there and let them carry me the rest of the way, but I did have a bit of a pride left, however small.

Darton paused beside me to wipe the sweat from his brow. The left sleeve of his jacket was soaked with blood from shoulder to elbow now, but he'd refused to release his grip on Excalibur. Hadn't even used the damned sword as a walking stick, as I'd have been tempted to do. But his face was nearly as pale as his knuckles where his fingers gripped the hilt, and I'd caught him swaying more than once during what had felt like the longest walk of my life.

At least the mists hadn't badgered us with any more warped memories leaving the pool. Excalibur had parted all those tumultuous emotions with a simple swipe here and there.

"My goodness, look at the two of you," Mavis said, and that was before her gaze fell on Arthur's shoulder. Her eyes widened. "Come on, come on, the both of you. Let's get you patched up before you bleed yourselves dry." She put her arm around Darton's back to lead him the rest of the way down the slope, ignoring his wordless protest.

"You didn't fare much better," Eric remarked to me, offering his own arm.

"I'm all right," I said. I didn't need the assistance, but I might have taken his elbow just for the break if I hadn't noticed the twitch of Darton's jaw. I waved Eric off and trudged the rest of the way by my own power.

The cuts on my arm were shallower than Darton's. I'd twisted the sleeve of my jacket to cover them, and only a little blood had managed to seep through. They still hurt like nettles dug under my skin, though. I'd have sealed his and mine with magic if I'd felt I could do that without collapsing, which wouldn't have done either of us any good for the trip back here.

In the stored daylight beaming from the van, my spirits revived just slightly. Enough that I could resist the urge to slump against its side as Mavis tutted over Darton's wound and then my own. She had strips of linen in the van which she wrapped around his back and shoulder and then my forearm, folded tight to reduce the bleeding.

"We'll take proper care of you back at the house," she said. "No arguments. That's where we're going now. You're not in any condition to be taking on more villains like this."

I wasn't sure I'd even been going to argue. I hadn't slept properly since what felt like at least a year ago, back in the other side of the ocean. The weariness filled my head, sloshing through my thoughts as if I'd been dunked in that ocean. A little sleep, and I could take care of us.

"House sounds good," I offered.

Eric cocked his head at Darton as Darton hauled himself into the van, pulling Excalibur after him. "That is *quite* the sword, mate."

Darton gave him a crooked smile that looked more pained than pleased. "Yes. Yes, it is."

* * *

The fae hunters' house, like Jagger's and the one I'd had modeled on his, stood off by itself on an isolated patch of land. Because this was England and closer in climate to our Pacific Northwest than Jagger's desert, like us they'd paved the yard around the house to eliminate shadows cast by grass or weeds, a sight that inexplicably pleased me.

The house itself looked slightly more homey than either back home: A chimney poked from its roof, and the sides of the building looked like wood. When we walked by, I touched one slat and realized it was actually ceramic.

"My mother believes that practical doesn't have to mean dreary," Eric said with an upward twitch of his lips.

The inside of the place looked like I'd have expected a stereotypical English cottage to, other than the absence of windows. Knickknacks cluttered the varnished shelves, and cushions lay across an array of oaken furniture. The kitchen, where Mavis insisted Darton and I sit for further tending to, smelled like fresh baked bread. I started to wonder if I'd fainted on the way back and this was all just a pleasant dream.

We unwound the hasty bandages and peeled off our jackets. The sting of my cuts confirmed that I was in fact fully awake. Darton sucked in a sharp breath as Mavis dabbed disinfectant over the gouges on his shoulder.

"I'm going to have to do some stitching on these," she said. "With your permission."

He set his jaw. "If they're that bad, go ahead."

Eric had been left to look after me, I supposed because I was the less urgent case. He grabbed the disinfectant from his mother and gave me a flash of a grin as he poured some out onto a clean cloth. "I'm only hurting you because I care."

I rolled my eyes at him. "Just get it over with."

He cupped one hand around my elbow as he wiped the cloth over the rents in my forearm. The sting prickled deeper, but it was bearable. His fingers squeezed reassuringly for a second before he let me go.

"I hate to see what the other guy looked like when you two were through with him."

My mind leapt back to the smoking mass of the snake-dragon. "Not great. We were thorough."

Eric chuckled. "I'll bet you were. No point doing a thing unless it's done right." Then he winked at me.

Darton cleared his throat. Mavis had just tied off her last stitch, but I had the feeling the tension in his face was in reaction to more than just her needle. "What's our next move, Em?" he asked.

I frowned as I considered. My head was still swimming with fatigue. He couldn't feel much better. And he wasn't likely to find his connection to the sword while exhausted and in pain.

"We'll work out how to confront Rhedyn tomorrow. It's no good rushing in when we can barely stand up." I turned to Mavis. "I assume this place has plenty of protections against dark kind."

She nodded. "It'd take a lot of effort to get in here. We're happy to put you up for the night. I already made up the spare beds downstairs."

"Downstairs?" My gaze dropped to the floor. Basements and avoiding darkness generally didn't mix.

She smiled. "The outer walls all through this place are two-layered. And in between the layers we stream stored sunlight against reflectors all night. You'll be secure enough down there, don't you worry."

"Of course," Eric said, "I happen to think *my* bed is super comfortable. And it's got room for two. Just pointing that out."

His mother cut a glance toward him, and he grinned easily. I wasn't even sure how much he meant the flirty advances. "Thank you, Prince Charming," I said. "But I do actually want to sleep."

"Well, if you change your mind, I'm down that hall to the left." He pointed.

Darton stood up abruptly. "She isn't going to be keeping you company tonight. Or any other night." His voice had gone harsh.

"Whoa, there!" Eric said, taking a step back with his hands up. "I didn't mean to step on any toes."

I touched Darton's arm, meeting his eyes for a second before I looked at Eric. "It's fine. But I don't think we're in much of a mood for joking around right now, after what we've just been through. We appreciate the hospitality given."

Nonetheless, Eric apparently felt it wiser to hang back while Mavis led us down to the basement sleeping quarters. Possibly he was right in that decision. Darton stayed close by my side as Mavis pointed to the foldout couch in the open main room and the twin bed in the smaller guest room beside it.

"I was figuring Emma would take the guest room,

what with girls generally preferring their privacy more, but really the arrangement is up to you," she said. "There are some drinks and snacks in the fridge if you get peckish. But I think sleep is what you need the most now. I'll leave you to it."

The stairs creaked as she headed up. I rubbed my eyes. My stomach twinged, but we'd gobbled down some of the fae hunters' stash of energy bars on the drive to the house. That should hold me until morning.

I drifted over to the guest room door—and Darton followed. When I stopped in the doorway to give him a questioning look, he touched my shoulder. His gaze held mine, intent with some purpose I didn't guess until he spoke.

"Em," he said, and his voice was so thick with a different sort of hunger that my knees turned wobbly. His other hand rose to cup my cheek. He stepped so close my nose would have brushed his if I'd turned my head even slightly.

My breath caught in my throat. The familiar smell of him, warm and musky, drifted over me. I managed to keep my own voice steady. "Yeah?"

"Tell me you aren't even a little interested in that joker upstairs."

I gave a hitch of a laugh. "I couldn't be less interested. The only bed I'm at all inclined to be in right now is that one over there."

His thumb traced my lower lip. "Are you 'inclined' to have anyone join you there?"

I swallowed hard. It was so hard to think straight, to remember the lines I'd drawn and intended to hold, with him so *there*, touching me, wanting me. Harder still when I was so tired of fighting so many battles. I wanted him. I always did.

Maybe this was one of those times when the rest of my concerns didn't matter. I didn't think his proposition was just about him and me. His sword had rejected him. He was battered and wounded, inside as well as out. And now he had come to me.

How could I turn him away too? I could give him this, ease that hurt, even if it hurt me later.

"No one but you," I said.

Darton let out a ragged chuckle and pulled my mouth to his.

There was nothing gentle in his kiss. It demanded, claiming me. His lips worked mine apart, and his tongue swept in to meet mine. I melted into it, into him.

He groaned, his fingers tangling in my hair, and kissed me harder. His body pressed mine against the doorframe. I could feel him, every inch of him, including the hot length already hard against my thigh. His hands swept up under my shirt to caress my breasts. I whimpered into his mouth.

He dropped one arm to my waist to tug me away from the doorframe and shoved the door closed with his foot. I nudged him toward the bed. He pulled me with him, guiding me down to straddle his lap as he sat. The bandage on my arm shifted slightly as he freed me from my shirt, but I barely had time to wince before his mouth closed over my breast. The wash of pleasure chased every other sensation away.

His tongue worked over the nipple, drawing a moan from deep in my chest. I arched against him instinctively, seeking the pressure of his hardness between my legs—

wanting it without all those layers of fabric still between us. Darton grasped my hip, matching my rocking rhythm with another groan. He turned his attentions to my other breast. Then he swung us around and flipped us over.

My head hit the pillow, and he sank over me, catching my mouth with his again. My hand trailed down his chest. It ventured over the hard-on bulging against the fly of his jeans. Darton gasped and bucked into my hand. Wanting. *Needing.* I curled my fingers around him, sliding them up and down against the thick fabric. He ducked his head against my shoulder.

"Em," he muttered. "God. You have no idea." He sucked in a stutter of breath, and every muscle in my body froze.

The sound drew up the memory of a similar one to a few hours ago. That suppressed snicker when he'd watched me—the first me, the me that should have mattered the most—watching him, my prince, my to-be-king, with open adoration. *Mooning like a schoolgirl with a crush. If I didn't know better...*

Darton had gone still over me. "Em?" he said. My throat constricted at the nickname. I could tell myself when he said it he was thinking of my real name, but right now... Right now he was only thinking Emma. Because he'd laughed to imagine Merlin could ever have wanted this, or wanted it with any hope of those feelings being returned.

Nausea churned in my stomach. I scooted out from under Darton and away to the side of the bed. My shirt was lying on the floor. I grabbed it, needing something to cover me. To make me feel a little less naked, even if my agony was written all over my face.

"We can't do this," I said. "I'm sorry. We just can't."

Darton sat back on the bed. His head bowed. He took one ragged breath and another, as if he were struggling to get himself back under control.

"If it's that you don't really want to—that you don't really want me—you should just say so," he said in a low voice, still not looking at me.

A choked laugh escaped me. "It's not *that*. I've told you—"

"I know," he broke in. "But we keep doing this back and forth anyway. All kinds of dark fae know where I am. There's obviously no getting away from them. So it can't be just about how 'woken up' I am. I wish you'd just tell me the truth."

I didn't know how to deal with the rush of emotion that surged up inside me. Some of it was frustration that he sounded so wounded, that he was making this all about *him* and his insecurities when I—

And that was the other thing. *Tell me the truth*. The very thought of doing that, of admitting out loud what I hardly liked to let myself think, made my gut twist into a massive knot.

"Darton..."

He shook his head. "Don't tell me it's okay. Don't tell me it's nothing. I know something's wrong."

I swallowed hard, pulling my shirt all the way on. The way I'd kept quiet so long was ridiculous, wasn't it? I'd been nagging Keevan to speak up to Izzy about his feelings, while here I'd hidden my own for fifteen hundred sodding years.

Maybe it was time. Because who knew how much time we even had left.

I stood up and turned to face him. My arms instinctively rose to hug myself. "You want the truth?" I said.

Darton looked up at me. "Yeah. Please." But his body had tensed. He was bracing, because he was so sure that truth would be horrible.

Of course, in his mind it might be.

My fingers dug into my elbows. I closed my eyes for a second, drawing up the courage to put the words into speech. Then I opened them again to gaze straight into his. My voice came out ragged.

"The truth is I have loved you, utterly, always. From that very first life until now. And you—you have only loved *me* some of the time. Generally dependent on what body I happened to be inhabiting at that moment."

Darton's lips parted silently. He stared at me, apparently lost for words. I made myself hold his gaze.

"It *is* okay," I said, even though my throat had gone hoarse. "I feel what I feel. You feel what you feel—or don't. It's no one's fault. But I have to—I have to draw the line somewhere, for my own sake."

"Em." The nickname came out in a rasp. He didn't seem to know what else to say, still.

I let my arms drop to my sides. "I'm going to be here for you as I always have been. I'm going to do whatever I can to save you and to serve you after I have. You don't have to worry about that. But this"—I motioned to the bed—"wrenches my heart around too much. I shouldn't have let myself try. I'm sorry." I backed up a step. "We should both get some sleep. I can take the other bed."

I walked out, shutting the door behind me.

25

I flinched awake on the pullout couch, my heart thudding in alarm. For the first few seconds, that racing beat was the only sound I could hear. Had it been a nightmare that had woken me, and not some actual threat? I inhaled slowly, willing my pulse to slow—and a skittering sound carried through the wall beside me.

I pushed off the mattress, snatching up the wand I'd left close at hand. An eerie warbling rose and fell all around the room. The hairs on my arms rose. I didn't like the sound of *that* at all.

Something had found us. And given who we were and what we were here to do, I felt pretty certain it wasn't anything good.

Swinging my purse over my shoulder, I hurried to the bedroom door. I pushed it open with a purposeful thump. Darton startled out of his own undoubtedly restless sleep. He blinked at me.

"What's—"

He hesitated, and I saw the memory of our last conversation in the tensing of his expression, the twitch of his eyes. There wasn't time to hash out that awkwardness now.

"Come on," I said. "Something's here. I don't know what, but I think we'd better find out."

"Right. Right."

He threw off the blanket. Like me, he'd opted to sleep fully clothed, probably remembering how many hasty escapes we'd needed to make in the past. Just as well that I wasn't faced with any more bare skin than that.

I jerked my head toward the stairs, and he followed. The noises grew louder as we climbed the steps. We emerged onto the first floor to a wavering groan, a hiss, and then a piercing shriek.

Lights beamed all through the rooms, but the kitchen and living room stood empty. The front door hung ajar. A human-sounding shout carried through the gap. I pulled another wand from my purse, gripping two at once, and nudged the door farther open.

A ring of electric light hazed the concrete yard outside, ending several feet past the edges of the house. The space beyond it was choked with pre-dawn darkness. A darkness that moved. Shadow creatures shaped like all manner of animals stalked along it, their shapes rippling across the border of the light.

"Eric, bird, ten o'clock!" Mavis's voice hollered from around the side of the building. A dark hawk-like shape dove down from above, jittering as it passed through the light but holding together—until a burst of flame shot up, engulfing it.

A panther-like beast leapt at the door where I was standing. I whipped my arm out automatically. "*Darkness begone.*"

Its shadowy form spasmed and vanished. My fingers

stayed clutched tight around the wands. The building's light defenses weren't holding the dark creatures back completely anymore. And I knew from past experience that it was only a matter of time before they found some other way to turn the tables on us.

Mavis came running into view. She pressed a button on the bulky metal device she was holding, and a flare of fire hissed from its mouth. It seared across a serpentine creature that had been darting toward the house.

"What's wrong with the lights?" I called to her.

She whirled, her jaw tight. "It's been too long with too little sun. The solar panels didn't draw enough to hold us with sun power all through the night. We're running off the back-up generator now—and some of these vermin are apparently strong enough to brave that."

Swine crud. I glanced at the sky, but not a hint of dawn had tinged the clouds yet. And even once it came, it would take time before the panels gathered enough sunlight to bring the lights to full power. The rain was holding off for the moment, but the air was damp and heavy. The dark fae's conjured storm wasn't over yet.

Rhedyn must have sent these creatures after us as soon as she'd realized her snake-dragon hadn't done the trick. Or else—

My pulse stuttered. I shut my eyes for a second to tune out everything except my internal senses and reached out with my awareness to the south. If the Darkest One was already free...

No. The chill I'd been braced for didn't come. No sense of her unbound presence leaked across the countryside. She was still trapped—for however little time longer.

"It's our fault those things are here," Darton said where he stood just behind me. "Like at Jagger's place. We have to help fight them off."

I nodded, my mouth pressing flat. The last thing I wanted was a repeat of our experience at Jagger's house. The house he'd decided he had to blow to smithereens just to get us out safely.

"No more casualties on our watch," I said.

"Exactly."

At a shout from Eric, Mavis dashed back around the house. A second later, a winged creature that looked more like a pterodactyl than any living thing I'd ever seen in my lives swooped down toward the roof. I leapt forward, jabbing my wands upward.

"*Darkness begone.*"

Darton brushed past me. I spun around to tell him to stay back, and the warning caught in my throat.

He'd grabbed Excalibur from where he'd left it near the basement door. The blade gleamed with unearthly power as he slashed it through the air at the edge of the light. He swung it as if it were part of his arm, part of him. The way he was meant to.

"Back!" he snapped at the dark rabble. "Get out of here, or I'll split you all apart."

He swept the sword toward them, and it cut through their shadowy bodies with a watery warble. The creatures hugging the fringes of the darkness scattered, several shattering at the touch of the enchanted blade. Darton sidestepped to press his advantage. A small smile crossed his face.

My heart squeezed, watching him find his rhythm. Watching the Arthur in him emerge. But I couldn't just stand around feeling pleased. This was my battle too.

I passed one of my wands to my other hand and strode closer to the edge of the light. Crossing my arms in front of my chest, I clenched my fingers around the sealed wood and pulled at the life energy inside it.

"*Darkness begone.*"

I whipped my arms out in matching arcs. A blast of light rippled from the wands through the shadows. More dark creatures wavered and blinked away—but there were still far too many lurking around the more distant parts of the yard, lit up briefly by my attack.

Rhedyn hadn't bothered with glooms. Either she'd learned from the mercenary's mistakes or simply was wiser than him in the first place. The larger, more conscious dark creatures were wiser too. They weren't going to simply pour in at us in a mass for easy slaughtering. Now that we'd shown our power, they were regrouping where it would take much more power to reach them. Regrouping and considering the best way to outmaneuver us.

The wands had turned dead in my hands with the effort of my large-scale casting. I dropped them, and they broke into dust at my feet. I had a few more in my purse. More still in my suitcase back in the house. But I needed some of those to face Rhedyn. I had to be strategic too.

As if sensing my hesitation, the darkness around us shivered as a fresh wave of creatures slunk toward us. I dug out another wand. Eric loped over to join us, a flame-thrower fixed under his arm from a harness.

"Was that *you*, with the light?"

"Yep," I said. "And it looks like you might be about to get a firsthand demonstration." I eyed the creatures testing the edges of the light, wanting as many as possible close by before I drew on my magic again. The hiss of Mavis's flamethrower carried from behind the house. No, we weren't finished here yet.

Eric's head twitched toward the area where Darton was walking the fringe. Excalibur flashed as my king swung it through another beast that ventured too close. Eric's jaw dropped. "Holy shit. I'm starting to see why you went through all that trouble for that sword."

"Let's just hope between the bunch of us it's enough," I said.

The swarm of creatures was thickening. I took a step forward to increase my range. As I raised my hand, a rumble echoed across the sky. Thunder.

All the creatures in the yard flinched. They scattered in an aimless fashion for a moment before drawing back.

Oh. That was interesting. I should have realized. If a little static electricity could fry a gloom, how many of the dark rabble could a single lightning strike sear apart? I might be able to clear the whole area with just one more wand lost.

I raised my free hand toward the clouds, stretching higher with my senses. Up, up, toward those thickly congealed clouds. The weight of them pressed against me, stewing with gathered moisture. I nudged at them for any hint of a crackle.

But even as I brushed up against a tingle of electricity, the sensation pulled away from me. The clouds quivered and calmed, as if some other force had combed that building energy out of them. The taste of rot crept through my mouth.

Rhedyn's colleagues were working their magic even now. They didn't want a full-out storm interfering with their work. Without their presence, I might have summoned a lightning strike or two, but I didn't have the strength to push back against all of them.

One reincarnated half fae against who knew how many full—I didn't stand a chance, did I? I didn't have any chance at all.

The chill of that thought washed over me, and for an instant my mind simply froze.

"Emma!" Eric said.

I snapped back to the present, my hand automatically brandishing the wand. Eric was already flinging himself toward a pack of shadow creatures that had sprung at me in my momentary distraction.

Eric aimed his flame-thrower. The spurts of fire ripped through two of the creatures. The spell I spat out blasted through two more. But I hadn't been focused or had time to aim. The fifth, an immense hound-like beast, clamped its jaws around my forearm before I could speak another spell.

Cold seared through my flesh. I clamped my teeth against a cry and wrenched backward. The creature opened its mouth to take a deadlier chomp at me, but I was ready this time.

"*Darkness begone*," I gasped out with a flick of the wand. A spark of light flared around the hound. The hound's form crumpled in on itself and disappeared.

I staggered backward, clutching my wounded arm with my other hand to keep the wand steady. The dark creature's fangs had sunk straight through my sweater. I knew when I let myself look I'd find the skin marred with dead gray streaks to match the slashes I already carried from earlier encounters.

Footsteps thumped against the ground. Darton was rushing to my side, his face pale. I waved him back.

"We need you," I said. "You and that sword. We have to keep them back. I'm fine now."

"I can't..." He hefted Excalibur again, but not with the ease I'd seen just a minute ago. The muscles in his arms strained the way they had yesterday, when he'd stumbled with its weight. The blade's gleam had dimmed. What in sodding hell was going on?

"Just try. You've scared them plenty already." I pointed to the fringes. "It was working with you."

Darton's mouth tightened, but he nodded. He strode back to the edge of the fray, heaving the sword into the air as he went. But it was a clumsier motion now. The blade cut through the creatures pressing their advantage along the border of the light—and they only flinched away. The ordinary blade, without its magic activated, wasn't enough to end them.

Eric hurried forward too, blasting a few of the nearest creatures with flame, but it wasn't enough. We couldn't stop to figure out Darton's problem now. The next wave of the dark rabble's assault was still gathering.

But even as my fingers closed around the wand, an ache spread up my arm into my chest. It wasn't just Darton faltering. I was tiring out fast without the sun overhead to lend me more energy. We needed to end this fast, or we might not end it at all.

The dark creatures pushed forward again, and Darton stumbled back. He gripped the sword with both hands, his face set with the same anguished determination as when we'd faced the snake-dragon in the Pool of Turmoil.

But we'd gotten through that. Because we'd

combined what powers we had.

I threw myself toward him. My first instinct was to reach for the amber stone I'd shoved back in my purse. But Darton hadn't bothered to pull on his jacket when he'd raced outside, and there weren't scraps of fur just lying around for my use.

Maybe that was for the best. I wasn't sure how to control the electricity all that well yet, and it would have taken quite a surge to blast it across the entire force around the house. I didn't want to hurt Mavis or Eric in the process.

I still had the light inside my wands and wound through the life inside my own body. Light that would sear apart the shadows but not our allies. Light Excalibur would respond to.

"Darton!" I set my hand on his shoulder. His muscles tensed at my touch. "We'll go at them like we attacked the thing in the pool. My magic and your sword's power, together. All right?"

He nodded, eyeing the creatures snapping at the fringes of the light. "What do you need me to do?"

"When you feel the energy coming, just swing the sword as wide as you can."

I thrust my hand into my purse, fumbling my fingers around all four of the wands I had left on hand. I might have to throw a year or two of my own life into the mix, but that was business as usual these days.

As I drew in my breath to cast the spell, a bear-like beast charged at us from the darkness. My heart lurched. I hardly had time to sputter out the ancient words.

"Darkness all around be gone!"

I grasped onto all the glittering energy I could catch

hold of and propelled it through my body and down Darton's arm to the sword.

Sparks crackled behind my eyes. Excalibur lit up like a beacon. Darton was already slashing it through the air. The blaze of light that rippled off it whipped across the landscape around us like a sonic boom. Even soundless, it knocked the breath from my lungs.

Somewhere behind us, Eric gave a yelp, but at least it sounded startled rather than pained. All across the yard and on the fields now lit beyond, the creatures of the dark rabble crumpled and washed away.

Darton and I had been tired, and the shadowy animals were stronger than glooms, so it wasn't the thorough victory I'd been hoping for. But the scattered shapes that remained as the magical light hazed away staggered, limping, away. There weren't enough left that they were ready to attempt another attack, at least. And the new day's sun was just starting to tint the clouds along the horizon.

Darton lowered the sword. "They'll be back, won't they?"

"They will," I said. "And sooner rather than later. But I know what we need to do now."

He raised an eyebrow at me. "Oh yeah?"

I squeezed his shoulder briefly before releasing it. "We're going to get lightning on our side. And I know just who can help us gather it."

I also knew that they weren't going to be the slightest bit keen to pitch in, but I'd deal with that problem when we came to it.

26

Somehow the trip out to the secluded forestland we'd visited yesterday felt even lonelier this time. I peered past the sweep of the windshield wipers at the gloomy woods lining the narrow road. The tires of the car Mavis had lent Darton and me bumped over the ruts and stray rocks. The heating system was whirring away, but I felt as chilled as if I'd just stepped into the fall rain.

The drive was lonelier in a totally literal sense too. We'd left Mavis and Eric back at their house, which at least was in one piece and not a smoking ruin. When I'd asked Mavis about borrowing a vehicle, she'd smiled and said Jagger had warned her to make sure she had something extra on hand.

"I picked this up from a friend of ours in the business," she'd said, leading me to their garage at the back of the yard. "He is hoping to get it back."

"Well, I did manage to take decent care of Jagger's van," I'd told her. "And our track record with fae hunters here is already a lot better."

She'd shaken her head, bemused. "Are you sure the two of you should be going off alone? We committed to helping you through whatever you need to do to stop these fae."

I'd had to smile at her offer. "What we've got to do right now, I'm the only one who can handle it. But if we need your help again, believe me, I'll be in touch. If any other strange readings or whatever get passed on through your network, you give me a shout, okay?"

She'd nodded, and Eric had come over to shake hands and give me one of those jokingly flirty winks. Five minutes later we'd been on the road.

Now, Darton shifted in the passenger seat beside me. He had that sword in front of him, propped so the end of the blade rested on the floor and the hilt leaned against his chest. Every now and then he gripped the hilt and seemed to test it. His expression had been as clouded as the sky overhead for the entire drive.

"Are you sure this is our best option?" he said. "I got a bad feeling from those fae when we were out here before. They *really* didn't like me being around. Not that I think they'd hurt me or anything, but... Can we trust them?"

I grimaced. He didn't know the half of it. But I'd stashed my father's journals away in Mavis and Eric's house for safe-keeping, and I wasn't going to spill the beans about his vague worries to Darton now. "I know they were jerks. I don't like it—or them—either. But I think I can convince them to get on board for this one thing. And if they give their word, they'll keep it. We don't have a chance at pushing back against the dark fae on our own."

"But maybe we would if I could get this damned sword to work for me." Darton frowned at the blade. He hefted it again, careful not to gouge the dashboard, and his jaw tightened. "It doesn't feel right. It's like it doesn't *want* to cooperate."

"That's just how a regular broadsword feels," I said. "You'd have worked up to getting comfortable wielding over several years when you were training the first time. But if we can solidify your connection to the enchantment on it, that won't matter."

"If." He set the sword back down. "You were counting on me being able to do that from the start. You didn't think I'd have this much trouble."

"I had no idea what to expect. That sodding thing has been hanging out in the Pool of Turmoil for centuries. We'll figure it out."

Darton fell silent. He traced his thumb back and forth along the leather-wrapped grip of the hilt. He'd been quiet for a lot of the trip so far, but somehow this moment felt more ominous. As if the weight of the question he was working up to was leaking from him before he even opened his mouth. My fingers tensed against the steering wheel.

He inhaled slowly. "What you said last night," he said. "Was it true?"

When I hesitated, he glanced over at me, his gaze searching. A lump rose in my throat.

I could have dismissed the question. Pretended my feelings vomit had been an exaggeration brought on by the stress of the moment. But... I found as I turned that possibility over that I didn't like it.

I didn't want to take my confession back. It was out there in the space between us instead of bottled up inside me now, and suddenly I had a little more room to breath, even if the breathing was a tad painful.

Darton—no, *Arthur*—deserved to know. I owed him at least that much truth.

"Yeah," I said. "It was."

He looked away, rubbed his mouth. "You never told me, back then. I don't think. I don't remember knowing, or having any idea..."

"No. I've never told you before at all. In any life before this."

His gaze jerked back to me. "*Never?* But I thought this... us..." He motioned between us as if the entirety of our bizarre relationship could be summed up in a wave of a hand. "I thought we'd, ah, hooked up in other lives before this. You made it sound like the attraction was normal."

My laugh came out hoarse. "There is a *small* difference between 'hooking up' with someone and professing your undying love for them. Just FYI."

"Well, yeah. I just mean... Why didn't you say anything, all this time?"

I swallowed hard. "You— No. It was me. I was afraid of how you'd react. I knew, back then, you would never have thought of *me* that way, and every time after... I've never known how much it was you and how much the spell."

I was still afraid. My pulse was rattling against my ribs. I kept my eyes trained on the road, but most of my attention was on his presence at the edge of my vision as he processed this information.

"Oh." Darton lowered his head as if to study his hands. "I can— From some of the things I remember, I can see why you might have been worried. The first time, anyway. But I really didn't have any idea. I'm sorry if I made things harder."

"Like I said last night, it's no one's fault. We feel what we feel."

"You also said that I only... In all the other lives, we've only ever gotten together like that when you were a woman?"

I wondered if he'd remembered something more, a sliver of sensation from some other existence between the first and now. I might as well be honest about that too. "No. It's been... Ever since we've gotten to be a certain age before the dark rabble would catch us, unless I've drawn a line, it's been pretty much always. But let's just say the times when I was in certain types of bodies have gone much worse than the others."

I only remembered one with any clarity, and even that was fragmented. A headlong rush from first kiss to fumbles under a blanket, alcohol tangy on both our tongues, and him waking up half sober some hours later, awkward and unsettled. He went to take a walk, to clear his head, so I had stupidly given him "space." And in that space the glooms had found him. That was how I'd lost him, three of these cycles ago.

"Ah." Darton's brow furrowed, but he didn't seem to know what else to say.

"We don't need to talk about it anymore. Things are as they are. I've had plenty of time to accept that, even if I haven't done the best job of it." I tipped my head toward the sword. "You found your rhythm with Excalibur for a little while this morning. I saw how it responded to you. Whatever you need, it's in you."

"Just not enough," Darton muttered.

"Well, you're still coming awake. You aren't entirely...

you. The you it's used to." I paused, thinking back to the moment in the fray when Darton's handle on the sword had slipped. Right after the one dark creature had attacked me. The gray gashes prickled on my forearm under my torn sleeve. "What was going through your head, when it stopped being easy? Or when you were trying to pull it out of the stone, back in the Pool of Turmoil?"

Darton leaned back in his seat, his expression pensive. "I was worried I couldn't do it, I guess."

"So it was doubts getting in the way."

"Maybe. I also..." His mouth slanted. "I don't know how to explain it. But this feeling came over me, when I was trying to pull it out, when I was trying to fight that dragon-ish thing, and today, when that monster attacked you... As if I *knew* I was going to fail you in some huge way, and it wasn't the first time. I was going to screw up all over again and let you down."

"Fail *me*?" I repeated, my eyebrows rising. "Art, it's not your job to look after me. So I don't really see how you could have failed at that. Failed yourself, maybe— whatever expectations you've got—but seriously, if we're going to talk about failure, should we get into my track record? We're only *here* fifteen centuries after our first lives because I've managed not to save us more times than I'd really like to count."

Darton made a dismissive sound. "You've kept us alive in the way that matters the most. We *are* still here fifteen centuries later. How much have I contributed to that?"

"That's not the point. My job was making sure you didn't get murdered by the Darkest One in the first place. The whole rest of this time I've been not-very-successfully trying to mop up the mess I made of that task."

"But you've fought, you've stepped up, you've done everything you could..."

"And you haven't?" I gave a disbelieving laugh. "Art, you don't give yourself enough credit. A couple of months ago you'd never have believed creatures like the things we've encountered in the last few weeks even existed. Yesterday you took on a snake the size of a house with nothing but a dagger. If 'doing everything you could' is the measure we're going by, I think you've got that covered."

Darton sucked in his lower lip. Abruptly I was remembering what those lips felt like against mine, which was really not what I needed to be thinking about right then. I trained my attention back on the road. The car's tires hissed through a particularly large puddle.

At least he knew now. I could draw my lines without having to lie anymore about why.

"It's always about me, though, isn't it?" Darton said after a moment, his voice low. "Even the first time, in our first lives, you came asking to serve me. You've spent so much of your life—your *lives*—trying to keep me alive."

"Well, yes. So?"

"How is that fair? For you to be tied to me like that, never getting to go after whatever it is *you'd* want?"

I shook my head. "You can't think of it that way. You— Do you remember that conversation we had on the plane? About being king, and whether you had a choice?"

"Of course."

"You said you did have a choice, and even if there hadn't been any pressure, you'd have made the same one, right?"

He nodded, and I drew in my breath. "I had a choice

too. I always have one. I could walk away, do my own thing, make the most of the time I have doing whatever the hell I want until the cycle starts over. But I always choose you, without hesitation. Because *this* is where I want to be. So don't you dare tell me that's unfair."

Darton looked at me for a long moment—so long my face started to warm at his attention. He let out a rough chuckle. "What in the world did I do to deserve you?"

My mouth twitched. "Something truly horrid, I've got to think."

He blinked, startled, and then he cracked up. A second later, I started laughing too. It felt like a release of so much tension—tension that maybe we'd both been holding inside for far too long.

When we finally stopped, gasping for breath, I reached over and briefly gripped Darton's arm. "You had so much greatness when you started, Art. You'll find it again if we can buy you enough time."

His smile fell. "I don't know. You say that, but— Every time I sleep, that memory comes back. That woman—the Darkest One—stabbing me. I just stood there and let her do it and it's only because of you we got out of it at all."

It was my turn to stare at him. I slowed the car to make sure I didn't drive right off the road.

"Don't be ridiculous," I said. "You did a sodding lot more than that."

His brow knit. "I can't remember anything else. It's all hazy and her face and the pain. And you yelling."

My stomach clenched. "And that memory has been coming back to you *every* night?"

"Not the whole time since we met. I first

remembered it, or at least pieces of it, in a dream that night when we were on the road, back home. I didn't have the same dream again for a while. But from around the time we moved into the new house, it's kept coming up."

"That would be around the time Rhedyn started paying attention to us."

He glanced over at me. "You think she has something to do with it."

"I think she could." My mouth tightened. "Because the way you're remembering it isn't accurate. And I don't think your mind would have distorted it like that on its own. It would be in Rhedyn's best interests to have you thinking of yourself as weak and helpless. Why didn't you tell me before?"

"I didn't know it was that strange. And..." His head dipped sheepishly. "I guess I didn't want to sound weak and helpless."

"Well, you're not." I paused, scanning the terrain around us. I hadn't seen any dark creatures since we'd left the fae hunters' home. This would only take a few minutes. And maybe it would make all the difference my king needed.

I eased on the gas completely and guided the car over to the shoulder. The engine sputtered out. I turned to face Darton. "Then I think you should see *everything* that happened."

27

Darton frowned at me. "How are you going to make me remember? I thought there wasn't any way to provoke a specific memory into coming back."

A hint of sunlight penetrated the thick clouds, but I didn't have any hope of that being suitable protection. I flicked a couple switches on the fae-hunter enhanced dashboard and the solar lamps blinked on all around the car. "I can't provoke a specific one of *your* memories. But I can let you see one of mine. If you're okay with that."

His eyes widened a bit, but I thought I saw more curiosity in his expression than apprehension. "All right. Are *you* okay with it?"

He was going to be seeing what I'd seen from right inside my head. With all the sensations and emotions that had passed through me in those moments. My body balked, but only for a second. There wasn't anything I'd said, done, or felt then that he shouldn't know. I'd already spilled my guts last night. Letting him see past the obscured visions Rhedyn had stirred up in his head mattered more than notions of privacy.

"I suggested it, didn't I? Hold on."

I pushed open the door and hurried through the

drizzle to the trees along the side of the road. Birch, that would serve this purpose well. I snapped a good, solid twig off one branch. The tingle of fresh life tickled my fingers. I dropped back into my seat and extended the twig toward Darton.

"You hold the other end and close your eyes. I can take care of the rest."

He gripped the twig. I let our hands come down to rest on the cup holder between the seats. Dragging in a breath, I pushed my mind back through time to that last, painful memory from our first lives.

I'd thought back to it so many times, trying to remember the exact words I'd said, the energies I'd drawn on, that it surfaced almost instantly. The sudden clouds scudding across the bright autumn sky. The smells of roasting meat and fresh-baked pastries carrying on the breeze. The chatter, punctuated with shouts and laughter, of hundreds of townspeople in the midst of their celebration, not yet realizing it was about to come to an abrupt and horrible end.

I closed my own eyes. *"From my mind to his,"* I murmured, reaching into the twig. A shiver of its energy shot from my fingertips to Darton's, and I propelled the memory through it.

The crowd jostled around me as I edged across the lawn outside the castle, keeping half of my attention on the dais where Arthur was to make his speech and the rest roaming the figures around me for anyone suspicious. I hadn't eaten since my hasty breakfast, but even though it was mid-afternoon, my stomach didn't have room for hunger. It was pinched tight with an anxiety I couldn't quite explain, but nonetheless trusted.

Something awful was coming. And I wasn't sure I was ready

for it.

A hush fell over the revelers as their king stepped to the head of the temporary stage. Arthur raised his hands and smiled that slightly crooked smile that never failed to make my heart leap, even now. A cheer rose up from his audience.

Less than a week ago, he'd sent the last of the enemy forces that had tried to invade fleeing home. It had been a long, painful war, but he'd seen us all through it, and it was over now. The relief in the crowd was so pungent I could almost taste it. Adoration for the man who'd accomplished it lit the faces all around me.

"My people," Arthur began as the cheer faded. "I can't tell you how overjoyed I am to be here with all of you, celebrating our victory over those who would have stolen our lands. We have all sacrificed and suffered, and now we all deserve to—

A cry split the air. I jerked around. The clouds were still thickening, and a figure had sprung from the shadows by one of the makeshift booths. He gripped the man in front of him by the head and neatly snapped his neck.

No. I hurried forward, pushing my way through the crowd. The people around the fallen man scattered with sobs and shrieks. Another shadow-clung figure and another wavered into view in the muted daylight. Their presence sent prickles over my skin. Dark fae, all around me.

The dark fae attackers lunged at the spectators with daggers and spears. A woman fell. A teenaged boy stumbled, clutching his bleeding arm. The fae who'd attacked him swung again—and Arthur was there, Excalibur gleaming in his hand, slicing through the fae weapon as if it were made of water.

"Back!" he shouted. "Back to the castle gates. My men, come to me!"

The castle guards who'd joined in the reveling were already hustling to flank him. The fae woman gnashed her teeth and sprang at him, dark sparks flaming between her hands. Before I could even spit out a spell to fling her back from a distance, Arthur had caught her with his sword. The shining blade cut through her dark-shrouded form, and she fell like a heap of fabric.

But more dark fae were emerging all across the lawn. Arthur raced to intercept a fae man who was aiming a blast of magic at a cluster of children. 'Shield them!' I cried out. A barrier of light energy snapped into place around them, but the king had already leapt to protect them in his own way. The dark spell glanced off Excalibur and sputtered out in the air.

I brandished my wand to push farther into the fray—and a woman stepped out of the shadows right in front of me. Her ash-blond hair was pulled into a knot above her tan face. Her eyes glittered menacingly.

"Where do you think you're going, Merlin?" Rhedyn asked.

"Through you, if I have to."

That part of the memory was a bit of a hash as far as Darton was concerned. If I'd had a fast-forward button I'd have zipped past Rhedyn's snarking, the bursts of magic we'd thrown back and forth at each other. I'd been too busy tangling with her to pay attention to my king. Which was why, when I finally heaved her to the side with a massive blast of wind I'd redirected around her counter-strike at the last moment, I'd been startled and horrified to see Arthur face to face with the Darkest One herself.

The tall, gaunt woman loomed over even Arthur's substantial height. A smirk curled her lips. A civilian lay near her feet, his skin deathly blue.

The king's jaw had set tight. He'd raised his sword high, the muscles in his arms flexing. I hurled myself toward them. Just as he shifted to deliver the strike, the Darkest One's hand flicked out. The knife she held split the plated padding of his jacket—

I yanked myself out of the memory. The twig snapped between my fingers. Darton flinched. He rubbed a hand over his face as the borrowed images must have faded from his own mind.

"That was... That was really strange," he said. "Like watching a home video of myself, except it wasn't just a camera I was watching through, it was *you*."

I hoped nothing I'd felt in those moments had been too discomforting. At least I'd been more focused on watching out for threats than admiring my king's physique, which I might have done from time to time on other occasions.

"But you see, don't you?" I said. "You can hardly say you just stood there. You charged right in, you stopped the Darkest One's people from hurting so many of yours. You were faster to leap to the defense than *I* was. You can't be ashamed of anything you saw there."

And yet he was frowning. I started the engine again, knowing we had to get going, and tried to figure out what I could say that would make him understand. Before I had, Darton broke his pensive silence.

"I wish I could remember what I was thinking, right before— To get into that memory properly, the whole thing, in my own head."

"Why?" I pressed on the gas and turned us back onto the road. "Obviously you wanted to protect everyone. You were fighting off the dark fae. I don't think there's any reason to believe you had any mysterious motives for that."

"Well, no..." His frown deepened. "It's just, that last glimpse I got, before she stabbed me and you pulled us out... There was something about the way I was holding the sword." He touched the hilt of that same sword where it leaned against him now. "The angle of it, or my grip. I'm not sure. It didn't look right."

"After watching you in battle innumerable times, I feel confident saying that you knew how to hold a sword properly."

"I know. That's why it seems significant." He shook his head. "Maybe I'm just overthinking it. Or I misunderstood what I was seeing. You were pretty far away, and it was just a glimpse. And I'm not really an expert on swords now. It's not like it matters at this point."

It might, but not enough that I wanted to delay our current mission any longer. "If it does, I'm sure it'll come to you, like the idea about the lenses finally did. In any case, you can see, can't you? That you saved so many lives, made so many better—and that was just on that one day. I've had centuries to catch up with your record of heroic deeds, and I'm still working on it."

"Okay. I get it." He relaxed back in his seat, and for the first time the corners of his lips curled a little upward. Remembering how brilliant he'd looked with that sword, I hoped. But then he added, "I'm sorry."

"What for this time?"

He laughed. "I'm not sure. It just felt important that I say that. Everything I should be sorry for, I guess."

"Well, consider yourself forgiven."

He looked as though he might have been about to say more, but at that moment a light fae woman sprang onto the road in front of us.

28

I hit the brakes. The tires squealed on the slick road, but the car jerked to a stop a foot shy of the fae woman. She didn't even flinch. I supposed if she'd judged the threat too much, she could have flashed away in an instant.

I shoved open my door and leaned out. "What are you *doing*?" We were still a half a mile distant of where I'd planned to stop to hike to the enclave. And while I'd expected a certain amount of resistance from my light fae brethren, nearly getting us into a road accident wasn't an approach I'd been prepared for.

The fae blinked her doe-like eyes at me. From her faint glimmer, she was a youngish one. But she didn't bow. I'd gotten more respect back in the New World than here in the place where they should have recognized me most.

On second thought, maybe that was the problem.

"You were told to leave," she said in a calm, silvery voice. "You and... him. You're not meant to be here."

Well, we could debate who got to decide where I was "meant" to be ad nauseam, but I didn't think it would be very productive getting into that subject with her.

"Stay here," I said to Darton. I switched on the sun lamps and pushed myself right out of my seat. The fae eyed me as I nudged the door shut and came around to speak to her face to face.

I leaned against the car's hood. "I need to speak to the elders," I said. "Cormag can come along if he likes, but I want at least two of the others as well. If protecting the enclave from the Darkest One and her plans here matters so much to them and the rest of you, I have a proposition they'll want to hear."

"*That one* is not to come any closer to the enclave," she replied, flicking her hand toward Darton.

"That's fine. You get a couple of your people over here to keep an eye on things, and I'll go talk to the elders wherever they want. But I *am* going to talk to them. You can't keep me out of the enclave if I want to get to it. I have roots there. The forest knows me, even if the rest of you don't like that."

She raised her chin with a little sniff, but she darted away, I assumed to deliver my message. Gritting my teeth, I got back into the car just long enough to park out of the way of anyone who might pass by, not that this road appeared to get a lot of traffic. I hadn't seen any other vehicles either time we'd come out this way. No doubt the enclave had set wards to encourage the average person to head in other directions.

"Is everything okay?" Darton asked.

"They're about as friendly as before. But I think I've gotten myself an audience with a few of the fae who can make the real decisions, and that's all I need to get started. Hang out with your sword some more. See if you can get better reacquainted."

He gave me a crooked smile and didn't protest when I got out again.

The light fae woman reappeared a minute later with two youthful companions in tow. "The elders say they will hear your proposal," she said. "As long as you go alone. We are to wait here to ensure no darkness passes this way."

I wasn't sure if she meant Darton or the dark fae who might come looking for him, but either served my purposes fine. "All right. Where should I find them?"

She pointed toward the woods. "Straight to the mothering ash, then seaward."

Directions in poetic form. I managed not to roll my eyes. "Thanks."

It took about a quarter hour of tramping through the forest before I spotted the "mothering ash." The large, aged tree loomed over a sapling on either side, clearly sprung from its own seeds. And seaward would be... I checked my sense of the sun and swung left. I guessed I was supposed to just keep walking until I bumped into the elders.

I was just starting to wonder if they'd decided it would be more worthwhile to watch me wandering around trying to find them than to actually talk to me when I spotted four shimmering figures amid the trees up ahead.

Cormag stood in the middle of the group, but the others were even more elder. They created a pool of natural light in their little clearing, streaming from the filmy edges of their bodies. In the dim daylight, it was as if a miniature sun had settled in the middle of the forest.

Cormag's face was tensed. "I thought you understood everything after our last conversation," he said the second

I'd reached them. "I was as clear as I knew how that we cannot tolerate—"

"I know, I know," I interrupted. "The dark fae got their dirty fingerprints all over Arthur's family line. Maybe there's some stain that's lingered. I haven't seen any sign of it since you brought it up, but sure, I'll accept it's possible. That's exactly why I'm here."

Cormag scowled. One of the elder women stepped forward with a beckoning gesture. "Tell us what it is you seek here, Son of Eóghan. Your father was wiser than most, and I hope some of his forbearance has passed onto you."

I was pretty sure my father had vented on more than one occasion that he felt it had skipped me entirely, but no need to get into that right now.

"You want me and my king gone," I said. "I understand that. But we *will* not leave until we've done everything we can to prevent the Darkest One's release. I was the one who imprisoned her. Keeping her in her prison is my responsibility. I assume you all can understand that."

"After all this time," Cormag tried again.

I shook my head. "Nope. I'm not getting into that argument again. We're staying and fighting, and there's nothing any of you can really do about that, is there? Unless you want to play dark fae and kill us."

The shudder those words provoked told me there wasn't any chance of that. I crossed my arms over my chest. "So the only questions left are whether the Darkest One will get free and snatch up Arthur's soul or whether we'll stop her. You'd prefer the latter, wouldn't you? And you *can* make a difference there."

"We will not fight your battles," the other woman said. "Our kind defends our ground, but we do not stir up conflict elsewhere."

"That's fine," I said. "I'm not asking you to go anywhere. But it's been wearing on you, hasn't it, all those clouds up there?" I pointed toward the sky. "No one in the enclave can have been enjoying that weather. And you have to be able to tell it's the dark fae keeping the sun hidden away."

"You want us to push back the clouds?" Cormag said.

I smiled. "No. I want you to crack them open. That'll be easier anyway, won't it? There's lightning brewing in them already. The dark fae have been calming it, but it's got to be a tricky balance. If the enclave works together, you can tip it. I want a full-blown thunderstorm over north Somerset by the end of the day. You get me that, I can destroy the fae working to free the Darkest One, no one touches my king, and this ends happily for everyone."

The second woman peered down at me haughtily. "Why should we expend our energy for one who has so little concern for our own wellbeing? You are bringing the poison straight to she who wishes to spread it."

"If she gets out, she's going to find him one way or another." I waved a hand in frustration. "But fine, fine, it really bugs you that this catastrophe might go down on your doorstep. I don't want it to happen here—or anywhere—either. That's what I'm trying to stop here."

"But if you fail..."

"I won't fail, if I have the lightning on my side." I hoped.

Cormag's eyes narrowed. "Even if the Darkest One escapes after all, there is one way to still protect us. To protect all those you claim to care about. If the king's soul passes from this world before she can grasp it, she will lose it for good."

I paused, my back stiffening. If Arthur died, he meant. Died for good, not just tumbling back into our cycle of rebirths. If the binding part of the spell was broken, the rest would fracture in turn. But there was only one way I could guarantee what Cormag was asking.

I raised my chin. "Is that what you need? My word that if she emerges, I'll take his life before she can?"

The fae's lips curled in disgust, but Cormag inclined his head, and none of the others argued. They couldn't bring themselves to destroy a life, but they could tacitly approve of me doing it. Bloody hypocrites.

I swallowed hard. I'd been ready to end Darton's life a few weeks ago when we'd faced the mercenary, if we'd lost control over that situation. But then I'd assumed I would be simply throwing us back into our cycle, *preventing* my king's final death—not bringing it about.

What if the magic the Darkest One had worked on Arthur all those years ago had faded away over the centuries? What if he wasn't a disaster waiting to happen after all? I *hadn't* felt anything catastrophic in him, ever. They wanted me to agree to kill him without even knowing whether it was really necessary.

"If you swear you'll sever his light before the Darkest One can spread her poison from it, we will bring your lightning," the first woman said. "I swear that."

Her words rang with a magical finality. She was bound to them now. I could have everything I needed, if I just agreed to this. This horrible task that I'd never have to consider as long as we took down Rhedyn in time.

With the lightning and the sword, we'd have all we needed. Without the enclave's help, we were almost certainly lost anyway.

"All right," I said, my voice rough. "If the Darkest One walks free, I will sever Arthur's soul before she can. I swear it."

I pushed a sliver of the life energy pulsing through my body into the last words. They spilled out into the air and solidified in my chest at the same moment. The oath hung there over my heart like a lump of stone.

The elders bobbed their heads. "It is spoken. It is so."

I clamped my lips back together, praying that the dread swelling inside me was only nerves and not an omen.

29

"Okay." Darton gestured with his phone. "Keevan has finally gotten a hold of his sister. *I'm pretty sure she thinks I'm crazy or involved in some kind of wacky science cult at this point. But I got all her physics Ph.D. lightning expertise out of her.*"

My hands tightened on the steering wheel, but the corner of my mouth quirked up. I could practically hear Keevan's voice in Darton's recitation of his words. "And what did she say in her expertise?"

Darton leaned back in the passenger seat. "He's getting into that... *Apparently there isn't a whole lot you can do to attract lightning, if for some insane reason you'd want to. I'm hoping your reasons aren't completely insane, Art.*" He chuckled. "I'm thinking it's probably a good thing Keev isn't around for this little expedition."

"Ah, he rose to the occasion just fine last time around." But, true, last time around we hadn't been messing with lightning bolts.

"*Anyway, unless you're a skyscraper or something, you're not likely to change the direction of a lightning strike unless it's already really close to you, she says. Within a few feet or so. But if it is coming down really close anyway, it will tend to hit the highest thing around. So if you're by a tree in a big open space—or by yourself in a big open space—you're more likely to get 'lucky.'*

I nodded. "Okay. I think I can handle the getting it close part." My affinity to the light would make it easy to call down the energy once it was ready.

"If the light fae come through with provoking the lightning in the first place, right?" Darton frowned. "Are you completely sure we can count on them?"

"They seemed persuaded by my arguments," I said. And by my oath, which I hadn't mentioned to Darton.

I glanced over at him. At the living embodiment of my king. He was peering at his phone now, waiting for Keevan's next text, looking every inch the modern college guy—the kind of guy who shouldn't have needed to worry about summoning lightning or fae magic.

The kind of guy whose possible murder I shouldn't have hanging over my head.

Darton had never asked for any of this. He'd been born with my king twined inside him, and he hadn't even known *that* until last month.

But he was still here. We'd gotten this far. I didn't have to fix all my mistakes right now. All I had to do was interrupt Rhedyn's meddling and shore up the bindings holding the Darkest One in place for a little longer. Buy us a little more time. The rest I could figure out afterward.

There was no *if.* I simply was going to do it, no other options allowed.

"You were right about the metal idea," Darton said. *"Any kind of metal will act as an attracter too. The bigger the better. I hope that helps. And that I'm not going to see any reports from England about some dude getting fried."*

I laughed at that. "Tell him I'm the one who's going

to be channeling the lightning."

Darton's fingers tapped against the screen. "He says he'd rather you didn't get fried either."

"Well, that's comforting. I guess we should be looking into buying a lightning rod."

He sent off one last message to his best friend and brought up his mobile browser. "You haven't heard anything worrying from Priya or Jagger back home, have you?"

I shook my head. "Our families are fine. The dark fae that were hassling them haven't made any moves since we left. It sounds like most of them have taken off—probably on a boat headed back here."

"But they won't get here in time."

"Not if we can end this today."

"Right." He skimmed through his search results. "There's a home improvement store in the next city we'll be passing. According to their website, they carry lightning rods."

"Perfect. Then we'll make a little detour." My heart started to thump. One more stop, and then we'd be returning to the ground where this all began to face our greatest enemy.

* * *

Darton had seemed calm enough strapping the lightning rod on its side on the car roof, which was the only way we could figure out to carry the thing, but when we exited the car a couple hours later, he eyed it as if he were worried it would start shooting lightning at us right there and then.

"Are you *sure* you won't get hurt with this spell?"

"Maybe a little," I admitted. "But a little hurt beats death and mass destruction."

"Yeah." He still looked pensive as he helped me undo the cables that had held the rod in place. I'd parked at the far end of the lot behind a country flea market a short hike from the overpass—the closest I could get the car to Rhedyn—but a few passing shoppers noticed and shot us odd looks anyway.

Just wait until they saw Darton hauling out his broadsword.

A sprinkling of rain dappled our faces and then faded. The damp breeze pressed against my face. A gathering tension reverberated through it, carried down from the churning clouds overhead. A hint of ozone tickled over my tongue.

The light fae were working their magic. The crackling power of the storm was building, almost ready to burst open. And I needed to be in the right spot when it did.

"Come on." I pointed to a low, bare hill just south of the overpass. "That looks like a good spot to tempt lightning."

Darton gave a hoarse laugh, but he heaved Excalibur out of the car with a smooth sweep of his arms. The blade beamed. He shifted his stance, angling the sword out in front of him as if ready to do battle, and the light lit in his eyes too.

"This is my sword," he said, and for the first time, he sounded as if he fully believed that.

"It is," I said. "And I think we'd better take it elsewhere before a whole lot of people other than Keevan decide we're crazy."

He lowered the blade as we left the parking lot behind and tramped toward the hill. My arm burned with the weight of the lightning rod, which was nearly twice as tall as I was. I leaned it against my shoulder for balance and pushed onward. My other hand dipped to my side, checking first for the two wands I'd shoved in my pocket for easy access and then for the rest of the supplies in my bulging purse.

The moisture on the wet grass soaked into my sneakers and chilled my feet before we'd made it more than halfway up the hill. The wind picked up, hissing over it in a way that reminded me too much of the snake-dragon Rhedyn had sent after us in the Pool of Turmoil. Light only knew what she'd throw at us this time.

But this time my king had his sword, really *had* it, and the most intense blast of light nature could provide would soon be at my beck and call. We had a chance, and I was going to wring it for all it was worth.

As we continued up the hill, the rumble of the cars on the overpass reached me. The twisting roads, raised up on steel frames so they could be routed over and under each other, spewed the vehicles traveling on them off in a bewildering number of directions. The hill lay in a wide V between two of those adjoining highways.

I squinted at the shadows beneath the nearest branch of the overpass. An unearthly tremor ran over my skin. Somewhere down there, the Darkest One was sealed away in the stone. Somewhere down there, Rhedyn was battering my ancient spell with her dark magic. I wished we didn't have to be here—I wished she'd never shoved her way into these lives of ours. But at the same time, an ache almost like homesickness had filled me.

My spell had propelled the Darkest One away from the spot where she'd confronted Arthur before sealing her away, but not terribly far. We were some half a day's ride from the site of my and my king's former home. We might have sat on this hill, fifteen hundred years ago, to break for lunch on the way back to the castle.

Maybe the same sense of nostalgia had struck Darton, because he sucked in the cool autumn air and said, "Somehow this feels like I'm *returning*, even though I don't remember ever being here before."

"Some part of you does," I said. And then my voice fell away, because a cluster of shadowy figures had emerged from the dark spaces beneath and around the overpass.

Maybe two dozen dark fae were striding toward us, with a host of dark creatures charging alongside them. My jaw went slack. Darkness take me—and it very well might.

I grasped Darton's arm and tugged. "Let's get the higher ground while we can."

We scrambled the rest of the way up the hill, our feet skidding on the slick grass. The end of the lightning rod thudded against the ground as I flung it out in front of me like a walking stick. We hadn't quite made it to the crest when the first warbling of dark magic sounded behind us.

I whipped around, drawing my wand and snapping out a spell at the same moment. My blaze of light crashed into the dark fury of energy that had been rippling toward us.

Both spells shattered apart in a spray of mingled light and shadow. My muscles trembled. I dropped the lightning rod and grabbed my other wand to hold it at the ready.

A few of the swifter creatures had already clambered up the hill. Darton slashed at them with his gleaming sword, and they fell, crumpling into the grass. A small, determined smile had crossed his face.

Yes. That was what we needed.

I hollered into being another blast of light at the brigade of dark fae heading our way. It swept over them, rippling their shadowy clothes. They didn't even stagger, but they did at least slow down.

I didn't have any hope I could destroy even one of them with just my own power, but as long as they were busy defending against my assaults and attempting to attack us, they weren't focusing their attention on the clouds. My enclave could work their own magic even faster.

A few of the dark fae spat spells toward us, but I cast those away between pants for breath. This bunch had been picking away at the Darkest One's bindings and holding their storm steady across half the country for days. They'd drained most of their energy by now. I couldn't have survived against even a couple of full dark fae who had all their power, but a bunch of exhausted ones? I might just be able to hold them off.

I hadn't seen Rhedyn yet, though. And she was not just full fae but ancient, with all the power that came with that age.

A thicker wave of shadow creatures was barreling toward us. Darton glanced back at me. "Together?"

I hadn't tried combining my magic with the full power of Excalibur before. The blade was practically singing with its connection to my king's soul. Voices rose by the base of the hill. The dark fae squadron was starting up the slope. I sprang forward, clapping one hand against Darton's back with the wand between us.

"Darkness begone!"

Darton sliced the sword through the air, and the light

blazed from its edge all the way down the hill, glowing brighter and brighter as it streamed on. It burned away every one of the dark creatures the fae had sent after us. The dark fae gasped and cringed, but stayed standing.

Both of my wands crumbled, drained of energy, but a fresh surge of confidence filled me. The two of us, together with the sword, were more powerful than they'd expected. And we had more power yet to come.

I snatched another wand from my purse. The dark fae at the base of the hill were pulling closer together, their murmurs echoing in a joint spell. I preferred not to give them the chance to finish it. "Again!" I said to Darton, gripping his shoulder. He nodded and swung the sword once more.

The blade arced with a brilliant glitter, and I pushed all the energy in the wand through me into that motion. *"Beams of light, twist and hold."*

The light that seared off of Excalibur's blade this time twined into a thick rope. It whipped down the hill and snapped tight around the huddled fae. A few tried to spring out of range at the sight of it, but the light spiraled on and on, winding loop after loop around every one of them.

Darton stared at the mass of struggling bodies. The shadows that clung to them licked and cringed away from the gleaming binding.

"How long can you hold them like that?" he asked.

I tossed away the now-dead wand. "They'll be able to work themselves free in a few hours, I'd guess. But in a few hours we'll be long done here."

Or long dead by Rhedyn's hand—or her master's.

I paused to take a breath, and that was my mistake. In

the instant while my guard was slightly down, three dark fae who must have circled the hill and crept up the opposite side sprang at us from behind.

One of the men leapt at Darton with a lash of dark magic and a knife. The other and the woman came at me.

Throwing myself onto the ground, I tumbled away from them. I didn't have time to grab another wand. My fingers dug into the grass. That thin green energy flowed into my palms. I snapped it up like a shield as the woman swung a whip of shadow at me.

"*Carry them, like to like!*" I called out. A wind whipped up from the grass and slammed into the man. It tossed him down the hill, right into the knot of trapped fae at the base. His pained grunt gave me a small twinge of satisfaction.

The woman had managed to dodge the blast. She lunged at me again, words in the old tongue spilling from her mouth. I battered away her smack of magic with a flail of my arm and a wrenching at the life energy inside me. Good-bye to another couple weeks of life.

Beyond her, Darton was matching blows with the other fae, Excalibur's blade deflecting knife and spells alike. The clouds overhead crackled but didn't split. So sodding close.

The fae woman flinched at the sound. I took advantage of her brief distraction to snatch at my fallen purse. The woman had just whipped her hands up to throw another spell when I spun with my second-to-last wand, calling up the wind again. The surge of air tossed her down the slope after her companion.

A chill quivered up through the ground into my body, as if from somewhere deep below. From the cavern where

Rhedyn was unwinding my work. The Darkest One's will was seeping through even stronger now. Was she that close to breaking free?

Pulse racing, I shoved myself to my feet. Darton was just swiveling to track his attacker's parry. The dark fae man leaned close and muttered something as he sliced out with his knife.

Darton smacked the narrow blade away, but his expression stuttered as if he'd been slapped. The glow that had lit both his face and the sword dimmed. My stomach lurched.

I scrambled over as he tried to swing the sword again. Its weight dragged at his arms, and his mouth twisted. The fae man cackled. He gathered a whirl of shadow between his hands—and I kicked his feet out from under him.

I grasped Darton's wrist. "I've got you." He let Excalibur drop toward the dark fae who was springing up again, and my fingers clenched around my wand.

"*Carry him, like to like,*" I said, channeling the magic through the enchanted sword. The wind stirred with the swoop of the blade. It sent the fae man careening down the hill to join the others.

"Art," I said, but I never got to ask the question on my lips. The ground shuddered and pitched beneath us. I fell to my knees, snatching at the suddenly crumbling soil.

The lightning rod. I couldn't lose it. I hurled myself up the hill over the sudden landslide. Pebbles and clods of dirt fell away under my scrambling feet. My hand closed around the metal post. I jerked around to call Darton to me, and the rod started to slide down the hill too.

Darton had dug his sword into the ground, but as I glanced over, the hill spit it back up. I caught his arm as another quake jostled us closer together, but then we were just hurtling downward side by side.

Down toward the dark space that gaped even wider now beneath the underpass. Movement stirred within the shadows as we tumbled toward it. A cold laugh carried from their depths, and then Rhedyn's raspy voice rang out.

"So glad you've come to meet me, Merlin."

30

The landslide jerked us to a stop a few paces shy of the base of the hill. Darton staggered to his feet. He hauled Excalibur with him, but the sword's blade was still dull, his arms still straining. Whatever that damned dark fae had said to him had clearly shaken him badly.

The blade had shone a little more for me, recognizing my magic, when we'd faced Rhedyn's snake-dragon. At the crunch of footsteps over gravel by the cave just below us, I scrambled up and grasped the hilt.

"Let me take the sword."

Darton stared at me. He opened his mouth with an expression that told me he was going to protest, but then a figure appeared at the cave's opening, and his grip loosened. I heaved the sword toward me and turned to face Rhedyn.

For the first few seconds, *I* could only stare. She wasn't the blond, tan-skinned fae I'd faced more than once in the past. It was her—I could sense it in the tendrils of shadow clinging to her like hazy vines—but this body was shorter, more solid, with a head of black curls and eyes nearly as dark.

A human body.

Rhedyn smiled at my surprise. "Not what you were expecting, wizard? I learned from you—how to cling on after death and find a new home, as you have so many times. It took longer to work the magic than I'd hoped, but here I am now."

That was why. That was why *everything*. Why I hadn't sensed her in so many lives before. Why it had taken so long for her to build up enough power that her efforts were finally affecting us. A human body would restrain some of the natural fae powers of her soul.

She must have been working to free the Darkest One through my entire current life, at least. Wearing down the barriers so more and more influence could seep out, until our mercenary had sensed it from across the ocean and made me realize something worse than usual was happening.

I didn't know whether to be angry or grateful for that. Darton could have had more time to live his life properly. But if the mercenary hadn't stepped up, Rhedyn might have carried on like this, scraping away at my spell, never worrying about me, until she'd broken the binding and we'd all been in an even deeper mess than we were now.

Thunder rumbled overhead. Rhedyn kept her smile, but it tightened. So very close. If I had the sword, I wouldn't even need the lightning rod. I could channel the lightning straight through Excalibur.

"It doesn't matter what body you're wearing," I said. "It won't stop me from doing what I need to do."

Her lips pulled back into a full-out sneer. "If you really think you can, go ahead and take your best shot."

I wrenched the sword off the ground. My magic sang

through it, but not enough to really lighten its weight. Gritting my teeth, I swung it at her. *"Darkness begone."*

I hadn't expected to do much more than propel her backward anyway. Her power might be dampened by the body she was in and all the magic she'd expended working at the Darkest One's prison, but I was working with a human body too, and full fae trumped half any day. But before the words had even fallen from my mouth, Rhedyn shoved out her hands with a snapped spell of her own.

Energy radiated from her body. The hill shook, and the ground tipped. She raised her arms. With a groan, the entire crest upended and poured down in a mass of earth toward us.

"Em!" Darton grabbed my arm and yanked. I stumbled with him, clutching the sword. He pulled me under a small, rocky outcropping on the hillside, just as the avalanche cascaded over us. In an instant, we were buried in that small pocket of air and darkness.

My breath stuttered. I pushed back against the more stable ground behind us until I was sure the dirt had finished falling. Darton crouched unmoving beside me. I couldn't see him, but his shoulder pressed against mine, hitching a bit with each inhale.

"Well, this is going smashingly," I muttered, and he choked out a laugh.

"What do you always say? 'We'll figure it out somehow'?"

"That sounds like me." I closed my eyes, not that it made much difference in our earth-bound prison, and started to reach my awareness out into the hillside to get to work on figuring things out. Then Darton's arm slid around me, tugging my mind back to him. To us.

"Em," he said, his voice rough. "Merlin. I don't remember if I ever said this before. I know I didn't say it enough. Maybe it *isn't* enough, in the end, after everything you've told me. But I want you to know that you have always been the most important person in my life. All of them. I'm pretty sure I can say that for the ones I don't remember too. And I will always stand by you, no matter what comes. No matter how this ends."

He hugged me tighter to him. I pressed my face to his shoulder, closing my eyes again, this time against the tears threatening to spring up. The ache that filled my chest now was only painful because of the thought of losing this. Losing him.

"It's enough," I said, past the lump in my throat. "It's always been enough." My liege. My greatest friend. "Now let's get out of here and show that dark fae what we're made of."

I grasped Excalibur's hilt with my free hand and shoved it into the loose earth that had covered our makeshift shelter. "*Batter and blast.*"

Energy blazed through the sword with a crackling power no wand had ever offered me. The barrier in front of us burst apart in a spray of soil. I threw myself forward, feeling as much as seeing Darton charging forward beside me, the fae dagger in his hand.

A blast of dark magic sizzled into my face. I jerked to the side just in time to only feel the singe across my cheek. Rhedyn was hissing words under her breath. I swiped the dirt from my eyes and dodged another shadowy projectile. The clouds overhead outright boomed.

I swung the sword, sending out an arc of light that forced Rhedyn backward a couple of steps. A half light fae against a full dark fae might not be much of a contest, but add a magically enhanced sword to the mix, and I had a sliver of a chance.

A flicker crossed the sky. The lightning had come. That would give us much more than a sliver. I just needed it to come down to us. To come down to us and blast our enemy away.

"Em," Darton said. He held out his hand. "Let me?"

His hair was plastered to his head with the damp and his face was smudged with dirt, but in that moment he looked every inch the stalwart king. My heart skipped a beat.

This was his battle too. He'd told me over and over again that he trusted me, had shown me he did so many times. He'd given me the sword bound to his soul just a few minutes ago, because I'd asked. Did I trust him to know he was ready to wield it? To stand by me as he'd promised.

Yes. With all my heart, I did.

I thrust the sword toward him, swiveling in the same movement to search the hillside for my fallen lightning rod. Rhedyn snapped out a spell, and Darton whipped the blade to shatter it. A gleam lit within the sword from hilt to tip.

"Are we ready?" he asked me.

"Almost." There. The metal staff with its pointed top protruded from the earth just a short dash above us. I hurled myself upward over the still crumbling soil and wrapped my hands around the rod. With a heave, I freed it.

I needed more than this to call the lightning to me. I needed a source of power.

My gaze fell to the matted grass at the base of the hill, just a few feet from where Rhedyn stood. I'd have to sacrifice height for that, but no matter.

"We need to close in," I shouted to Darton. He nodded and pressed on down the hill, cutting off every blast of shadow Rhedyn threw his way with a slash of his sword. Her eyes narrowed. She stood her ground, hurling another spell at him, and another. But I thought I could see her tiring more. Her arms shook, just slightly.

I skidded the rest of the way down the hill, landing ungracefully but on my feet on the flatter ground at its base. Rhedyn's army of dark fae was still thrashing at the binding of light I'd cast around them, but she either didn't have the energy or the interest to try to free them.

She whipped a searing ball of shadow my way, and I leapt to the side. Darton charged at her at the same moment, jabbing his blade at her stomach. She batted it aside with a swift muttering, but her face had pinched with strain.

She'd given up so much of her strength trying to free her master. And despite it, the Darkest One was still sealed beneath the mountain, stirring but stuck.

The clouds above let out a massive rumble. It was time to finish this. To prove that we could.

I stabbed the lightning rod's base into the ground and dropped down with my knees braced on either side of it to hold it upright. Digging my hand into the limp grass, I flung out my other arm. "Arthur! Now!"

He parried one last surge of Rhedyn's magic and dashed over to me. The sword sang in his hand as he extended the other to clasp mine. I tipped my face to the sky, clenched the grass and his fingers, and cried out with every shred of life in me.

"Light of the skies, blaze to me, blaze true. Break the darkness and cast it away."

The clouds boomed and flashed. Not one but three streaks of lightning raced down to meet me. They snapped against the head of the lightning rod in a single mass of energy. The rush of light and electricity smacked into me, rattling my teeth. I held it with all my strength and balled my will around the coursing, shuddering power. Then I threw it from me into Darton, into the sword he held.

Darton thrust Excalibur toward Rhedyn. Light blazed and arced all around its blade. In that last instant, I thought I saw Rhedyn turning to flee and catching herself. She spun back toward us, meeting the blast of pure light energy with her arms raised as if in surrender.

The immense bolt seared straight into her gut. Her lips jittered, but her body fell. She slumped over on the ground. Her eyelids stuttered, her eyes gone pure black right through the whites. Her arms lay spread in her last pose, now limp with death.

A wisp of shadow drifted up from her chest. My pulse hiccupped. Oh, no, I wasn't letting her essence flee again to cling to some other human form. I swung the lightning rod down, calling on the last flickers of electricity still humming through it, and tossed them at that wisp.

It sizzled and popped in a burst of sparks. And with that, my old enemy was fully gone from this world.

31

I dropped the lightning rod. My skin stung as it fell to the ground. I raised my hand and found myself staring at a bubbled scarlet burn streaked across the center of my palm and the inner knuckles of my fingers. My nerves were jangling as if a shot of that electricity were still bouncing around inside my body.

A wash of relief swept those uncomfortable sensations away. Rhedyn was gone. The Darkest One was still bound. We'd done it. Again.

A laugh I couldn't pretend wasn't a bit startled jolted out of me. Darton gripped my shoulder.

"Is it done?" he said hoarsely. "Is she— Are we safe now?"

Not even hardly. I dragged in a breath. "Not yet. Rhedyn has still weakened the seal that was keeping the Darkest One locked away. I have to do my best to rebuild it." I glanced up at the sky. "Maybe the lightning can help with that as well."

Maybe, if I absorbed a little more of that power, worked it through my will, I could create a binding that didn't require the tangling of our souls to hold it in place.

And then we could really be done, for good.

I raised my hands to reach out to the sparking clouds—and an ear-splitting *crack* rang out from the cave before us.

The earth jumped and broke open between us. From the depths of the darkness in the cave, a screech pealed out, as pleased as it was furious. My heart stopped.

"Em?" Darton said, his eyes wide. He threw his hand toward me. The chasm in the ground between us gaped wider. I scrambled and leapt across, catching hold of him just before the edge crumbled under my heel.

"It can't— *She* can't—" I was mumbling, but I knew even as the protests spilled out that it wasn't true. The image of Rhedyn with her arms spread flashed through my mind.

I'd destroyed her, but she'd turned her death into a sacrifice to her master. And that last burst of sacrificial magic had been enough for the Darkest One to wriggle free.

Before the thought had even finished passing through my mind, a tingling raced over my skin. An itchy tingling, as if a layer of my skin were sloughing off. I stared down at my arms, and then at Darton, who was shuddering as if he felt the same thing. The itch dug all the way into my chest, between my ribs, pinching and scratching. I choked on a breath.

My spell. Fifteen hundred years of binding, of deaths and rebirths, of finding each other. The Darkest One had finally wrenched it all apart.

With another *crack*, the entrance to the cave shattered apart. A wave of darkness spilled out, crashing toward us like a tsunami, surging up toward the clouds to sputter against the flashes of lightning. My lungs seized up.

I couldn't fight her. I'd never been able to fight her. The only way I could save my king was to get him far, far away. But I was capable of that.

I threw my arms around Darton and called out a spell down to the depths of my fragile, mortal life. The wind whipped up around us, whirling us away. It tore away my sight. My mind spiraled into darkness. I felt us land, stumbling on grassy ground. Heard Darton's voice saying, "What— Em, where are we?"

"Somewhere safe," I mumbled. "Momentarily." Then the effort hit me over the head, and I blacked out completely.

ABOUT THE AUTHOR

Eva Chase lives in Canada with her family. She loves stories both swoony and supernatural, and strong women and the men who appreciate them. Along with the Legends Reborn series, she is also the author of the Demons of Fame paranormal romance series, beginning with *Caught in the Glow*. You can visit her online at **www.evachase.com**.